SEE ME

A SHE'S MINE NOVEL

Jennifer Ryan

For those who persevere, hold on to hope, and never give up on love.

This book contains...

stalking, violence, rape (off the page),

a baby's death, murder, suicide, trauma,

sex, true love, and a happy ending.

Chapter One

4th **of July – Another event his parents dragged him to...**

Wow! He hadn't seen her in two years.

She'd changed. Filled out in all the right places.

His gaze traced her curves. Those legs. That ass. Damn.

He wished he could go up to her and say hi.

Lame.

She'd never talk to him. What would he even say to her? No one ever really talked to him. Not unless they wanted something. Usually from his father.

He hated being used. He hated that he couldn't just go up to her, strike up a conversation, and have her begging him to take her out, take her to bed. He wasn't that guy. He didn't know how to be that guy, even though right now he'd do anything to be that man for her.

She made him hard. She made him want.

Then he got lucky and spotted some friends from school, who were friends with Brooke's best friend. He could use them to get close to Brooke. Then maybe he'd have a chance.

Yeah right!

It could happen, he argued with himself.

Maybe it was meant to be.

Chapter Two

4th **of July picnic at Brooke's home...**

Brooke Banks stared out at the crowd of people milling around the garden and seated at the picnic tables on the patio. Her best friend Mindy Sue was holding court by the pond with her boyfriend, Marco, and several of their college friends. They were entertaining themselves playing cornhole and horseshoes on the grass. They'd all come to support Brooke through this happy but difficult event.

"Brooke! Is that really you!" Mrs. Ellis's mouth hung open as her gaze went from the tips of Brooke's cowboy boots, up her legs and her slightly curvy body, to her green-eyed gaze. "Wow! You were always a pretty girl, but now you're a beautiful young lady."

She appreciated the praise. At least someone had noticed she'd grown up. "Thank you."

"I'm so sorry about your stepfather. We've missed him these last two years." Mrs. Ellis's husband, the mayor, had been friends with Harland since they were boys in school.

Two years ago, her stepfather had died of a sudden heart attack. He'd held the annual picnic for all his friends, fellow ranchers, and community leaders. She missed him every day. She, her mom, and his son, Cody, hadn't been ready to carry on the tradition after Harland's passing. But this year, Brooke insisted they revive it. It was important to keep Harland's memory alive. Traditions mattered and kept them together.

Plus she hoped it would help Cody look toward the future and see this place as *his* now, because he was the one carrying on in his father's absence.

And it didn't hurt that some of the most influential people in the state were here.

As a lawyer, Cody could use the connections with his father's cronies. You never knew when you'd need a favor from someone with the kind of clout many of the individuals here today flaunted.

She nodded to the governor and his wife, who were chatting with her mother, Susanne, nearby. Mindy Sue's father, Doug Wagner, was one of the most highly respected and successful defense attorneys in the state. There were three judges, plus the district attorney and several of his associates here, too, along with most of the business owners from three nearby towns. Everyone they'd invited showed up out of respect for Cody and his father.

And she'd been the one to pull all of this together, from the invitations to the catering, decorations, the music, games, and fireworks show. Every detail, she'd conceived and executed.

She hoped it showed everyone on the ranch that she'd grown up, because from the second she'd arrived home from college, she'd had to remind everyone she was twenty, not ten.

It started with their ranch hand the day she arrived home for summer break calling her little one. Paco didn't mean anything other than affection, but it made her feel like a little girl and not the woman she'd grown into. It didn't help that Cody refused to let her have even half a glass of wine at dinner. He never missed an opportunity to exercise his overprotective streak when it came to her.

Even more annoying, his girlfriend was *Team Cody all the way. UGH! Of course she sided with him to score points.*

Mrs. Ellis pressed her hand to her heart. "Time passes so quickly. We blink and..." She waved her hand up and down in front of Brooke. "Little girls turn into young ladies. Friends pass." She waved at her misty eyes. "Sorry. I miss Harland."

"Me, too."

"And I haven't seen enough of your mother. How is Susanne doing? She must be so proud of you."

"She is." Brooke was lucky to have such a supportive mom, even if she was having trouble giving Brooke her freedom. "And she's well. It was hard in the beginning, but now we're all just trying to keep Dad alive in our hearts."

Mrs. Ellis patted Brooke's forearm. "That's the way, now isn't it? You must be close to finishing college."

"One more year to go until I graduate with my bachelor's degree." She couldn't wait.

Mrs. Ellis leaned in. "And is there a special young man?"

Brooke's cheeks warmed. "No." Just Cody. But he wasn't hers. No matter how hard she tried or wished it were true.

"Well"—Mrs. Ellis nudged her shoulder—"the right one will come along soon enough."

Yeah, I already found him. He's just not into me. Not in that way.

Her mom, Susanne, made her way over to them. "Betty, don't you look lovely."

Mrs. Ellis's sleeveless, fuchsia-colored sheath dress complemented her dark hair and green eyes while showing off a nice pair of toned arms. Mrs. Ellis must work out, because she was in good shape.

Mrs. Ellis waved off Brooke's mother's compliment. "Thank you, Susanne. You're as beautiful as ever. That turquoise dress just makes you glow." The women shared a quick embrace and kiss on the cheek.

"I've missed you," Susanne confessed.

Her mom had retreated from her friends after Harland's death, lost in her grief. But over the past year, she'd slowly started to really live again and reconnect with old friends.

Brooke loved that the party had brought these two back together.

Mrs. Ellis held her hand out toward Brooke. "I nearly didn't recognize your beautiful daughter."

"They grow up so fast." Her mom smiled, even if a bit of sadness crept into her eyes that time had passed too quickly and soon Brooke would be off to school again.

"Yes, they do." Mrs. Ellis was probably thinking of her two children. "Thank you for inviting us to the party."

"Oh," her mother said, "I'm so happy you're here, but the event"—Susanne looked around at all the people, decorations, and buffet nearby—"this was all Brooke's doing."

And today Cody would see she could handle a party of this size and scale and make it enticing for all these people to show up and be here for him. All she'd had to do was call up the governor's wife and tell her how much she hoped she and her husband would attend, and that her stepfather Harland had loved her pecan pie. Mrs. Harris had won first place in the state fair three years in a row and took great pride in showing off her version of the official state pie. She had graciously agreed to not only come to the picnic but to bring a dozen of her homemade pies herself. From there, it had been simple to let others know the governor would be attending, and the RSVPs had rolled in. Not that these people wouldn't come because they respected Harland and Cody. They would. They did. But it never hurt to have a little incentive for those who thrived on being seen in the right circles.

And she'd do anything for Cody.

Mrs. Ellis's smile grew as her gaze shifted to Brooke. "I should hire you for the mayor's next event."

Pride swelled in her heart. She'd worked hard on this picnic. And Mrs. Ellis's approval meant a lot. She attended a ton of events each year. She'd know if something was done well, or fell short. "Unfortunately, I'll have my nose stuck in books for the next couple semesters."

"You should think about becoming an event planner."

Mrs. Ellis's suggestion was nice, but Brooke had other plans. And they included running the ranch with Cody.

Unfortunately, she wouldn't have Cody all to herself. His girlfriend, Kristi Randall, beelined it across the patio toward her and she inwardly cringed.

Kristi barely got out, "Sorry to interrupt, Susanne, Mrs. Ellis." She turned to Brooke. "Have you seen your brother?" Kristi stood before her, searching the crowd with barely a glance for her.

Kristi had never liked her. The feeling was mutual. Kristi wanted all of Cody's attention on her. Brooke? Same. Still, you'd think Kristi would want to befriend Cody's best friend.

Not Kristi. She saw other women as competition.

And while Brooke loved Cody, she also knew she wasn't in the running to be anything more than what she already was to him.

And referring to him as her brother. Yeah, no. She and Cody didn't call each other brother and sister. Their seven-year age gap meant they hadn't been raised together. Brooke and her mom arrived on the ranch when she was ten. Her mother hired on as the cook before Harland fell hard and fast for Susanne and they married. And while Harland had felt like the father she'd never had, she and Cody treated each other like good friends, not siblings.

She'd never, not once, thought of the charming, temptingly hot Cody as her brother.

Kristi huffed out her frustration. "I've been looking for him everywhere." In her long, flowing white dress, pink strappy kitten heels that Brooke hated to admit were super cute, and a tan sunhat over her long golden hair, Kristi made Brooke look like a ranch hand and not the hostess of one of the most sought-after invitations in the state.

Brooke should have put more thought into her outfit like her mother suggested. Not once, but like four times.

She never really paid much attention to what she wore on the ranch or at school. She went for comfort over fashion.

Today she'd thought she'd upped her game by wearing a faded denim skirt that hit mid-thigh and showed off her tanned, toned legs, a short-sleeved, fitted red T-shirt that had lace detail around the arms and hemline but now felt like it wasn't anything special, and her black cowboy boots. She'd pulled her hair up into her usual ponytail to keep it out of the way and off her neck in the hot sun. She could have tried something different. Maybe keeping it down and using some pretty clips to keep it out of her face, even if it would be heavy and hot draped down her neck and back.

Compared to Kristi, she looked plain.

Not exactly showstopping for this who's who party.

Standing next to Kristi, seeing how everyone else around her had dressed in what Mindy Sue would probably call resort chic, suddenly made her uncomfortable. Nervous butterflies battled in her belly as her cheeks heated with embarrassment. She'd tried so hard to make today perfect for everyone. Now, she felt out of place. Not the first time.

Changing now would look too obvious. So she let it go with a heavy heart and tried not to let herself think about it again.

Brooke glanced at Mindy Sue and her other friends out on the lawn, all of them in sundresses or skirts and pretty blouses, hair done, makeup on. Brooke had swiped on some ChapStick and mascara and called it done.

Even the guys were in khakis and slacks with short-sleeved button-up shirts.

She scanned the crowd again and noticed the ranch hands had put on their finest boots, dark denim, and cowboy shirts with pearl buttons, belt buckles shining.

She sighed, thinking that instead of spending the whole morning helping the caterer set up, she could have taken time to actually think about what she wanted to wear and put together something a bit more...sophisticated. Maybe then Cody would look at her like he looked at other women. And she wouldn't feel like the lovesick shadow who followed him around all the time, hoping he'd see how much she loved him.

Ugh. Pathetic. And yet she couldn't squash the undying hope that lived inside her that one day...

Kristi tapped her on the shoulder. "Brooke. Hello. Cody?"

Right. Brooke looked out across the patio, gardens, and grass area where the just-over-two-hundred guests were mingling. "I haven't seen him since we came out to greet everyone."

Kristi huffed out a breath.

Trouble in paradise?

One could hope. Because Kristi had this way about her. She liked getting what she wanted and seemed to be the kind of person who'd do anything to get it.

An only child. Spoiled.

But Brooke had also gotten the sense that pleasing her parents really mattered to Kristi. Brooke got that. You wanted them to be proud of you. It just seemed like Kristi really needed it more than most.

Still, Brooke recognized the longing in Kristi's eyes. She felt it in herself every time she thought about Cody or even looked at him. He had this quality that drew her in.

Kristi and others weren't immune to it either.

But Cody was different with Brooke than he was with the other women who came and went. They could talk for hours or just chill and watch a movie with nothing said. She knew him so well, she could read him like a book. And he was always there for her. Since the day she arrived at the ranch with her mom, they just clicked.

They were friends.

She wanted them to be more.

He ignored all her attempts to get his attention in that way.

She had half a mind to tell Kristi he was off talking to some ex, but that was petty and immature. She'd long since grown past trying to sabotage Cody's girlfriends by conveniently forgetting to deliver messages, or telling them Cody liked something that he hated. He always caught on and gave her a disapproving look that made her feel terrible. She didn't want to be on the wrong side of Cody. She definitely didn't want to lose the amazing connection they shared.

She was really trying to be the grown-up no one on the ranch saw her to be, including her mother and Cody.

Maybe she could do a better job by thinking things through first, like dressing appropriately for the party and presenting herself as the adult she felt like on the inside. Then everyone would see it. Right?

It sucked that everyone still treated her like a child. Well, at least a teen with no sense, despite her stellar grades and the twenty years she'd kept herself alive and well, thank you very much.

Maybe she'd made some mistakes along the way. Thinking Jamie was her friend at middle school summer camp, only to find out that Jamie had hidden a bottle of vodka in Brooke's bag and she got caught during inspection the first day and sent home. Luckily, her mom believed her that she hadn't stolen it from the bar at home. It was a cheap brand they didn't keep in the house. Then there was the time she'd played spin the bottle at Brent's house freshman year with a bunch of friends. She really wanted her first kiss to be with Cody, but Joe came in second, and then the bottle landed on Chris. She'd been disappointed but game to kiss him just to get it over with. But Brent, the asshole trickster, who she'd turned down in front of several of his friends for the spring dance, told her to close her eyes. She did and puckered up to kiss Chris but got a face full of dog tongue instead. Brent got his revenge. Everyone laughed at her. The next day at school, everyone snickered behind her back about her French-kissing Brent's mini poodle. Yeah, high school was not fun with that hanging over her head.

Kristi frowned as she continued to scan the crowd. "If you see him, please send him to me. Tell him my father would like to have a word with him? It's important."

The demand wrapped in the request rubbed Brooke the wrong way. "We're supposed to give a speech while everyone is eating. The lines are forming now. I'm sure he'll find me soon."

"That can wait. This can't. It's an opportunity Cody won't want to pass up. Not if he's smart."

Cody was the smartest guy she knew.

"What's it about?"

"The future. One I think Cody wants, which is why I worked so hard to set this up."

Brooke cocked her head, concerned and suspicious. "What did you set up?"

Kristi huffed. "My father is waiting. Will you just help me find him?"

Mrs. Ellis and Susanne both raised a brow, though Kristi didn't see their curious gazes.

Brooke couldn't let the snappish tone go. "You know, a straight answer would get better results."

"Cody wants to make a name for himself. I can make that happen." Smugness was not becoming on Kristi.

The muscles in Brooke's shoulders tensed. "He doesn't need anyone to make him look good. He's smart, driven, and good at everything he does."

Kristi smirked. "Oh, I know he is."

Brooke didn't like the innuendo. She avoided Mrs. Ellis and her mother's stares. "Whatever." She tried to walk away, but Kristi snagged her arm and halted her.

"Don't mess this up for him."

She turned and looked Kristi right in the eyes. "I want what's best for him."

Kristi grinned again. "Good. Then send him over to me." She smiled smugly and walked away.

Brooke wanted to tear Kristi's pretty blonde hair out.

Mrs. Ellis gave Brooke the same sympathetic look as her mom. "Don't let her get to you. Women like her end up with no friends, wondering why no one likes them."

"I guess. Excuse me. I have to find Cody." She decided if whatever Kristi was talking about would really help him, then she'd do the right thing.

She found him in the garden, sitting in an Adirondack chair next to his buddy Brad Whitlock, the district attorney's son. They'd grown up together and went to college together.

Brad saw her coming and grinned. "Hello, beautiful." He took her hand and tugged, putting her off-balance so that she landed in his lap. He hugged her close. "Where have you been all my life."

"Right under your nose. But the B word you use for me is usually brat." She elbowed him in the gut, making him laugh as she smiled back at him. Brad was like a brother to her.

Which was weird to think of him as when she'd never seen Cody that way.

And the object of all her desires frowned at his friend.

Brad ignored it. "I think gorgeous suits you better now."

Cody pounded his fist into Brad's shoulder with anger in his eyes as he reached out and took Brooke's hand, pulling her up and out of Brad's lap and into his. "Hands off, asshole."

Brad held up his hands. "I was just saying hello."

Cody narrowed his gaze. "You know the rule. No flirting with *her*."

Brooke cocked a brow. "Is this like the bro code?" She had to admit, she liked seeing Cody possessive over her. And sitting in his lap gave her all kinds of shivery feelings and indecent ideas.

Brad chuckled. "You don't mess with your best friend's sister."

Cody nudged her off him. "Is it time for the speech you want us to make?"

Brooke stood beside him, knowing he'd changed the subject on purpose, but not understanding the wince he'd given at Brad's words or the strange look in his eyes when she left his lap. Regret?

No. That's wishful thinking and my imagination.

She tamped down her hormones and adoration for him and focused. "Uh, Kristi ordered me to find you."

"Excuse me?" Cody didn't look happy about that.

Brooke let it go. "Her father wants to talk to you. Something important."

"Better hop to it," Brad teased. "Don't want to keep the future Mrs. Jansen waiting."

"What?" Brooke nearly choked on the word and the idea that Cody planned to propose.

Cody punched his fist into Brad's arm again as he stood. "Stop joking about shit like that."

She grabbed his forearm and stopped him from walking away. "Are you..."

"No," he said emphatically.

She breathed a sigh of relief that he wasn't planning on asking her to marry him.

Yet.

Shut up, she yelled at that voice in her head.

Cody glanced at the crowd. "Where is she?"

Brooke looked past him. "By the bar."

"How about I get you a drink, Brooke?" Brad offered.

"No," Cody snapped. "Brooke isn't of age."

Brad shook his head. "Come on, old man. We were drinking way younger than she is now."

Cody met Brad's taunting eyes. "Go find one of the couple dozen available women here today. She's not for you."

Brooke wanted to break the tension between these two friends. "I mean, I could do worse."

Cody's lethal gaze landed on her. "Are you serious?"

She rolled her eyes. "No. I'm going to make sure everyone is heading to the buffet line." She walked away, but not before she heard Brad tell Cody, "I was just messing around."

She knew it was to keep his friendship with Cody on good terms, but it kind of pinched her heart, too, that he wasn't serious about her being beautiful, or that he would be interested in her.

Not that she wanted to date Brad. It would just be nice if he thought she was worth Cody's wrath.

You're being ridiculous.

She knew that.

Still, the whole interaction with all of them felt weird. Like maybe Cody didn't want her with anyone but him.

Now that's really ridiculous.

Or was it?

She really needed to stop this train of thought and get a grip.

She made it through the garden and to the buffet line just in time to catch the moment Cody found Kristi and slipped his hand around her waist, pulling her close to his side as he used his free hand to shake her father's hand.

Kristi looked up at him adoringly.

Cody glanced down at her and smiled. People close to them noticed the happy couple.

Was he really thinking about marrying her? Or had Brad really just been joking?

Brooke's heart sank. She was too used to this feeling when it came to Cody. Maybe one day he'd see her as the woman she'd become.

The one who wanted him and only him.

Chapter Three

F^{*uck!*}

What the hell just happened?

Cody tried to rein in his...what the hell was he feeling?

Rage at his friend for pulling Brooke into his lap.

Possessiveness because he'd wanted to keep her in his.

Fucking lust for getting hard as her lush ass brushed against his dick before he moved her.

Regret that he'd had to let her go.

Brad was lucky he'd hit him in the arm and not the face. He still wanted to pound the shit out of him for calling Brooke beautiful, making her smile.

And what the fuck was with her saying she could do worse than Brad? Did she like Brad? Did she want to date him? Fuck him?

What the hell was going on?

It felt like his world turned upside down all of a sudden.

"Honey, there you are! I've been looking for you." Kristi hooked her arm through his and snuggled up to his side with a wide grin and bright, happy eyes.

Guilt hit him all at once, even though he hadn't really done anything.

Except get jealous over your best friend paying attention to Brooke.

He wasn't jealous. He was protective.

Yeah. Right.

Fuck.

"Smile. My dad is watching us."

Cody plastered on a smile.

Kirk started in their direction.

"You need to seriously get over whatever happened with Brooke and Brad and you turning into the overprotective big brother."

"You saw that?"

Kristi eyed him. "It's not hard to miss the way she looks at you. But she's your stepsister and you need to shut that down. People notice. It's...not right."

"There's no blood between us. We weren't raised together. I was grown when she and Susanne moved in. They had a hard life before they came to the ranch."

Susanne had taken a job as the new cook and housekeeper for him and his father. She'd arrived with next to nothing and a spindly little girl, so painfully shy and quiet, Brooke had trouble making friends at the fourth new school she'd attended in her short life. Cody saw how much she liked the ranch and the horses, and he'd made a point to try to help her fit in. Maybe she got a little carried away by his attention and didn't see the reality of their situation the way he did, but it wasn't his fault she'd been lovestruck.

Just like his dad, who fell head over heels for Brooke's mom, Susanne. The normally stoic, hard man had melted like butter every time Susanne came into a room. Cody had never seen his father's cold eyes soften with what could only be described as love like they did when he looked at her. After his wife walked out on him, Cody understood why he'd hardened his heart, even if Cody had been hurt by it as a child. He couldn't remember his father ever being soft or kind to anyone if a rough demand got him what he wanted faster. Susanne changed him. And Cody.

In his last years, his father had seemed happy for the first time in his life. He'd been different. Cody might not have wanted a stepmother and stepsister, but he'd thank Susanne every day for giving his father the best years of his life.

He'd even told Cody he was proud of him at his law school graduation. For the first time, Cody felt connected to his dad, like he'd finally measured up. It had made a huge difference in his life. And when his father passed away of a heart attack only two years ago, he was able to say goodbye to the man without regrets. Susanne had taught a tough old goat how to love, and he'd loved them all well before they'd lost him.

His father, who in the past would have looked at a little girl as useless on a ranch, took a shine to Brooke and taught her everything he knew about ranching. He'd treated her like his own, and Brooke tried so hard to earn his praise and pride. Her own father had abandoned her and Susanne years before, leaving them with nothing but a lot of hard days ahead of them. Until they'd come to the ranch and found two men who understood what they'd been through. They all healed each other by taking care of each other.

His father found love, and Cody found the best friend he'd ever have.

"The people here...they can make or break a career. Stay focused on what and who is important right now."

Cody didn't like what Kristi implied, but he didn't get a chance to say anything as Kirk arrived at Kristi's side and held out his hand to Cody.

"It's good to see you again."

Cody took his hand, shifting gears back to being in control, and gave Kristi's father a firm handshake. "Thank you for coming. I hope you're enjoying the party."

Kirk scanned the crowd. "Harland would be proud you're carrying on tradition."

"The credit goes to Brooke. She organized everything."

Kristi pressed her lips tight and eyed him.

Kirk acknowledged his statement with a nod. "Kristi told me Brooke is home for the summer."

"She'll head back to school in mid-August to finish her senior year." One more year of college, then she'd move back home for good. She'd be where she belonged.

With me.

That's not what he meant.

You sure?

He was losing his mind.

She'd be home. Things would go back to the way they used to be.

Is that what you really want?

"Then what?" Kristi asked, probably because she thought he and Brooke were too close to each other.

"She's studying business. She wants to help run the ranch and take some of the weight off my shoulders. She's smart. Driven. Knows what she wants and goes after it."

"That's for sure," Kristi said under her breath.

Cody knew exactly how Kristi felt about Brooke. They would probably never be friends. It would make things easier if they got along. He tried to stay neutral but sometimes he wished they liked each other. Of course, the last thing he needed was for them to gang up on him.

To keep him from commenting, Kristi prompted her father. "Daddy, tell him why you wanted to talk to him."

Kirk gave his daughter an indulgent look. "So impatient."

She beamed. "I'm excited."

Kirk focused on him. "Kristi tells me things between you two have been really good these last many months. Her mother and I like seeing our girl happy."

"So do I," Cody agreed. What else could he say? He and Kristi got on well. They enjoyed each other's company. The sex had been better in the beginning but was still good. They'd settled into a sort of routine. One Kristi didn't always appreciate or like because his busy schedule dictated when he could see her. But what guy wouldn't want to be with someone who went out of their way to accommodate them? He liked that Kristi made allowances for him with minimal grumbling when plans had to change last minute because he was stuck in court or needed to be at the ranch for some emergency.

"And are you looking toward the future?" Kirk sipped his bourbon and eyed him.

"I feel like I'm in the thick of building what I want that future to look like." It probably wasn't the answer Kristi and Kirk wanted, but it was the truth and they could make of it what they would, because he was with Kristi, even if he hadn't put a lot of thought into their future. She was convenient, available to him when he wanted to see her, and he simply didn't have the time to contemplate where things were going to end up when he was content enough with right now. His thoughts didn't flatter Kristi.

She was considerate, smart, helpful, and affectionate. He appreciated her easy manner, especially when he was in a mood.

Kristi hugged him tighter and stared up at him with excitement. "You work really hard. And while I love the time we spend together, I wish you'd enjoy life a bit more." That was her nice way of saying she wanted him to spend less time at work and more with her.

"Young men on the rise don't have the luxury of leisure time, darling." Kirk gave Cody an approving nod for focusing on work. "You two will have plenty of time together in the years to come."

Cody wouldn't touch that statement with a ten-foot pole. While he didn't have a lot of long-term relationships under his belt, he knew he and Kristi needed a lot more time to see if this thing could go the distance.

Kristi blushed and nodded at her father. "Cody and I are solid. I'm excited to see his plans come to fruition in the near future. He's working hard and winning his cases." Her eyes shone with pride.

So supportive. He rewarded her with a soft kiss. "Thank you, sweetheart."

Kirk nodded again, like he'd come to some decision. "As you know, I have a lot of connections in this state. An opportunity has come up that I think you'd be perfect for"—he pointed his bourbon glass at Cody—"and would make your rising star shine a bit brighter."

Anticipation and excitement fluttered in his gut. "I'm open to hearing about it." Though cautious, because he wondered if whatever Kirk had in mind came with conditions and strings attached.

"Governor Harris, as you know, is extremely excited about the new children's hospital that opened several months ago. He and I, and others, including your father, were instrumental in pulling the funding together for the project. Of course, the governor ran on a platform that included helping children, especially in getting the healthcare those most vulnerable need."

"My father would have been proud to see the new hospital open. I've heard nothing but good things about it and how it's impacted the community. The previous clinic wasn't able to keep up with the demand for care. Families had to drive into the city to get the services they needed."

"Exactly why it was so necessary. And to make sure the hospital is run well and thrives for years to come, we as board members take our job very seriously." Kirk sipped his drink again, letting it hang there that he was on the board, which gave him clout and power.

Cody wondered what any of this had to do with him. "Lives are on the line, along with jobs. And having community support means people care about the hospital, the patients, and those supporting and running it."

Kirk grinned. "I knew you'd see the big picture. That's why I spoke to the governor about who we should tap to fill the upcoming vacant board member seat. While he doesn't serve on the board because of his political position, he's still very active with the board members who do. Since he and I were longtime friends with your father, and you and I have an even more personal connection with you seeing my daughter, I recommended that the upcoming vacant seat on the board should go to you."

Cody gasped at Kirk's offer. "I'm..." *Speechless.* "Intrigued. And honored." He'd never thought about taking on a board position. He'd been too focused on building his reputation as a lawyer. But being a part of something his father had invested his time and resources into would be so rewarding. He'd do his father proud watching over the hospital, its patients and staff, making sure it ran smoothly and provided everything the community needed.

"You'd make a great addition to the team with your legal expertise. The pro bono work you do for children hasn't gone unnoticed." Kirk looked from him to Kristi, letting Cody know Kristi had filled him in on his extracurricular work.

He didn't talk about the work he did for a legal aid foundation. He was a criminal attorney. Sometimes kids got into trouble and needed someone to see that they deserved a second chance. Most of the kids he helped came from low-income households with parents who were struggling to get by. Kids did desperate things when life felt dire and hunger was a way of life. He tried to turn things around for the kids he helped before they ended up in gangs and as career criminals.

Kirk went on. "I'll put your name forward to the board. With Governor Harris backing my recommendation, too, you'll be a sure win for the seat."

Overwhelmed, he said, "I'll need more details about the job." He didn't want to put Kirk on the spot in the middle of the barbecue, but he needed specifics before he got too caught up and agreed without knowing exactly what he was getting into.

"Well, my daughter won't thank me for adding a few more hours and responsibilities to your plate, but I think you're up for the challenge."

"Of course he is. And he can always cut back on his hours at the ranch," Kristi interjected.

Cody kept his attention on Kirk, not wanting to upset Kristi by reminding her yet again that he enjoyed being on the ranch, outdoors, doing manual labor. It grounded him.

"The board meets once a month. Depending on what's on the agenda, it could be anywhere from four to eight hours of work. We handle a lot of time-sensitive things via email and video conferences." Kirk smirked. "And the pay is more than fair. The only thing is, I need your answer now. I want to put your name in before anyone else on the board submits someone else and it turns into a pissing match. But like I said, with the governor backing you, too, it's a sure thing."

Cody thought about how his father spent a great deal of his life giving back to others and helping those around him, including the opening of the hospital before his death. His father would want him to do this. And in this moment, he felt as close to his father as he had before his death.

He held his hand out to Kirk. "I'm in. Thank you for recommending me and having such faith in me to take on this task. I won't let you down. I'd be proud to carry on what my father started in supporting the hospital and its workers and patients."

Kirk pumped his hand then held on. "Not only did I do it because I respected your father and I see a lot of him in you, but hell, son, we're practically family. In fact, I'd love for you to come to dinner next Sunday."

Kristi beamed with joy. She'd been trying to get him to spend time with her parents at their family dinners for the last month.

"I'll be there." Cody barely had time to think about what he'd have to rearrange on his schedule at the ranch to make it happen when Governor Harris and his wife approached and Kirk called out, "Come meet our new board member."

Governor Harris smacked Cody on the back. "Well, all right then, son. I knew you were smart and savvy enough to seize the opportunity. Your father always told me you had big plans beyond the ranch. He liked to dabble in this and that, as you well know. He was always looking out for the community. He had my back during my campaigns. Now, I get to repay the favor through you." He held out his hand. "I hope this will be a long and prosperous friendship."

Cody shook the governor's hand. "Thank you."

He received another smack on the back from Kirk. "Now you're playing with the big boys."

Governor Harris laughed and jabbed Cody in the ribs. "Watch yourself. This one always has something up his sleeve."

Kirk smirked and shrugged like he didn't know what the governor was talking about, but Cody knew what Kirk wanted. His daughter happy. And he thought that happiness came from Cody. They were together. But Cody now felt the tug of obligation where he used to simply be pleased to have her by his side. He tried to let it roll off him but the way Kirk looked from him to Kristi's beaming face, their hands clasped together, then back at him, said everything about the situation and what it meant going forward.

Kirk wanted Cody to keep his daughter happy. In return, Kirk would support him for the seat on the board and any other things he could use to boost Cody's standing in the community and in his career to ensure his daughter got the life Kirk felt she deserved.

Since everything aligned for Cody at the moment, he didn't let the sense of obligation weigh too heavy on him. Right now, he thought about the good he could do on the hospital board.

He couldn't wait to tell Brooke about it.

The party was in full swing. Most of the guests had already gotten their food and were spread out among the tables. Brooke and her friends were still out on the grass, most of them with plates of food and drinks. Brooke and Mindy Sue were talking while Mindy Sue's boyfriend hovered nearby.

Cody said a quick goodbye and thank-you to Kirk and the governor, who were already in conversation with the Whites, who owned three car dealerships in the two nearby towns.

Kristi gripped his arm before he headed toward Brooke. "Where are you going?"

"To tell Brooke the great news."

A flash of annoyance lit Kristi's blue eyes. "You can tell her later. Let's grab our plates and eat before we watch the fireworks together with my mom and dad." That sounded nonnegotiable.

Cody bristled, but let it go. He didn't want Kirk or the governor to see them bickering. Not now. Not right after

Kirk had plainly made it clear he wanted Cody to keep Kristi happy.

She pulled him toward the buffet. "We can talk about you coming to Sunday dinner and figure out our schedules for next week and set up a couple of dates."

He didn't miss the implied order.

"I miss you, Cody. Now that you're going to have even more to do, we're going to have to work that much harder to spend time together so this works out."

Did she mean their relationship or the board member seat her father offered him?

"Well, it sounds like we'll be having Sunday dinner with your folks for the foreseeable future."

Her smile lit up her whole face. "I knew this was what you wanted and would bring us closer together." She wrapped her arms around his neck and kissed him. Slowly. With the sultry vibe that had been ever-present in the beginning of their relationship. "This is the start of something more for both of us. I always knew we were good together. Now, I feel like we're really a couple. Partners. And that means so much." She kissed him again, this time with a hint of the passion they'd had when they first got together. A promise for what was to come when all eyes weren't on them. Because Cody could feel everyone staring. And when the kiss ended, he caught the satisfaction in Kirk's eyes that matched the one coming from his daughter's as she smiled at him, locked in his arms.

But there was someone else he wanted to share his good news with. He caught Brooke's eye and tilted his head toward the house.

She nodded and started walking in from the grass to the patio.

Cody brushed a quick kiss on Kristi's lips and held both her hands in his. "Get a plate and find us a seat and I'll join you in a few minutes."

"Where are you going?"

He spotted Brad and two of their friends standing on the patio. "I just want to say hi to my friends and use the restroom before I sit down to eat with you."

She looked past him at Brad, John, and Juan. "Okay. But don't get all involved talking about sports and horses or whatever."

He chuckled. "I promise. Back in a few." He headed toward his friends, noting that Brooke had just gone through the French doors into his study. He didn't dare look back to see if Kristi was watching to see if he joined her there.

He wasn't sneaking around. He was just trying to spare Kristi's feelings. She didn't need to be jealous of Brooke.

Are you sure?

Yes. Because maybe his feelings for Brooke were a little mixed up right now, but he'd get his head on straight and things would go back to the way they'd always been.

Right?

Fuck!

He said hi to his buddies and shot the shit for a moment before excusing himself and heading into the house through the living room French doors, then made his way into his study, where he found Brooke waiting for him, looking too tempting in that tight-as-hell denim skirt.

I'm in so much trouble.

Chapter Four

B rooke was waiting in Cody's office, wondering why he'd asked her to meet him alone.

Did something happen with Kristi? Did they have a fight? Break up?

She couldn't be that lucky.

She paced in front of his desk, wondering if Cody was thinking about him pulling her into his lap. It wasn't the first time she'd done it over the years. When she was younger, she'd climb into his lap all the time to talk and be close to him. At some point, he'd told her she was too big and she'd transitioned to sitting by his side, as close as she could get to him. He didn't mind. He never minded.

Until today.

No. She wasn't going to make a big deal about it.

He'd been annoyed at Brad for flirting. If that's even what he'd been doing.

She'd known him forever. Brad was just trying to get a rise out of Cody.

"What's that face for?" Cody asked walking into the study and closing the door behind him.

"It's just my face. What did you want to see me about?"

"First, I'm sorry I haven't done the whole welcome speech you wanted to do."

She waved that away. "People seem to be having fun. The caterers are serving dinner now. The fireworks show is sure to cap off the night with a bang." She gave him a cheeky grin. "We can say something in between to thank everyone for coming."

He leaned back against the front of his desk as she stood in front of him. "You really outdid yourself on the party. I know I wasn't excited about having it, but…"

"Go on, say it." She smirked.

He mock glared and grinned at the same time. "You were right." The words came out with a reluctant but amused sound.

She chuckled. "There it is."

He hooked his arm around her neck and pulled her into a hug, kissing her on the forehead. "Don't gloat."

She grinned up at him, her hands on his chest. "Don't ruin my moment."

He squeezed her tight, then let her loose and grinned so big she knew something was coming.

"What is it? Is this about whatever Kristi set up with her father?" She hoped it was something good.

"He offered me a seat on the board of directors of the new children's hospital."

"The one Dad helped build?"

Cody's smile grew. "Yes. I'll get to help steer its course and oversee that it's being managed well and growing with the community."

She leapt back into his arms and hugged him. "That's amazing. I'm so proud of you." She leaned back to look him in the eyes. "*He'd* be so proud of you."

"It makes it even better to know that he'd want me to do this." He gently set her away from him, though it felt a little slower than usual, with a reluctance she was sure couldn't be real.

She pushed down her skirt, drying her damp palms. "He'd know you'd have the best interest at heart for everyone involved, from the patients to the workers to the community needs. This is amazing." She lost a bit of her smile. "I bet Kristi is excited."

"Yes and no. It means I'll be working even more."

"For something that is so worthy of your time and attention."

"I know. And she knows that, too. She just wants us to spend more time together."

Brooke dropped her gaze to the floor. "She's here often enough."

Cody eyed her. "What's that supposed to mean?"

She shrugged. "It's just an observation."

Cody folded his arms over his chest, making his biceps strain his shirt sleeves and stretch over his wide shoulders. *Have mercy.* "Why don't you like her?"

"*She* doesn't like *me*. She treats me like an annoying gnat, which I find odd considering I'm the closest person to you."

Cody's eyes took on a thoughtful look, like he hadn't thought about the fact that the woman in his life didn't want to befriend the person who loved him the most.

Brooke looked at Cody from under her lashes. "Because of how she acts, I'm not inclined to try too hard to like her, because she doesn't seem right for you."

They didn't seem to click. Not in the forever kind of way. He wasn't desperate to be with her. He didn't spend all his time talking to her on the phone or texting her.

Maybe that wasn't their thing.

Still. Where was the need and passion?

She never saw it between them.

Well, except Kristi desperately trying to keep Cody away from Brooke.

And he'd have told her if their relationship was different. Special. He told her everything.

Well, most everything. Cody kept his relationships with women, for the most part, private to spare her feelings.

Feelings they didn't speak about or acknowledge outright. It was their not-so-secret secret.

And everyone who knew them knew about it.

So embarrassing.

But it didn't change how she felt. Or some of the impulsive things she did, that in hindsight could be termed cringeworthy.

Cody didn't meet her gaze when he admitted, "Kristi and I are good together. She gets me and what I can give and what I can't."

She wanted to put her hand on his arm in comfort and feel the corded muscles in his forearm bunch beneath her hand, but controlled her impulse. "I assume you're referring to your insane schedule."

Cody unfolded his arms and put his hands on either side of his hips on the edge of the desk. "I can't help that. She knows it. And I like the way things are between us. It's...uncomplicated. For now, that's enough."

Yeah, she and Cody would be all kinds of complicated. But wouldn't it be worth it if they loved each other?

Did he have that with Kristi? "So you guys have that thing?"

Cody raised a brow. "What thing?"

"The thing you can't explain that connects you and makes you want to be with that person all the time. Like not being with them isn't an option." *Because that's how I feel about you. And if that's how you feel about her...*

Please don't feel that way about her.

Cody ran a hand over his neck, letting her know he was uncomfortable. "Why are we talking about this?"

"Everyone wants something. If you don't have it with her, then what is the thing you want?" If she knew that, then maybe she could give it to him and be what and who he wanted.

Cody hesitated for a moment. They'd never been shy about opening up with each other. It was something he only did with her. So it didn't surprise her that he answered her very personal question with a truth that floored her.

"I want something and someone real. Someone who stays even when things are hard."

With both of them sharing a parent having walked out on them, she understood what he meant. "You deserve that, Cody, and so much more."

"That's what you and I have." The quiet sincerity in his voice made the words sound even more emotional.

The words hit her right in the heart.

If they had that, then what did he have with Kristi that made him stay with her and not even look at Brooke as someone he couldn't live without? In that special way. Not the friendship way he always boxed them into.

They'd forged their connection over the years based on unbridled truth and open honesty in all things. She felt like they could take that foundation and turn it into something even more intimate and amazing.

But just like all the times she flirted and tried to show him how she felt in the past, he turned away and didn't say anything about seeing the hope and yearning he couldn't miss in her eyes as she stared at him, wondering if he would ever see her as something more than his friend.

Cody pushed around folders on his desk, not meeting her gaze now.

She tried to put him at ease again. "I'm really excited for you and this new opportunity. You're going to be great."

A slow grin grew on his too-handsome face as his blue eyes lit up. "Maybe you were right about throwing the party and inviting all these people."

She eyed him and smirked. "Maybe? Come on, you can say it again," she teasingly taunted.

He stepped closer and stared down, directly into her eyes.

Her breath hitched whenever they were this close. Which was never often enough, in her estimation. He had to hear her heart thundering in her chest and feel the anticipation she couldn't hide, even if it was for something he probably had no intention of doing. Though her lips and heart begged for it.

"Is that really what you want? For me to pour out my gratitude and tell you, you always know what's best for me?"

It wouldn't hurt. But... "I want you..." She paused for the barest of seconds. Long enough to see his eyes flare, then narrow on her mouth. "To smile, like you used to before we lost him."

His expression softened. "What's there to smile about? I've been working my ass off since he died climbing the ladder at work and keeping this ranch running." His gaze shifted to the window behind her as he whispered, "And you're not here most of the time to give me something to smile about."

Oh how her heart lit up with joy, but she hid her grin. She didn't want to make him uncomfortable about reluctantly admitting that he missed her while she was away at school. In little more than a month, she'd be back on campus in the dorms with Mindy Sue.

But this moment... She'd never forget it.

While he shared most things with her, his feelings about her were never spoken. Though she knew how he felt. He loved her. He liked her. He trusted her.

All the things you needed as a foundation for a relationship. One Cody made sure she knew was as a friend. But maybe after three years of her being away at school, he felt something more than just her absence. Maybe more than missing her, he wanted her.

She took a chance, stepped in closer to him, put her hands on his wide shoulders, and rose on her tiptoes, bringing their faces close.

His breath hitched.

She slowly leaned in, her heart jackhammering in her chest.

A second before she kissed him, his hands clamped onto her hips. He held her immobile, fingers digging in.

She liked the bite of his fingertips and wondered if he'd leave his mark. She hoped so.

His gaze darkened. "I should go find Kristi and her father." Several seconds passed with their mouths inches apart. Her holding him. Him holding her. Then he stepped back, his fingertips scraping off the denim of her skirt. Like he could hardly bear to let her go? Her hands dropped off his shoulders. He walked past and out the door, slamming it, like he couldn't get away fast enough.

The rejection stung. Her heart throbbed with the pain of coming so close and not getting her chance to prove to Cody how much she loved him.

This was the first time she'd gotten that close to what she wanted and he'd touched her in a way that wasn't friendly and innocent. That grip he had on her...the way he looked at her...it felt like he'd been holding himself back.

Why? Couldn't he see how good they could be together?

No. Not if he walked away like that.

Maybe it was time to grow up and face reality.

If she didn't stop throwing herself at him, she might end up losing him.

What was the point anyway when he kept walking away?

Cody didn't know what happened. One minute Brooke was teasing him that she'd been right about throwing the party even if it brought up too many memories for him about his father, the next she was so close he could smell her favorite strawberries on her breath and the coconut sunscreen she used to keep her pale skin from burning. The cocktail of her scent went right to his head. His hands shot out and gripped her hips. The feel of her under his hands made him hold tighter. He was probably hurting her, but he couldn't seem to release his hold. And another part of him liked the feel of her too much to even think of the consequences. His dick perked up. It wasn't the first time in the last month since Brooke had been home from college that he'd looked at her and his body stirred with a desire he shouldn't feel or want.

Did she have to come down to breakfast every morning in nothing but flannel shorts and a tank top? When did her jeans start molding to her perfect ass like that? Why did seeing her smile make him think of other things she could do with those full lips?

When did she stop being just Brooke and start being a temptation?

Why the fuck had he said those things to her about wanting something and someone real, who'd stay even when things got hard?

You certainly are. For her.

But he'd meant it.

Brooke was the one person he knew would never turn her back on him or leave. She would always be there for him no matter what.

That meant everything to him.

She was his friend. Probably the best one he'd ever have.

Off-limits to the sensual thoughts he was having about her.

She was too young. Too inexperienced. Too naïve. Too lost in the puppy love she'd had for him for years to see that she had no idea what it would really mean if Cody gave in and gave her what she thought she wanted.

She was too important—too special—to fuck it all up with...well, fucking her.

Because if he did...he feared he'd lose her.

That could not happen. He needed her. Without her...his life was...dull. Faded. She brought the light and fun into his life.

She wanted and deserved a fairy tale happy-ever-after kind of thing. He was too cynical. He had far more life experience than the girl he'd watched grow up before his eyes, who'd never even had a serious boyfriend.

He didn't want to think about the guys she probably dated at college.

None of his damn business, even if he kept a close eye on her.

Thinking of her showering all her affection and joy on some other guy made him feel too raging bull and possessive.

There needed to be a line between them.

His father had asked him to continue to look out for her before he died. He made Cody the executor of the estate and in charge of Brooke's inheritance until she came of age.

He swore he'd take care of her always.

And her mother, too.

And putting his hands on Brooke that way was crossing a line.

This wasn't some welcome home hug, an affectionate kiss on the cheek. This was...more.

She knew it, too.

He needed to get his head on straight and stop thinking the things he'd been thinking about and desiring lately.

It needed to stop before he did something stupid. Something he couldn't take back. Something that crossed a line and might make her turn away. Something that might make her hate him. Something that hurt her.

That was the last thing he ever wanted to do.

Nothing was worth losing what they'd shared these last many years and what they'd always have if he just kept his head—and his hands off her perfect body. The one she'd grown into the last few years and he'd ignored until recently.

If she wouldn't think of the consequences, he had to do it for both of them.

He didn't look at her as he left. "Fled" probably described his action better than anything. But he had to do it. Because one more second of her being that close, of her warmth seeping into him, her scent filling him, his desire rising, and he'd have lost all sense and given in to the temptation she'd suddenly become.

He found Kristi at one of the picnic tables and pulled her close as she smiled up at him. He didn't much feel like smiling back but he did because it was expected. The woman at his side didn't feel half as good as the one he'd just left. He'd barely touched Brooke. And yet it cracked something open inside him.

He focused on Kristi and told his brain to fucking stop thinking about Brooke and that breathless moment they shared in his study.

A moment he would always remember without regret. A moment filled with promise and yearning and potential and possibility. A moment he could hold her and the notion that for a brief second they were of the same mind and heart before reality hit, the breach Brooke opened inside him sealed, leaving this persistent ache, and he had to do the right thing.

Brooke wasn't for him.

He had a beautiful woman here, not headed back to college, and her family was helping him achieve the success he'd been dreaming about and working hard to reach. Did it matter that his relationship with Kristi helped to make it happen? No. Not really. Because in life, sometimes it was who you knew, not your experience or expertise, that opened doors.

How he got the job didn't matter as much as how well he did it. And Cody couldn't wait to show Kirk and the governor that their faith in him wasn't misplaced and he deserved it.

He settled into the embrace with Kristi and the bond they were forging.

When thoughts about that moment in his office with Brooke, how it felt good and right to have her in his hands—even if it had been on the precipice of cheating—popped up, he ignored them.

Well, he tried.

Chapter Five

I'*m such a fool!*

Cody wasn't interested in Brooke like that. She should know better after all the times she'd pushed and he'd stepped back. She forced this unfair dance on him. Again.

He had a girlfriend. He wasn't a cheater.

Yet *she'd* put him in that position.

It wasn't the first time either.

Her hand went to her roiling stomach.

I sure know how to mess things up.

What he must think of her.

She wondered if he ever teased her behind her back with his friends. Or worse, if they'd teased him about being pursued by a kid. Because that's what she'd been compared to him, just a few short years ago. Seven years older than her, his twenty-seven to her twenty didn't seem so great now. But she imagined Cody at twenty might have been embarrassed on several occasions to have a thirteen-year-old girl hot on his heels when he came home and hung out with his college buddies on the ranch.

Oh God!

Her face flamed with embarrassment.

She needed to start acting like the adult she was and think about others. Cody would hate himself for cheating on a girlfriend. Kristi would be hurt and angry, too. And while Brooke didn't think Kristi was Cody's forever, she was who he'd chosen to be with right now.

Every time Brooke presented him with the choice to be with her, he didn't take it.

Apparently, she couldn't take a hint. Or an outright dismissal.

It ends now.

She needed to stop this merry-go-round before she hurt Cody and lost him.

She loved him. And if that was really true, then she needed to accept him as he was. Her friend.

The weight of that settled on her, heavy and sorrowful.

Things needed to change.

She needed to change.

Time to be the grown-up, not just pretend she was.

Mindy Sue met her on the grass as Brooke approached their group of friends. "What's wrong?" Mindy Sue studied her, concern in her eyes.

Brooke frowned and confessed. "I nearly screwed everything up with Cody."

Mindy Sue shook her head. "It can't be that bad. You two are so close."

"I tried to kiss him, thinking we were having this amazing moment. But like always, it was all in my head, and he stepped away."

Stormed away, you mean.

He kept the line between them firmly in place. He never scolded her. He acted like an adult. She was the child, always trying to take what she wanted without thinking of the consequences.

Mindy Sue wrapped her in a hug. "I'm sorry." Mindy Sue knew all her secrets, including the one about how much she loved Cody and dreamed of a life with him here on the ranch.

You mean a fantasy.

One that would never come true.

"I made a fool of myself. Again. And it stops now."

Mindy Sue hugged her and whispered, "Maybe it's for the best. There are so many guys at school who would love to take you out. Guys who are...less complicated than dating Cody."

Less complicated than her stepbrother, Mindy Sue meant.

Mindy Sue held her by the shoulders. "So many you've already turned down because you're waiting for him."

"Not anymore." Because she was waiting for something that would never happen. Cody cared about her, but not that way. Never that way.

Oh how it hurt.

A tear slid down her cheek.

Mindy Sue saw it and wiped it away with her thumb. "You deserve someone who will love you back."

She pressed her lips tight and blinked back the tears. She wouldn't cry over him anymore. "You're right. It's time for a change. I think I need a back-to-school shopping spree. A new look to go with the new me. You in?"

Mindy Sue beamed and jumped up and down, excited. She excelled at shopping. "Yes. Definitely."

"And I'll take you up on the salon day you always offer and I decline. Hair. Nails. The works. But when we get back to school." She didn't want Cody to think she was doing it to catch his attention. She wanted to settle into the new her away from everyone here. She didn't need anyone teasing her about trying to be different when all they saw was the same old her.

The next time she came home, she'd be who she wanted to be.

Mindy Sue bounced on her toes. "It's going to be so much fun."

Marco walked up and hooked his arm around Mindy Sue's shoulders. "Are you two going to join us or what?"

Mindy Sue leaned into him. "Yes. We were just making plans for when we get back to school."

"Ugh," Jeramiah groaned. "Let's not go there. It's summer. No school talk. We're here to have fun."

Brooke settled on the grass and took the plate of food Mindy Sue handed her. "Thank you."

"I wanted to be sure you actually ate at your own party." They bumped shoulders.

Brooke glanced at Simon beside her. "Who won the cornhole match?"

"Believe it or not, Adam." Simon glared at the guy next to him, who had that kind of cute geek vibe. "Dude smoked us."

Adam pushed his empty plate away. "Do you know how many county fairs and summer picnics I've been dragged to over the years by my old man?"

"Sorry you had to be at this one, too." Brooke didn't know Marco's friends well, but Adam she'd seen several times at various get-togethers, usually lurking in a corner or out of the way of everything as his father, the governor, took center stage. He'd been to the ranch a few times in the past, though they'd never really spoken.

Simon, on the other hand, spent a lot of time with Marco, and with Brooke by extension of Mindy Sue dating Marco. She liked Simon. He was laid-back and addicted to coffee and his phone. The biology student was obsessed with plants and their medicinal uses. He loved researching other cultures and the plants they used for healing.

Brooke found it interesting, but also a little creepy that he could name ten plant toxins that could kill you off the top of his head.

Adam draped his arms over his knees and clasped his hands. "At least I've got you guys here to give me an excuse to ditch the parentals and their bullshit. Fake smiling and feigning interest in everyone is exhausting."

Marco rolled his eyes. "Everyone fucking kisses your ass because you're the governor's son."

Adam rolled his eyes, too. "Exactly. They don't know me. They don't give a shit about me. It's all about him."

"So what are you into?" Brooke asked. "Are you a poli-sci major?"

His gaze dropped. "Yes."

He didn't seem happy with his choice. "I guess you'd have to be with a governor as your father. So, is it an expectation or a calling?" She'd bet expectation based on his tense shoulders.

"Mostly it's an expectation. I like it though. My background makes it easier to relate to the material in my classes."

"Are you thinking of following your father's footsteps into public office someday?"

Simon and Marco scoffed.

Marco explained why the idea seemed ludicrous to them. "You might be the first girl our boy Adam has ever spoken to without some liquid courage."

Adam's cheeks flamed red and Marco laughed.

"You're so fucking awkward, dude." Marco flinched when Mindy Sue tapped him in the gut. "What was that for?"

Mindy Sue stared daggers at him. "Be nice. Adam's shy."

"Yeah, he and Simon are going to be virgins for life at the rate they actually interact with the opposite sex."

"Fuck you," Simon barked.

Mindy Sue scooted far away from Marco. "What is wrong with you? That's not just rude. It's mean."

"Babe." Marco reached for Mindy Sue but she swatted him away.

Mindy Sue's frown sank deep. "No. Apologize."

Marco fumed, but turned to Adam and Simon. "Sorry." Under his breath, he added, "Even if it's true."

Brooke heard him, but Mindy Sue and their friend Julie sat behind him and missed it.

Adam and Simon both looked at Brooke and flushed with embarrassment.

Mindy Sue stood and stared down at Marco. "Let's go get something to drink."

He held up his half glass of lemonade. "I'm good."

Mindy Sue huffed out a frustrated breath. "Come with me." She started walking away.

Marco reluctantly stood and went with her.

Julie gathered up the empty plates. "I'll take care of these. Back in a sec."

Jeremiah followed her with the empty cups.

Brooke found herself with the two uncomfortable guys. She tried to make them more relaxed and went back to her original conversation with Adam. "So if you're not interested in being the candidate, what do you want to do?"

Adam stared at the grass but answered her. "I prefer the behind-the-scenes aspect of politics. Campaigns, fact-finding on causes and legislation, analysis of the viability of being for or against something, finding the best way to give the masses what they want in the most economical and fair way. Those kinds of things."

Brooke gave Adam a smile as he glanced her way finally. "You're a numbers guy. I envy you that. I'll bet you aced your calculus and statistics classes."

He tried to hide his grin. "That's where I excel."

"It's where I fail," she confessed.

Simon's gaze shot to her. "You failed your math class?"

"Well, not literally. I think the highest grade I got in any math course was a B plus, and that took many sleepless nights studying until my eyes were more red than green."

Simon set his phone down for once. "Me, too. I prefer facts to figures."

Adam offered, "If you need a tutor, I'd be happy to help."

"Thanks," she said sincerely. "But I've actually completed all my math prerequisites. I got them out of the way early. I figured if I pulled my hair out all in the first three years, then nobody would remember me as the bald graduate next year."

"Your hair looks good to me." Simon's shyness flared as his gaze dipped away, then came back to her.

"Thanks. I didn't have to take a math class this past semester. It gave me time to grow it back," she teased. She glanced past Simon to Adam, who'd gone quiet. "It must be hard to excel at anything and be recognized for your accomplishments when your father is such a high-profile figure."

Adam's head snapped up. His gaze met hers. "It's like living in the shadow of a huge cloud. He starts rumbling and everyone turns to stare at him to see what he has to say and what he's going to do. It's like I don't exist."

Simon bumped his shoulder to Adam's. "Tell me about it. Everyone kisses my dad's ass."

"What does your dad do?" Brooke was happy she had this chance to get to know them better.

"He and his family own Opal Oil."

Damn. They were billionaires. She didn't know what to say, except, "Wow. How does he feel about you studying biology instead of business or something?"

"He's more interested in my older brother, who's happy to join the family business."

"That must be hard."

Simon shook his head and wrapped his arms around his knees. "Trust me. I prefer it that way."

"At least you've got someone to take the focus off you," Adam said, reminding them he was an only child.

"I guess I'm lucky," Brooke said. "My mom supports everything I do."

"What about your dad?" Adam asked. "Not Harland Jansen. I know he passed a couple years ago. But your real dad?"

How does he know that?

She didn't like thinking about how her real dad left and never looked back. "I don't know anything about what he's doing now. He left us a long time ago. It's just me, my mom, and Cody now."

Simon scrunched his mouth. "Do you get along with him? Everything between me and my brother is a competition. And he wins all the time."

"I'm sure that's not true. And Cody isn't my brother. We're friends. And he's older, and a guy, so I never felt like I had to compete with him. He always felt like someone I could count on to help me."

"Must be nice," Adam commented, and Simon nodded his agreement. "What are your plans after graduation?"

Brooke had put a lot of thought into what came next but didn't have an actual plan. "I own part of the ranch, so I'll help Cody run it."

"Really?" Adam looked skeptical. "Is that an expectation or what you really want to do?" She smirked at him. "I see what you did there, throwing my question to you back at me."

"Answer it," he cajoled with a knowing grin.

"I love the ranch. Especially the horses. But there is something else I've thought about doing. But...it's a silly idea."

"I bet it's not." Adam stared at her, waiting.

"Putting together this party brought up a lot of memories of my stepdad and made me think." She paused, unsure if she should say it out loud.

Adam and Simon stared, their gazes open and earnest for her to go on.

"I want to continue what my stepfather taught me. Community is everything. He supported local businesses.

I want to do that, too, to keep our small businesses alive and thriving. I have some money. I thought I'd maybe open my own business or something." Her heart pounded. She couldn't believe she'd spoken that tiny little seed of a dream out loud.

Adam perked up. "My dad was talking to someone when we arrived. She was telling him that her local bookstore was probably going to close because she wants to retire next year and she can't find anyone interested in buying or running it. You could do it."

She had her inheritance. Cody managed it until she turned twenty-one next year. Investing in a small business sounded like a great idea. She loved reading romance and all its subgenres, fantasy, and thrillers. She could turn her love of books into a job she loved.

Adam shrugged. "I'd like to ditch my parents' expectation and spend my days being a bookworm in a quiet shop."

Brooke grinned. "It does sound lovely." She imagined it in her head. "There's a vacant space next to the bookstore. I could turn it into a café."

Simon sat up straighter. "Now you're talking. Coffee, tea, cupcakes and other treats."

Brooke cocked her head toward the buffet. "They're setting out dessert right now. Let's head over and get some before all the double chocolate cupcakes are gone."

They all stood and Brooke met Adam's gaze. "Thanks for the suggestion. I'm going to look into the bookstore idea."

Adam smirked. "Okay. Good. I think you'd be really good at it."

Brooke looked from Adam to Simon. "You guys are really cool. I'm glad I got to know you better today."

"Maybe we can meet up at school for coffee or something," Simon suggested.

"I'd love to. With both of you."

Adam's anxious gaze dipped away with shyness but he nodded.

Simon's cheeks pinked.

"And the next time we're all together with Mindy Sue, Julie, Jeremiah, and Marco, I'll be sure to pay more attention to the group and not get lost in just the girls." She wanted them to be more comfortable around her. "Maybe I can even be your wing-woman when we're out and find you both a date."

Simon and Adam's eyes went wide with trepidation, then they both hurried their steps to the dessert table.

She grinned at their bashfulness.

This was what she needed, to focus on school and friends. Maybe soon she'd be ready to open her heart and start a relationship with someone new—instead of waiting for something that was never going to happen with Cody.

Chapter Six

She's amazing!

He stood in her dark bedroom. He wasn't nervous about being caught. He could make up some excuse about Brooke asking him to grab her a sweater. Being in here, amongst her things, energized him. The room felt like her. Warm. Inviting. It smelled like her. Roses and honey. Heady and sweet. He'd taken his time looking at all her stuff and realized a few new things about her. She liked soft comforts, like the chenille pillows and oatmeal-colored cashmere throw on her bed. She kept pictures of friends and family scattered everywhere around the room. Several of them—too many in his estimation—were of her with Cody.

They were obviously close and did a lot of things together. Horseback riding. Vacations. Eating out.

It irritated him. But there were just as many of her with Mindy Sue, too, so he didn't hold it against Brooke.

He didn't have such close connections to people. But he felt one to her.

He'd like to fill his room with pictures of her. And them together. Soon.

She'd promised they'd see each other more when they were back on campus.

He couldn't wait.

They'd finally connected.

It wasn't just him.

She sees me.

He watched her out the window, standing with everyone else waiting for the fireworks to begin.

She wanted him.

He knew it in his bones and down to his soul.

She was beautiful. Tempting. He wanted her to look up and see him, then rush in to be with him. She'd put her hands on him, her mouth. God, those fucking plump lips of hers were a distraction. He thought about them closing over his hard dick.

He stroked his hand over his shaft, wishing it was her hand on him. Falling into the image in his head, he unbuttoned and unzipped his pants and pulled out his aching cock.

Look at her! So fucking gorgeous!

And mine!

She stood with Mindy Sue and the rest of them, chatting away. Smiling. Fucking shining with joy. She glowed.

He bet her skin was soft as a flower petal.

He pumped his aching cock again.

He wanted to know what it felt like to slide inside her wet, hot, welcoming cavern.

Stroke.

Would she beg? Oh, he'd make her beg.

Stroke. Stroke.

He rubbed his hand from base to tip to the image of her doing it in his mind with her hand fisted around his shaft. Faster. Harder.

His cock felt like a steel rod.

His balls tightened.

Just thinking about her, looking at her standing there, oblivious to what she did to him, got him off.

Would she scream when she came?

He wanted her to.

He'd heard it could happen. Could he get her there? He'd need to figure out how.

He could do it. He wanted to do it.

He wanted to know what it felt like to be deep inside her, instead of jerking off with his fucking hand.

She was the one. His one and only.

Stroke.

At least, she would be. He'd find a way to make it happen.

It couldn't be that hard. She liked him.

He stroked himself again and again. So close.

He'd show her he could treat her right.

He couldn't wait to get back to school, back to them hanging out. He'd have to spend more time with Marco. He liked the guy well enough, though Marco could sometimes be an ass. Especially when he was drinking. But he offered the most important thing: proximity to Brooke. He'd suffer through anything to be with her.

She brushed a wisp of hair behind her ear and laughed at something Julie said to her.

Fuck. This girl is killing me with need.

It made him even harder. He spit into his hand and stroked himself while he took out the pair of panties from his pocket with his free hand. He'd stolen them from her dirty laundry. Purple with white polka dots and lace trim. So sexy.

He stared at the beautiful woman who didn't even know how pretty she was and came with a grunt as he bit his bottom lip so no one would hear him moan for her, though the house was quiet. The orgasm rolled through him, his cum staining her cute undies.

That was so fucking good.

Her wet, hot pussy would be even better.

He should get out of here. He didn't want to be found lurking in her room with purple lace and his cum wrapped around his dick.

He stuffed the panties in his pocket and tucked his junk back in his pants.

Brooke had stepped away from their friends and headed for her mom and stepbrother. He'd seen her with Cody before, all smiles and whispered words as her eyes ate him up. But this time, she didn't stand as close as she could get to him like he'd seen her do before. This time, she stood by her mom as Cody held the microphone, thanked everyone for coming, and then bid everyone to enjoy the show.

He was right. He'd stolen her attention. Now, she only wanted him.

I bet she's thinking about me right now?

Brooke suddenly looked up to where he stood in the window.

With the lights out, she wouldn't be able to see anything but his dark silhouette.

But she knew he was here.

In her room.

Soon, they'd be together.

You're already mine.

Chapter Seven

C ody couldn't believe how well the party turned out. Best of all, he and Kristi were having a good time together. They worked well as partners in conversations. There seemed to be a new easiness between them. She stayed by his side and smiled up at him every time an encounter with guests ended well, like she was proud of him. Proud to be with him. It stroked his ego and made him want her even more. They were like his dad and Susanne, sauntering around the party, making sure the guests were having a good time, but always aware of each other in the stolen glances and whispered comments shared only between them. Kristi had been the perfect companion as they made their way around the backyard, greeting guests. Her father had caught up to them multiple times to talk him up to one person after another.

Cody knew everyone here because of past parties, but he'd never interacted with them like a peer. That's what he was to them now that he'd established his career.

It seemed so strange and also like the very thing he'd been working toward the last several years.

It also made him miss his dad.

Cody wondered what he'd think of all this.

He looked at Brooke, standing beside Suzanne. Not him. She didn't even look at him.

Fuck.

He'd handled that thing—that fucking weak moment he'd had when she'd made a move—badly. He should have stepped away and ignored it like all the other times.

But this time had been different. The look in her eyes, filled with such innocent desire. He got caught up in it. No one looked at him the way she looked at him. Yes, it fucking made him feel good. Needed. Wanted. Like he was her everything.

It was too much and not enough all at the same time. He couldn't remember another woman ever looking at him like that.

Brooke, she did it all the time. And when she did, it was just different. It hit him in some amazing way he couldn't describe.

She wasn't shy or coy with him. She didn't hold back. She put it all out there.

He loved that about her.

He didn't want to tame that or shame her for wanting something she shouldn't.

He was too old for her.

She was too young to know that she'd eventually fall for someone less complicated and more suitable.

Did he want that?

He should.

But he loved the attention and the way she made him feel, even if he shouldn't.

Fuck.

What was he thinking? This couldn't happen. Especially not now.

He was with Kristi. They were looking toward the future. Sure, that was a new thing, but it was the start of something.

That's what the board seat was about. Him stepping into a bigger life.

He'd need a partner who knew that world and could stand beside him. Kristi had proved she was that person for him today.

Brooke was headed back to school soon. She'd barely begun her life as an adult.

Yes, she'd pulled off this amazing party. She'd gotten all these folks here for him.

But she wouldn't be here for dinner parties, charity benefits, and client dinners.

The house would go back to being too quiet. Lonely.

And after each long grueling day, he'd come home and spend the night missing her, because she wasn't here to sit in his office and talk about everything and nothing like they did when she was home.

One more school year and she'd be here for good. They'd share the house—she owned a third of the ranch. They'd work it together.

Right?

He couldn't imagine things going any other way.

She had to come back. This was where she belonged.

With me.

No, not like that.

Fuck.

Cody focused on the crowd and not Brooke standing away from him instead of by his side. "Thank you all for making this Fourth of July as special as the ones my father used to throw. And just like he used to do, we'll end things with a bang. Enjoy the fireworks." Cody hugged Susanne to his side and glanced over at Brooke just as the first explosion went off overhead in an array of red, white, and blue sparks.

Brooke gasped and stared up at the house instead of the sky, her eyes wide with shock.

"Brooke? What's wrong?" He followed her gaze but didn't see anything. "Brooke." His sharp tone got her attention.

She frowned, shook her head, then barely glanced at him as she said, "Nothing," and went to join her friends.

Susanne looked up at him. "What's going on with you two?"

"Nothing." The word shot out of him too fast to be believed.

Susanne's gaze narrowed, but she didn't push for more.

"We're fine." He said it to soothe her, but maybe he needed the reassurance more, because it felt like he'd hurt Brooke, even though that was never his intention.

As Kristi pulled him to her side near her parents and the governor and his wife to watch the show, he told himself it would all blow over in the morning. Everything would go back to the way it was.

But that's not what happened.

Brooke stayed at Mindy Sue's house for a week.

He was so busy he might not have noticed except that every night when he dragged his tired ass to bed, he saw her empty bed as he passed her room.

He hated the distance between them.

And then she was back and it felt like nothing had happened. She was her normal self, riding the horses during the day, helping the ranch hands when something needed to be done, chatting with him and Susanne at dinner when he made it home in time, and spending time texting and talking with her friends.

He got glimpses of her as he rushed to do one thing or another to keep up with work and prepare for the board member vote. Kirk invited him to several dinners to introduce him one by one to the other board members. Kristi had gone with him, talking him up just as much as her father did. He appreciated their support. And he and Kristi grew closer. He spent some of his nights in her bed, lost in her lush body, releasing all the tension he carried day to day. Within a month, it all seemed to be falling into place.

Except something still felt off with Brooke. He couldn't pinpoint exactly what it was, but it nagged at him.

The knock on his downtown office door surprised him, since he'd told his assistant an hour ago that he planned to spend his lunch break taking care of a personal matter, which basically let her know he wanted some time to himself. He'd been going nonstop for weeks. He'd like one lunch break where he wasn't going over a case or meeting a client.

"Come in," he reluctantly called out, knowing he was about to lose the quiet solitude he desperately needed.

The door opened and his jaw nearly dropped when he spotted Brooke, looking anything but like the girl he was used to seeing. She'd dressed up, done her hair and makeup, and carried a leather satchel in one hand and takeout from his favorite taqueria in the other. "I know you're not expecting me, but after weeks of waiting for you to finally have a break in your schedule, your assistant took pity on me and let me know you were spending your lunch hour alone." Before she even stepped all the way into the office, she added, "If you want to keep it that way, all you have to do is say so and I'll go."

"Come in," he growled with impatience. He waited for her to close the door and walk toward him before he asked, "What are you wearing?"

She stopped short and looked down at herself. "Clothes."

He shook his head. "That's not your normal look." And it threw him because she looked...lovely. He couldn't remember the last time he'd seen her with her hair down. Thick and long, it hung past her shoulders and brushed the tops of her breasts over the pretty white blouse she wore to go with a pair of black slacks and a killer pair of black heels. If he didn't know any better, he'd think she could be one of the interns working here.

"Like I said, I need to talk to you. I thought it best to dress appropriately to meet you in your office. Plus, I had a meeting in town that I wanted to be taken seriously for, so..." She held her hands out to emphasize her point.

He didn't like the self-conscious look on her face and tried to ease her mind. "You look really beautiful, Brooke."

Her whole body went still.

He meant what he said, but he hoped she didn't take it to mean more than it did. Though he was still taken aback by her appearance and the strange pull it made him feel toward her on top of the feelings he'd been resisting since she came home for summer break.

"Thank you." The sincerity in her voice surprised him. She seemed to catch herself staring at him and moved forward again and set the food bag on his desk as she dropped her satchel in one of the client chairs. "I got you your favorite carnitas fajitas with rice and beans." She pulled out his container and set it in front of him with a plastic fork and napkin.

"How many chicken tacos did you get?"

"Just two. I've got a lot to talk about, so I won't have a lot of time to eat and do that before your one o'clock meeting."

"Brooke, you don't need to make an appointment to talk to me. You know that."

She tilted her head and studied him. "When's the last time your day ended before the sun went down?"

He stared at her for a long moment, recognizing the emotion in her eyes. "You're worried about me."

"Yes. But that's not what I want to talk to you about." She handed him an orange Mexican soda.

He took the first bite of his food and groaned out his pleasure. "You want to talk about what happened between us at the picnic." His stomach knotted. He didn't want to say the wrong thing and hurt her again.

She shook her head. "It's not about that. But I do owe you an apology."

No, I owe you one.

But she continued before he could say anything. "Probably a lot of them for the stunts I've pulled over the years. I'm sorry. It won't happen again."

Disappointment washed over him. *What the hell!*

"You're with Kristi. I need to respect your choice and the boundaries of our relationship."

What?

"That's so...very grown-up." And it pissed him off. He didn't know why. But he didn't like any of this.

Brooke went on like he wasn't floundering inside. "Which is why I'm here. I need some money from my trust fund."

He smirked and shook his head. "Did you already spend your allowance going out with your friends?"

She thumped her soda bottle on his desk, her eyebrows narrowing. "Don't do that. Don't treat me like a child."

He sat up straighter and stared at her. "I'm not. I was joking."

She raised a brow. "That was very condescending. I'll be twenty-one next May. At which time, the trust fund will be mine without restrictions."

He didn't know what to do with this too-serious Brooke. "Until then, I decide how you spend the money."

"Exactly why I'm here. I'm going to graduate next June. I've been thinking about what I want to do next."

What? Really? "I assumed you'd help on the ranch, like we always talked about." Unless she'd changed her mind. If she did, she would have told him. They talked about everything. Didn't they?

She's here right now, talking to you. Listen!

"Yes, but with my business degree, a job as a project manager at some company seemed like the most likely thing to do aside from the ranch. But while I was planning the Fourth of July picnic and thinking about Dad and all he did for the community, I wondered if I could carry that on in some way."

She had his full attention. He leaned against his forearms on the edge of his desk, fajitas wrap in hand. "What are you thinking?"

"I want to help revive some of the local businesses downtown, starting with the bookstore. I learned from a friend at the barbecue that the owner is interested in retiring soon." She pulled out several folders from her bag and set them on the desk. "Mrs. Walters has run the place for thirty years. The store is cramped and the stock hasn't kept up with times and what's most popular, particularly when it comes to younger readers. I think I can revamp the store and make it more appealing to a wider audience of readers." She handed him the green folder. "In there is my business plan and proposed offer for the bookstore. Mrs. Walters is happy with the price and that the sale won't go through until March of next year."

"Why March?"

"Because she wants to do one more holiday season here in town and I'll need a few months for renovations before I open the store after I graduate."

"It's a small space, if I remember correctly. I doubt the renovation will take more than a month or so."

She handed him her red folder. "Inside there are four bids for not only renovating the bookshop, but also the empty space beside it. I want to turn it into a café attached to the bookstore. The second-story office spaces—four to be exact—need an overhaul, plus the four apartments on the third floor."

"Wait. You want to buy the whole building?"

"Yes. If you'll look at my business plan, you'll see that it makes the most sense to buy the distressed building, where the apartment tenants have long since vacated and only two of the four office spaces are in use. Their leases are up this December. I've had the building inspected and appraised. Mr. Scott, who has owned the building for sixty years and has no heirs and is willing to sell just to get rid of the headache of taking care of the place, has also agreed to my terms." She handed him the yellow folder. "Now, the building does need some big repairs and upgrades. The initial three bids I got for the work were okay. One low, one slightly higher, and one astronomically high. Then I remembered Dad used to talk about his friend Danny, who could fix anything."

Cody nodded, trying to get his bearings as she supplied him with information and awed him with her business acumen. "Danny Quinn. Quinn Construction. One of the biggest firms in the state."

"Well, I called him. He sent a guy. That's the fourth bid, which is much more detailed and below the highest bid I received. I assume the lower bids would have gone up as the project went on. For me, Quinn wins the bid, but you can take a look and determine that for yourself."

He held up the folders. "You did all this on your own over the last month?"

"Yes. I did my homework, consulted the right people, and put together the information needed to attain the money to buy the property and start my own businesses. Once I've got this up and running, I plan to take on the pizza place in town. They used to have the best food and service, but things have gone downhill over the last ten years. I think it could use a refresh."

He gaped. "You want to buy a restaurant?"

"Yes. Mrs. Marino has been running it since her husband died years ago of a heart attack. He ran the business. She doesn't really have the heart for it. And her kids have grown up and the last is about to go off to college. She hasn't had the money to invest in the business because she needed it for her kids. I think an infusion of cash, a fresh look, and an updated and more upscale menu will be welcomed downtown, especially now that there are several office buildings close by. With delivery, the restaurant could do a really nice lunch and dinner rush."

Cody had abandoned his food and simply stared at Brooke in front of him, wondering when she'd changed into...this smart businesswoman. "You're serious."

She stared right back with a scowl on her face. "Yes. When Mom and I moved here, Dad took me everywhere with him. He made this place feel like home. He made me love this town and all the people he introduced me to. I want to be a part of it. I think revitalizing downtown will draw other new businesses and help keep small business as the norm instead of them dying out like they've been over the last decade."

"This is what you want to do with your life? Own a bookstore and pizzeria?"

"Well, I was thinking it would be really cool to have a salad and pasta bar to go with the pizza. Italian classics like spaghetti and meatballs, ravioli, pasta Alfredo, and other dishes. Not like a buffet, more like Italian fast food. It's already prepared, you just tell the server what you want by the bowl or plate kind of thing."

"That's..." He couldn't believe it. He loved the idea and so would the hundreds of downtown workers. "It's an amazing idea."

She shifted in her seat, uncomfortable with his praise.

He hated that. He, better than anyone, knew Brooke was smart, kind, empathetic, surprisingly wise for her age, and enthusiastic about the people and things she loved. He had no doubt she'd make this venture a huge success, because Brooke didn't give up. It just wasn't in her nature.

She leaned in. "I know it's a lot of money, but I know I can do this, Cody. It will be a fresh start for me and help the community."

"I think so, too."

She sat back, her eyes going soft. "Do you think Dad would have liked my plans?"

Cody choked up and tried to hold it together. "He'd love this idea. He'd want you to use the money to make you happy and also ensure your future. You're doing both. I'm really proud of you, and touched that it's, in part, because of him."

Her eyes softened with grief mixed with a whole lot of affection. "I loved him, too. He was the only dad I knew."

"Your mom is the same for me. Without her kindness...the way she changed my dad...softened him...I don't think I would have loved him the way I did at the end. We were better for having you both at the ranch and in our lives."

"You sure about that?" She raised a brow. "Because it feels like lately we're growing apart."

He knew it. He hated it. But he couldn't tell her that and make her think there could be more between them. Not after that moment they shared in his study. The one he couldn't stop thinking about.

How about when you pulled her away from Brad and into your lap?

So fucking stupid. He should never have touched her. Because now, all he wanted to do was reach for her. Was her skin as soft as it looked? What would it feel like to have her body pressed up against his?

Stop! Danger!

It wasn't that he'd never touched her. They hugged. He kissed her on the head sometimes. She kissed him on the cheek as often as he let her get away with it.

Yeah, because you're an idiot.

It didn't used to be anything more than a friendly hello. Now...it meant something it shouldn't.

She's going back to school. You have Kristi.

Still didn't stop him from thinking dirty things about the woman in front of him. He forced himself not to adjust his raging hard-on.

Fuck. I'm so screwed.

He lost his train of thought.

Brooke stood abruptly, grabbing the bag that still held her tacos and her satchel. "I've taken up most of your lunch. Eat. When you have time, look over the information. I need an answer by the end of the weekend before I head back to school on Monday."

"Wait. What? You're not supposed to go back for a couple more weeks."

She gave him a lopsided grin. "Mindy Sue and I have plans. I'll be back at Christmas. In the meantime, if you okay the funds I need, we'll correspond via email and text to finalize all the paperwork and finish the deals. I really appreciate your help with this, Cody. I promise you, I'll work really hard to make the businesses a success. For Dad."

He shook his head. "This is all you, Brooke. I'll look over the stuff, but I know you can do this."

For a moment, her gaze filled with all the love and adoration he used to see in her eyes all the time. He never wanted to see anything but that and joy.

"Thank you, Cody. That means a lot."

His words had touched her.

And then, she headed for the door, leaving him feeling desperate to call her back.

He couldn't let her leave like this. Like it was some business meeting and not...more. "Brooke, wait." He rushed to her and pulled her into his arms. She stood there, unmoving at first, and then it was like she gave herself permission to do what she'd never hesitated to do in the past and wrapped her arms around him, holding him tight. He inhaled her roses-and-honey sweet scent, feeling drunk on it as it invaded his system and he became aware of her body pressed down the length of his.

Fuck. This feels so good. Too good.

He couldn't keep her this close. He stepped back and held her at arm's length. "Everything is going to be okay."

Are you saying that to her or yourself?

Right now, he didn't know. He couldn't even decide if it was the truth or not.

She stepped out of his reach. "If I don't see you before I leave, I'll see you at Christmas."

He felt oddly adrift without her in his arms. "Don't leave without saying goodbye."

"I know you're busy. I don't want to be a nuisance."

He stuffed his hands in his pockets so he didn't pull her close again. "You're not. Ever. And I'm sorry if I've sometimes made you think you are." He meant it. "We're friends." He reminded her as much as himself. "That will never change."

Something warm and tender washed over her eyes and made him yearn for more. "Then you know it's never goodbye, just I'll see you later."

He wanted to say, *please stay*. Because these last thirty minutes had been confusing and somehow life altering. Something had changed. She had. And if he let her go, he knew they might not ever go back to the way things had always been.

But the only thing that came out of his mouth was, "See you later." He made it sound like an order, because it was.

She walked out and he watched her go, noting that one of the paralegals stared at her ass as she walked to the elevator. He glared at the guy and made him scramble away.

That's right, asshole, stop staring at my Brooke.

What. The. Fuck?

He needed his head examined.

Brooke turned in the elevator car and gave him a wave.

Maybe it was good she was leaving, because if he gave in to what he wanted to do, he'd ruin them. And he couldn't lose Brooke.

Not now.

Not ever.

He didn't let himself think too hard about that dangerous and enticing thought.

He stared until the doors closed on her beautiful face and he closed his office door, went to his desk, stared at the food she'd brought him, and wondered again when she grew up to be so smart and poised and business savvy.

Don't forget sexy.

That outfit...*Fuck.*

Needing a distraction, he opened the first folder and dove in, knowing he'd approve her request and be waiting like a child for Christmas to come so he could see her again.

She hadn't even left yet and he missed her already.

I'm so fucked up.

Chapter Eight

He couldn't stop thinking about *her*. Brooke. He hadn't seen her since the picnic. The start of school seemed so far away. He spent far too many nights with her on his mind, in his heart, a ghost he saw but couldn't touch.

He wanted to call but didn't know what to say. Overwhelmed by his need for her, the words stuck in his mind, evaporating in his throat before he could speak them.

He'd called a dozen times, hanging up before she answered.

Anxiety sucked. It made him second-guess himself. It made his thoughts spin.

The shyness he'd always felt around others trapped him in loneliness and a box he couldn't escape.

Desperation to do something, be something else, find the strength, the bravery, hell, a single word to tell her he needed her, overwhelmed him and left him wanting and disheartened when he couldn't find the courage.

He was weak, just like his father thought.

Soft.

But he was a problem solver.

She'd seen his number on her phone, how he kept calling and hanging up. If he found his voice and called her, she'd ask questions. He needed another way, a direct but private and easier way to reach her. She needed to know how he felt. He needed to tell her how he felt. Then she'd see. She'd know. He was the one who could be her everything.

She was that for him.

And she was anxious to see him again. That's why she returned to school early.

He'd found her walking downtown with Mindy Sue a week ago. They'd gone into the salon and come out an hour later and he'd gasped with surprise, even as he went hard as a rod.

Gorgeous didn't begin to describe her. Brooke had changed her hair. It framed her beautiful face. And her smile...she knew she looked good. She glowed with happiness and confidence.

Mindy Sue had hooked her arm around Brooke's shoulders and pulled her along toward the drugstore.

He'd pulled out his new burner phone, tapped into his new social media account, and commented on a picture she'd posted of her and Mindy Sue eating pasta the other night.

@youseeme: You look even better today! The new haircut... gorgeous!

He'd kept it simple. He didn't want her to block him. He just needed her to know how he felt.

Chapter Nine

B rooke didn't post often, but every time she did, @youseeme commented. She wondered who they were. Was it the same person who called all the time, even at odd hours during the night, and hung up before she ever answered? The calls had stopped. Maybe whoever it was finally realized they had the wrong number?

Maybe it was just an annoying telemarketer.

She didn't think so. Then again, those calls had really amped up her imagination. Especially after she could have sworn she saw someone in her bedroom window the night of the picnic just as the fireworks went off.

She'd checked her room that night, afraid she'd find something creepy. She didn't notice anything out of place or missing.

Was she hallucinating? Not likely.

So who would be in her room?

Some random guest who got lost trying to find the bathroom, heard the fireworks, and rushed to her window to get a look?

Yeah, she made a lot of excuses for that sighting and the calls.

Now she had some random person leaving her comments. They were nice comments. Not threatening in any way. Except for the subtext. Because the comment that she looked better today than when she had dinner with Mindy Sue implied that they knew her. Saw her before and after her new haircut.

The account only followed her, no one else. Odd. Maybe creepy. For the most part, she didn't engage except to heart the comment, so they knew she appreciated it, like when she posted a picture with her new haircut all styled to perfection and her new makeup highlighting her green eyes and long lashes months ago.

@youseeme: Love those grasshopper-green eyes. I see the happiness in them. And the satisfaction that you know you look hot!

The comment made her smile. It made her feel good. It made her feel seen.

When she posted a picture of her stack of books for this semester, they commented...

@youseeme: Smart and beautiful! You're killing me.

That gave her a sense of satisfaction. She wanted to be seen for more than her looks.

"Are you going to take the pic or what?" Mindy Sue asked.

They'd just finished getting dressed up for the Halloween frat party they were going to tonight. Mindy Sue dressed in a sexy devil costume, accentuating her bust and ass with the long forked tail coming from the back of the body-hugging pants and bustier. Brooke rocked a sexy white micro-miniskirt and belly-baring halter top that showed off her boobs to perfection. White wings and a golden halo floating atop a headband completed her sexy angel outfit.

"Brooke?" Mindy Sue bumped her hip to Brooke's.

"What? Sorry. I got lost thinking about how @youseeme always comments on my stuff."

"Don't give him another thought. He's had weeks to ask you out and he hasn't. Which means it's probably not a *he* but a *she*. Someone you know but aren't that close to who's just being nice."

Brooke blew it off and held up her phone. Mindy Sue put her arm over Brooke's shoulders, narrowed her eyes, and gave an evil look with pouty red lips, holding up her hand in the universal rock-on sign with her middle and ring fingers down, thumb, forefinger, and pinky up.

Brooke smiled angelically, her eyes soft and bright and twinkling with joy.

She snapped the picture and they both laughed at how they looked the part for their costumes.

Brooke immediately posted the pic, telling herself to just have fun and not think about anything else.

Mindy Sue checked her phone. "Let's go. Julie and the guys are all waiting downstairs in front of the dorm."

They grabbed their stuff and headed out.

The second they walked out the dorm's double doors, they heard Julie, Jeremiah, Marco, Adam, and Simon cat-call and whistle.

"Smokin' hot, babe." Marco gripped Mindy Sue's hips, pulled her close, and gave her a deep kiss. Luckily she wore a really good red lip stain or it would be all over her and Marco's faces.

Simon and Adam spoke at the same time to Brooke.

"You look amazing."

"Sexy as heaven."

She laughed, turned, and moved her shoulders up and down, showing off her wings. When she looked over her shoulder, they were both checking out her ass, which was barely covered by the miniskirt.

Their comments and the look made Brooke feel really confident. So different from the girl who used to wear baggy T-shirts over her jeans to hide her shape. She hadn't even realized that's what she'd been doing, because she didn't want the guys on the ranch to tease her about how she'd filled out. But she wasn't a little girl. Not anymore.

And she rocked that costume with sass in her step and a swing in her curved hips as they all walked over to the frat house to join the raging party.

And her admirer had appreciated it.

No sooner had they walked into the crush of partygoers and grabbed a round of shots and drank them down with a "Let's party," a notification lit up her phone.

@youseeme: DAMN! THAT BODY IS ROCKIN'. YOU SURE KNOW HOW TO STRUT YOUR STUFF.

The comment made her think, definitely a guy. It also made her smile. And wonder if whoever sent it was looking at her right now.

She scanned the room, looking for anyone staring back at her.

A few people. Mostly drunk frat boys.

She didn't have time to worry about it. Mindy Sue and Julie pulled her into the crowd dancing and she got lost in the music and the beat and having fun.

Five songs later, they all grabbed a beer and watched beer pong.

Julie, who was dressed as a cheerleader, bumped into a guy dressed as a football player. They seemed to hit it off immediately and were doing a shot together. Must be fate.

Jeremiah, Simon, and Adam had snagged seats on a sofa and were scoping out all the girls in the room.

Mindy Sue and Marco were making out next to her.

She was wondering how long she'd be the third wheel to her two girlfriends and downed the last half of her second beer.

She tapped Mindy Sue's shoulder to get her attention. "We need a group pic." She pointed to Adam, Jeremiah, and Simon on the sofa and Julie and her football hero doing yet another shot.

"I'm going to get us more shots. Back soon." Marco took off for the booze. She and Mindy Sue went over to the other guys.

"You guys having fun?"

Adam nodded and sipped his beer. He didn't seem to be a big drinker. He looked cute in his Harry Potter costume. It suited him.

Simon grinned up at her. "I like watching everyone get wasted."

"I'm wasted." Jeremiah gave her a dopey grin.

Marco arrived with the shots on a paper plate.

Brooke took one. So did everyone else.

"Happy Halloween, fuckers!" Marco called out, holding up his shot.

They all drank.

Brooke snagged the arm of one of the girls nearby. She didn't know her name. Didn't matter. She was too drunk to care. "Hey, can you take a picture of all of us." She handed the girl her phone and turned to her friends. "Group pic. Now!"

Mindy Sue pulled Marco close and kissed his cheek, his hand on her lower belly, indecently close to being right over her girl bits. Julie snuggled up to the side of her football player. His name was Mike. Maybe Mark. Something with an M. Brooke was two shots and two beers in, so it was hard to remember, let alone hear anything above the din of the party. Anyway...she somehow ended up lying across the laps of Adam, Jeremiah, and Simon on her side while they held their hands up like they didn't know if they were allowed to touch her. She was smiling and laughing as the girl with her phone said, "Cheese," and snapped the pic.

Brooke tried to figure out how to get off of the three guys without shoving her ass into Simon's crotch, kicking Jeremiah, or gripping Adam's thigh, and ended up belly flopping on the floor in a fit of giggles.

Some guy in a toga rushed over, took her hand to help her up, then kissed her right on the lips, surprising her and sobering her up a little.

He grinned with glazed eyes. "If you kiss a fallen angel, she has to grant you a wish."

She was working without a filter thanks to the alcohol. Knowing what guys could be like at these parties, she answered with, "Let me guess, you want me to fuck you."

His eyes gleamed with mischief. "Oh, I definitely want you to take me to heaven."

She couldn't help it, she cracked up. And so did everyone around them. It was a joke. He was being silly. The moment passed with that seriously cheesy line. Though in that moment she'd thought of the one man who made her feel like being with him would be heaven and it killed her mood.

The girl who took the picture handed back her phone. "I hope you like it."

"Let me see," toga guy said.

She pulled up the picture and loved it. It showed them all having fun as a group. They'd gotten together a few times because Marco brought his friends, so Mindy Sue brought hers. It worked. It was fun when they all got together.

She posted the pic.

Toga guy was still next to her. "Want to get a drink?"

She shook her head. "I've had enough. Thank you though." She turned to Mindy Sue. "I'm ready to head home."

"I'll walk you," toga guy said, holding out his hand again.

She hesitated.

Mindy Sue leaned in. "Marco and I are ready to go."

Toga guy raised a brow, silently asking her again if he could walk her home.

She shrugged and said, "Why not," because Mindy Sue and Marco would be with her.

They said goodbye to Julie, her new friend, and the three guys, who promised to look out for Julie.

She walked out with toga guy, blissfully happy to be out in the open air and quiet after the din of the party. "So, what's your name?"

"Rob. And you're Brooke."

"How'd you know?" She slurred most of those words.

"I heard your friends call you that."

Mindy Sue and Marco walked just a few paces ahead of them. Mindy Sue kept looking back and grinning at her.

Rob bumped her shoulder with his. "Listen, I'm sorry if I came on too strong back there with the kiss and that line. I was just having fun."

"It's fine. I get it."

He asked about her major, her classes. She asked about his. It was nice. Normal. But she just wasn't interested.

She didn't get that funny feeling in her belly.

Well, her belly did feel funny, but that was all the booze she'd drunk.

Outside her dorm, they stopped just far enough away from Marco and Mindy Sue to give them privacy while they face fucked and said goodnight to each other.

Rob stared at her like he could see right through her skimpy clothes. "I'd like to see you again."

She let him down easy. "I appreciate that but I'm really swamped right now with school and starting my own business. Thank you for walking me home. I really appreciate it and it was nice meeting you."

"Maybe we'll see each other again and I can change your mind about a date."

She grinned and headed for the door, not wanting to encourage him further.

The next morning she woke up to a comment from her admirer and it chilled her.

@youseeme: WHAT THE FUCK WAS THAT, LETTING THAT GUY KISS YOU LAST NIGHT? YOU'RE MINE!

How did they know about that random kiss?

She should have ignored the comment. But she couldn't let it go.

@brookebanks: YOU WERE THERE? DO I KNOW YOU? WHAT'S YOUR NAME?

It took two hours to get a response. She wondered if whoever was sending the messages realized their mistake in letting her know they were close enough to be at the same party.

@youseeme: I SAW YOU THERE. YOU SAW ME. I WAS RIGHT IN FRONT OF YOU AND YOU KISSED THAT DRUNK ASSHAT INSTEAD. THEN YOU WENT HOME WITH HIM!

He added a red rage face to that comment.

She shouldn't have felt like she needed to defend herself, but she replied...

@brookebanks: THE GUY WAS A GENTLEMAN AFTER KISSING ME WITHOUT PERMISSION AND WALKED ME BACK TO MY PLACE, APOLOGIZED, THEN LEFT.

Another reply came through right away.

@youseeme: I've only ever been nice to you. I care about you. I'll show you. And when it's the right time, I'll reveal myself to you, and you'll know what I know. You're mine.

@BrookeBanks: If you know me...if we're friends...then tell me who you are.

@youseeme: Soon

Now she was really creeped out. And annoyed.

She gave up. She wasn't interested in someone who couldn't answer a simple question. If he liked her, wanted to be with her, then say so. Let her make the choice if she wanted something more. But this...it felt childish. It felt a little...not exactly creepy, but definitely off.

But this person knew her. They obviously liked her. A lot. But why not just ask her out?

She assumed they were shy. Maybe even that they thought she wouldn't return their feelings for some reason and wanted a chance to let her grow to like them without them having to put themselves on the line in such a big way.

Great. Now I'm making excuses for them.

After that exchange, they still commented on the photos she posted. She let them know she saw them by hearting them. But she didn't comment back to them specifically anymore. If they wanted to talk, they needed to step up and make the effort in real life and not hide behind their screen.

And truthfully, she was still trying to figure out life without the possibility of a romantic relationship between her and Cody.

They'd barely spoken the last few months, but he had agreed to let her use her trust fund money to start her businesses. That was something.

He believed in her enough to let her risk the money, not that it was that big of a risk. The building was a good investment all on its own. Still, she wanted to prove to herself and Cody that she could make this work.

Too bad she couldn't make him see that they could work together, too.

Chapter Ten

Cody couldn't believe it was almost Christmas. Where had the time gone? Why did it feel like an eternity since he'd seen Brooke? Oh yeah, because she'd been gone for months and practically radio silent.

You've been too busy to call her, too, so...

What was she doing?

What was she thinking?

Was she even coming home for the holidays?

Of course she is. You're being an idiot.

Susanne had already told him she'd be here.

Still, his uncontrollable thoughts made him doubt.

This was her senior year. She was busy, studying and making her last year count by focusing on what she needed to do before she returned home for good. Of course she was taking advantage of everything school had to offer, including being with her friends and making connections that could potentially be as beneficial to her future as her stellar grades.

And he couldn't blame her for the lack of communication. He hadn't been much better. After getting the position on the children's hospital board, he'd barely had time to breathe between the hours he worked on projects for the board, taking care of his clients' legal troubles, the ranch, and dating Kristi. Not that seeing her felt like a job. Well, okay, sometimes it did because she could be as demanding as his clients.

Actually, that wasn't fair. There just weren't enough hours in the day for him to be everything to everyone.

He didn't want to think about Kristi right now. Things were...strained. Was that the right word? He wasn't sure. She constantly praised him for being such a great lawyer, for working so hard to ensure the children's hospital met the needs of its patients and staff, and for how good he made her feel when they were together.

He felt like he spent most of his time apologizing to her for being late for a date, missing a date, not having enough time to give to her, always rushing, never taking his time when they were together. He liked being with her when she was in an understanding mood. But when she wasn't...it felt like all her wants—for him to be more attentive, available, understanding of her needs—were just another item on his long-as-fuck to-do list.

He needed a vacation but didn't have the time to take one.

The bright spot had remained his interactions with Brooke. Though they were few and far between, she still found a way to make him smile.

Like when he'd sent her a text about her request...

CODY: I've gone over your detailed and thorough business plans and will approve the funds for your project. I'll get started on the contracts. Once they're ready, I'll send them for your review and signature before I present them to Mrs. Walters and Mr. Scott.

BROOKE: Thank you for the prompt response, Mr. Jansen. I appreciate your time and attention to this matter.

The professional response had made him frown and wonder what the fuck was going on with her.

But then she sent another text.

BROOKE: Now take the stick out of your uptight lawyer ass and remember that we're friends and you can say I'm fucking brilliant and the project is a go.

He laughed so loud in his office, his assistant came in to see what was going on. And for the life of him, he couldn't remember doing that in a long while. When had his life gotten so serious?

CODY: You're more than brilliant. Never forget that.

BROOKE: Can I get that on a plaque I can mount on my wall? Cody Jansen thinks I'm brilliant!

Before he could think better of it, he sent...

CODY: I think my life is dull without you in it.

BROOKE: I'm the gift that keeps on giving.

BROOKE: Now tell me what's wrong?

Of course she read what he hadn't even said.
Nothing. Everything. He was discontent and didn't know why or what to do about it.

CODY: I'm fine. Just tired and busy.

BROOKE: Mom told me you donated your obscene client fee to the children's hospital, so they could get a new MRI and CT machine. Get a company off on pollution charges and heal sick kids why don't you!

Cody laughed at that, too, but also felt incredibly proud of what he'd done to compensate for defending his client so well they got away with a slap on the wrist for that shit. His firm had gotten their cut, but his portion had gone to the kids.

Brooke understood his need to do good in the world. They had that in common. He didn't always get to pick his clients. Some of them he didn't like. Others he loathed. Especially those who used the law to get away scot-free with doing bad things.

BROOKE: I see your cape showing under your bespoke suit.

He chuckled again.

CODY: But you'll keep my secret, right?

BROOKE: Word is out. You're running with the big dogs now. You've got the money, the woman...next you'll be too famous for the likes of me.

CODY: Never. You keep me grounded.

BROOKE: Because I know you better than anyone.

Yes, she does. Because he didn't open up easily to others. Not even with Kristi.

She was starting to feel that. He was trying to be better, but it wasn't easy for him. He guarded himself after his mother walked out. He didn't need a therapist to know he had trust issues.

Not with Brooke.

Maybe because she was just a kid when they met. You couldn't hide things from kids. They saw right through you. And Brooke had been so eager to be accepted by him and his dad.

Brooke was his best friend, but Kristi was the woman by his side, the woman who complemented his life because she was a part of his work world. They shared friends and acquaintances, many of whom they ran into on a regular basis.

CODY: But will you help me bury the bodies?

BROOKE: I'll bring the shovel, you bring the beer.

He grinned at that, too.

CODY: Deal. And if you need me, I'm just a call away. Day or night. I mean it.

BROOKE: I know you do. But I also need to learn to stand on my own.

He hoped that didn't mean she didn't need him anymore.

BROOKE: I have to run to class.

BROOKE: And Cody...work isn't a life. You deserve to have a really great life.

BROOKE: Have some fun. That's an order from your partner in the ranch. And your friend.

That's when it hit him. This feeling he'd been having since she left. Guilt.

He shouldn't have touched her the way he did. He shouldn't have looked at her the way he did. He definitely shouldn't be thinking the things he thought about her all the time.

She cared about him. She wanted more with him. And for a brief second, he'd given in instead of stepping back. For a split second, he'd seen in her eyes how happy she'd be if he reciprocated her feelings. For that brief moment, even he thought it could be so, so good to let her unleash all her desires and love on him.

And then he pulled away. In rolled the familiar disappointment he saw on her lovely face. He knew every soft curve, every expression she made by heart. He'd seen them all. Well, most of them. But he didn't let himself think about what she looked like in ecstasy.

Okay, he did. But he tried not to.

He hated himself for always disappointing her. He felt guilty for giving her that moment and taking it away. Yes, he cared every time he hurt her.

But it had to be this way.

She'd barely lived outside of the life she had on the ranch. Safe. Protected. She'd dated some but never had a boyfriend. She majored in business but had never had an actual job outside of helping out on the ranch.

She had opportunities awaiting her, life experiences to live. How could she know with such certainty that if they were together it would all work out? She couldn't. Because she'd never been with anyone and lost them. He couldn't take that chance. She was too important, too necessary in his life to risk it.

And the last thing he'd ever want to do was break her heart.

Better to keep her as a friend than an ex.

And she deserved to have a full life, one where she got to experience all the things he'd already been through to get to the point where he was ready to settle down and have a family. She was too young to clip her wings before she'd ever soared.

She'd come home for Christmas and everything would be the way it was supposed to be.

Chapter Eleven

December 20ᵗʰ – Christmas Party at Brooke's home...

Cody tried to tamp down his excitement by sucking in a deep breath and letting it out as he pulled on his dress shirt and called out, "I've been waiting to see you," as his bedroom door opened.

He really tried not to show his disappointment when Kristi walked in.

Her bright smile dimmed and he knew she knew he was expecting Brooke.

He tried to cover. "You're early. And you look amazing." She did. The gold strapless dress made her skin glow and her blue eyes stand out.

Her gaze swept over him, landing on his chest where it was exposed between the two sides of his unbuttoned shirt.

"You keep looking at me like that, and I'll have to do something about it." He went to her and kissed her cheek, not wanting to mess up her lipstick.

She stepped back and eyed him. "Who were you expecting to walk through your bedroom door?"

Like she didn't know. But he wasn't going to play this jealous game. Not tonight when they were expecting a houseful of guests.

"You." He started buttoning his shirt.

She raised a golden brow. "Brooke's home, right?"

"Yes. She arrived the day before yesterday." He kept his voice neutral.

Kristi narrowed her eyes. "How is she?"

"Good. I think. I haven't gotten a chance to really catch up with her. I've been working to clear my desk before the holidays and she spent time with Susanne, riding her horse, and catching up with everyone on the ranch." His anticipation grew until it felt like a need he could barely contain. He missed her so much.

"I bet you're excited to spend time with her tonight."

He couldn't lie. "I am."

"Even though you promised we'd stick together and greet all the guests as *the* couple who are throwing this party. Right?"

The holiday party was a big deal in their social circle. People were busy this time of year. Getting everyone who RSVP'd together here tonight was a sign of just how well everyone respected and liked him and how far he'd come in his career and standing in the community.

Cody could write off the summer picnic as everyone just being nice after his father died. But for them all to show up again tonight spoke to the fact that they considered him important and part of their social circle.

And Kristi wanted to be with him in that.

So does Brooke. She made the summer picnic a success.

Yes, but he couldn't take advantage of her feelings for him. Not when his life would hold her back from exploring all the opportunities available to her.

Cody hooked one arm around her waist and drew her close. "As promised, I'll be a gracious host with you by my side."

Even though Susanne had done most of the work setting up the party with him, Kristi had asked if they would entertain their family, friends, and colleagues as a couple. He didn't see why not. They'd been dating for almost a year. Everyone knew they were together, but this would somehow show them how devoted they were to each other in her mind.

Like they didn't already know.

Kristi sometimes obsessed about what others thought about her. She especially wanted her parents' approval. Since they were coming, he guessed she wanted them to see her in the role of his partner.

Okay. Fine. He didn't see the need to put on a show. They'd do what they always did at work functions and dinners and be each other's support. They'd become good at that over the last few months. Especially when they had dinner with her folks, who always seemed to have a few extra guests at their table. CEOs, the mayor, council members, judges. Kirk surrounded himself with influential people and introduced Cody to a lot of them. Connection. Kirk was all about making them and using them.

Cody sometimes felt like Kirk used those dinners to make sure Cody was keeping his daughter happy.

And Cody wondered if her insistence on being seen together tonight as a united front had anything to do with the fact that she'd been dropping hints about them getting married the last few weeks. She never seemed secure enough in what they had to just be in it with him. She was always looking toward getting to the next milestone in their relationship. First date. First time they had sex. Six-month anniversary. First big holiday together. Hosting a party together. Their one-year anniversary coming up. Marriage. A family.

He was in no hurry.

She was anxious to have it all.

Kristi handed him his tie. "And what about Brooke?"

He tucked in his shirt. "I'm happy she's home. I can't wait to hear about school and talk to her about the plans for the businesses she's opening next year."

Kristi folded her arms. "I'm sure she can manage that on her own."

"She can, but I control her trust fund, so I need to know how much money she needs, when, and for what."

Kristi let loose her arms and her hands slapped against her thighs. "She's months away from being twenty-one. Just let her handle it." She was getting worked up over nothing.

"It's a big project. I want to be sure no one takes advantage of her."

Kristi huffed. "Is this how it's going to be tonight and while she's home on break? You're going to spend all your time with her instead of me?"

"What? No. I just haven't seen her in months and I want a chance to connect with her."

Kristi's blue eyes turned glacial. "Right. Like the texts you guys send each other aren't enough?"

"It's not the same as a real conversation." He draped his red tie over his neck, pulled his collar over it, wound the tie into a knot, and pulled it up to his neck, all while Kristi eyed him. "Look, I know you're nervous about the party. It's going to be a big crowd. A few of Brooke's friends will be here with their parents, so she'll be occupied while you and I tend to *our* guests. At some point, I'll have a moment to talk to Brooke. It's not like I'm going to spend the whole night with her."

Kristi's shoulders and face softened. "You're right. It's just..."

"What?" Didn't she trust him?

"You've mentioned her a lot over the last few months. You always seem to find the time to worry about her, think about her."

He smirked as he pulled on his suit jacket. "Do you want to know the truth?"

"Always."

"Brooke has been unusually quiet these last few months and it makes me nervous."

"Because you think she's pulling away?"

Yes. "Because I worry that something is wrong and she's not telling me. I'm responsible for her. I promised my dad I would always look out for her. And yes, I admit, I care about her. I miss her."

"Tonight is about you and me and our relationship and what it's grown into, and I don't want anything to ruin our night, including Brooke distracting you like she always does because she desperately wants your attention."

He closed the distance, put his hands on her bare shoulders, planted a kiss on her forehead, then looked her in the eyes. "I'm all yours. I promise."

Chapter Twelve

There she is!

He watched Brooke descend the stairs. She looked amazing. He hadn't been this close to her in weeks. Not since just before Marco and Mindy Sue broke up last month. Six long weeks ago. Now he didn't have an excuse to hang out with Brooke and their group. He missed their exchanges, when he got up the nerve to talk to her, mostly when she spoke to him first.

His anxiety always got the better of him, damnit.

He blamed Marco for fucking everything up and him not getting to have those too-few moments with Brooke anymore.

Marco had fucked up with Mindy Sue too many times by acting like a jerk in front of her and to her. The girls had rallied around their friend. Marco was already dating someone new. The rest of them still met up when their schedules permitted, but it wasn't the same without the girls.

Tonight he could be in Brooke's company and it wouldn't be odd at all because his family had been invited to many occasions here over the years.

Now if only he could talk to her without stumbling over his words or making a fool of himself.

God, he missed her. He needed her.

He wanted to touch her, to know the feel of her soft skin against his, the taste of her, the way she sounded when she liked all the things he wanted to do to her in bed.

Just thinking about it made him hard as rock.

He'd kind of worn out her panties. Maybe he'd sneak upstairs and steal another pair.

Maybe she'd give him the ones she was wearing right now if he could figure out how to get her alone. He'd kiss her, then slide his hand up that killer dress and between her legs. She'd be wet just from him being near her.

Fuck he was horny.

He pulled his cell phone from his jacket pocket, pretended to check his email, and snapped a photograph of her beautiful face. Unable to help himself, he snapped another of her long, golden legs. He saved both pics to his *Brooke* folder and tucked the phone back in his pocket before anyone noticed.

Not that anyone would.

One day, he'd be someone. He'd step out from behind his father's massive shadow and show them they'd underestimated and dismissed him for the last time.

Everyone in the room noticed her though. Who could miss such beauty?

The men's gazes tracked her every move. Their eyes locked on her curves. His hands fisted at his sides, but let loose when she simply smiled and kept walking, an ethereal glow about her that made everyone notice her and stand back at the same time.

They all noticed *it*, too. She'd changed over these last many months. Bloomed. That's the only way he could describe it. She owned her new look and confidence.

Both were sexy as hell.

He followed her, staying to the outskirts of the crowd.

She was the woman for him. He'd be the man for her.

Soon, she'd see how perfect they were for each other.

She'd regret not saying anything to him when he commented on her posts. She'd apologize and tell him that she'd always hoped it was him leaving her messages.

She'd be so happy. They'd be happy together.

Fate fucked him with his family. She owed him big time, and he wanted Brooke.

Brooke would make everything in his life right.

Time to up his game.

She's mine.

Chapter Thirteen

B rooke wound her way through the crowd, smiling at old friends and trying not to laugh at the double takes and outright gawking as she passed. The woman who returned home for Christmas break didn't resemble the tomboy girl who'd gone back to campus months ago, restless and ready for a huge change.

She noted friends' amazed expressions and let them bolster her confidence and pride.

The changes on the outside were the direct result of the changes she'd made on the inside. She no longer looked in the mirror and saw all the things she would never be.

Though she was still a tomboy at heart, she finally felt like a pretty girl.

She wasn't used to this kind of attention. At all. But she wasn't an awkward kid anymore and everyone *finally* noticed.

Her future looked bright. She couldn't wait to graduate college and start her new businesses.

"Brooke, is that really you?" Gloria stared at her, wide-eyed and grinning. "You look fantastic. So...so not the you I remember from two years ago."

"Time flies."

Gloria lived next door on a neighboring ranch. She was three years older than Cody. Brooke had a hunch that at one time or another they'd either fooled around or been a thing for a little while. Maybe he just liked sneaking over to her place to party. Gloria had that kind of reputation back in the day. Now, she was married with a little one.

"How are David and Lucy?"

"Amazing. David's here somewhere, probably having a beer with Cody. And Lucy...there's nothing like that little ray of sunshine. You'll find out when you have one of your own." Gloria looked happier than Brooke had ever seen her.

She envied Gloria's happy life.

She wanted that with Cody. But being an adult meant putting childish dreams away. Dreams she'd held on to far too long and too hard.

She'd never hidden the fact she was head over heels in love with him. She didn't care who knew it, or how she'd embarrassed not only herself, but him. She'd never seen her behavior as anything but expressing her feelings. She'd never seen that she'd been throwing herself at a man who would always look at her as a child, and heartbreakingly worse, only his friend. Though he always made time for her. They'd go on long rides, swim, play games. He'd even take her into town for a movie, or out to eat. They had such good times together.

Older, wiser, she had a much clearer picture of what she'd put him through, and she was sorry for it. His patience showed that under it all, they really were good friends.

The best of friends.

He'd had to be a good friend to let her get away with some of the stunts she'd pulled to get his attention.

"Oh, there he is." Gloria pointed over at Cody. "Now don't those two make the picture?"

She spotted Cody across the room, standing beside Kristi. *The golden couple.* Cody stood six-two, blond hair, his skin tanned to a golden brown thanks to a life spent working the ranch. The navy suit he wore set off the light blue color of his eyes.

Kristi was shorter than him at five-six with her perfect hair, perfect teeth, perfect boobs, perfectly slender, and perfectly smiling beside her man. Kristi had also proven to be the perfect snob and master manipulator with her pretty pout.

Brooke rolled her eyes with her back to Gloria.

"They look happy together." Gloria stuck the knife right in her back without knowing it.

They did look happy. Cody seemed content with Kristi pursuing him for her single purpose in life: to marry Cody Jansen and live the life of the successful lawyer's wife.

Oh yeah, let's not forget he's a board member for the children's hospital, too.

She wouldn't let anyone in this room forget it. Heaven forbid she remembered Cody owned a successful ranch as well. Though he spent more time in his downtown office now while the ranch manager ran things here. Still, he spent plenty of nights and weekends tending to ranch business.

To Kristi's way of thinking, it was a smelly, dirty business he should put aside and concentrate on being a lawyer and pillar of the community. Brooke thought Kristi was more interested in the money, power, and influence Cody was just beginning to wield, and Kristi could use to spend the rest of her life lunching on with her high-society friends.

"I'm glad he found someone and is happy after Harland's passing. That must have hit him hard. Both his mom and dad gone."

Brooke faced Gloria, appreciating her kindness toward Cody. "He took it really hard. We both did."

"Of course. Harland loved you like you were his. And your mom...I can't imagine how hard it is to live without the man you love."

It's hard. Really, really hard.

"She's doing better, too. She'd love to catch up with you, I'm sure. And you know she's going to want to not only see some baby pictures but get her hands on Lucy soon, too. You should bring her over to see the horses sometime."

"I will. Thank you. You know she loves them."

"Just like I do."

Gloria squeezed Brooke's forearm, then headed off, to find her husband most likely.

Brooke took one last look at Cody, abruptly turned, and headed for the buffet table.

He's not yours.

Before, she'd have made a beeline for Cody and sidled up to him to steal a kiss on the cheek. On Cody's part, kissing her hello was purely a friendly gesture. For her, it had been a way to touch him and be close.

Now, she gave him space to be with *her*.

Kristi had his full attention these days. He'd barely spared Brooke a glance since she arrived home. Tonight it seemed he was blinded by Kristi to anyone else in the room. Including her.

Brooke sighed. Sometimes, life wasn't fair.

"Hey beautiful, where've you been all my life?" Charlie smiled down at her with a strange look in his eyes. His gaze roamed over her before landing on her mouth.

They'd known each other forever, but he'd never looked at her quite like that.

To dispel any notion she was interested, she rolled her eyes and scoffed, then went with sarcasm and reminded him of their history. As friends. "Shoveling manure right beside you." She handed him a plate with a smirk and took one for herself.

Heavily laden platters and brimming bowls of decadent food covered the buffet table. Little Santa, elves, and angel figurines sat in between the abundant fare with twinkling white lights wound around evergreens. She loved Christmas and all the trimmings.

Her mother had helped Cody plan the party, using Brooke's contacts for catering, decorations, and the invitations. It was basically the same guest list from the summer picnic.

"Nah. The girl who worked beside me in the stables was a skinny kid with stringy hair, baggy jeans, and chapped lips."

She planted one fist on her hip and gaped at him. "Are you saying I'm not skinny anymore?"

He eyed her up and down again. "You filled out in all the right places." He winked at her.

For real. A wink.

Laughing it off, she filled her plate with pesto pasta salad and a slice of prime rib. She expected some attention, but not like this. Not from a guy who'd given her noogies and teased her like a kid sister.

Maybe she should look at Charlie in a different way, too. She discreetly gave him a once-over. Cute. Tall and lean. His dark hair a little long, just right for sliding her fingers through the soft-looking strands. But there was no spark.

Still, she appreciated that he'd noticed her and flirted with her.

Her confidence swelled.

Every bud opened into a flower. She'd just taken a little longer to bloom.

Chapter Fourteen

T he second Brooke walked down the stairs to join the party, everything inside Cody screeched to a halt. Wow! Just, wow!

His heart started pounding as he took her in.

Breathtaking. Gorgeous. Absolutely mesmerizing.

He wasn't the only one to notice. He couldn't take his eyes off her. Neither could anyone else. Self-assured, she glided across the room with a soft smile, her lips tinted a deep berry color. In contrast, her eyes were lined in black with a subtle pink shadow. Her dark hair fell in layers around her face and down her back and made her cheekbones and green eyes stand out all the more.

Perfect.

He'd seen a hint of this woman when she came to his office to discuss business just before she left for school. But this...he never saw coming.

Cody wanted like he'd never wanted anything more. It opened that crack in his chest, the one that opened when he'd touched her in his study at the picnic. Something wanted to come out, but he tried to hold it back. If he let it loose, it could ruin everything.

He'd spent too many years taking care of Brooke, treating her like a best friend. Because that's what she was.

Now? She'd changed. Maybe he'd changed, too. Because he shouldn't feel this kind of pull toward her.

And he definitely shouldn't feel the possessive punch to the gut when he caught other men staring at her in that little black dress. Strapless, her breasts rounded softly above the top.

Too tight. Too short, even if it did hit her long legs just above the knee and looked absolutely perfect on her.

Brooke wasn't supposed to look like that. Men weren't supposed to watch her while she walked by.

Charlie wasn't supposed to stand that close, or smile at her like some horny teenager.

He better shut it down before Cody put him face down in the Caesar salad platter.

Cody's chest shouldn't tighten when she smiled. His blood pressure shouldn't rise when she laughed at something Charlie said. He sure as hell shouldn't feel the tug and pull pushing him to go to her, but he did.

God, look at her. So confident. All he wanted to do was tell her how amazing she looked. And keep her all to himself. He didn't want all the men in the room looking at her. She was his.

No, she's not.

She stopped by her mom, who took Brooke's hands and held them out, so she could admire Brooke all dressed up and looking fantastic. Susanne smiled with pride and released her, so Brooke could take her plate out to the tables on the veranda.

He caught her eye, but instead of making her way to him, she acted like she still didn't see him. What the...

Why?

He didn't like it. It hurt. More than it should. The distance she put between them made him ache. And worry. What did this mean?

"Cody was the perfect addition to the board at the children's hospital. He's got all the others trying to outdo him in bringing in donations and top talent. I knew he was the right man for the job," the governor gushed about him.

Cody could care less right now.

Kristi beamed beside him. "There's no one better."

Governor and Mrs. Harris nodded their agreement. He barely noticed or cared what they thought. He did what he did for the hospital because it mattered, not to get people like the governor and other influential people in the room to pat him on the back. But he'd take it with a smile, because that's what it took to keep men like Governor Harris happy—because they thought you owed them, even though he was the one busting his ass. "Thank you for the praise and continued support." A diplomatic statement given expectation.

"You're going to do big things."

Funny, he thought he was already doing pretty damn well for himself.

Except Brooke still hadn't looked his way. Not once.

Mrs. Harris tilted her head toward a couple across the room. "The Hendersons have just arrived. Let's go say hello."

The governor and his wife made their way across the room.

He caught Brooke kissing his ranch manger, David, hello. Then she almost lost her plate when another ranch hand grabbed her from behind and hugged her to his chest while he kissed her bare shoulder and teased her about something.

He saw red at the way the guy manhandled her and had already taken two steps to put a stop to it when Kristi's hand snaked out and caught his forearm in a viselike grip. Her smoldering blue eyes told him she wasn't happy about something.

He'd become accustomed to receiving that look.

Lately, she wasn't happy with him about anything. He couldn't blame her. Work had never seemed busier. He had cases piling up at his office. The ranch had one problem after another, including the loss of a few key people. He needed to hire more workers for the ranch, so he wasn't filling in on his off hours.

He needed some relief from all the stress, not Kristi constantly hounding him.

"Where're you going, honey?" Her sweet tone conflicted with the anger building in her eyes.

"To say hello to Brooke. I've barely seen her the last few days."

"You live in the same house. You've seen her plenty. I'm sure she'd like to spend time with her old friends. Seems she's drawn attention from many of the male guests. It's nice to see her spreading her wings and her social circle."

He got the hint. Kristi didn't like Brooke taking up his time. They'd already had this conversation upstairs.

Brooke was his friend. She'd always be his friend.

Kristi should understand that by now.

"I wonder if she's got a boyfriend back at school."

He recoiled at the thought and his gut tightened painfully. No way.

Why not? Look at her, she's gorgeous.

He didn't want to think about her making someone else feel the way she always made him feel. Special. Needed. Wanted. "She's too busy studying to date."

If she had a boyfriend, he'd know about it.

They told each other everything.

At least, that's what he'd thought until this past summer when she'd...pulled away.

He didn't think they would end up like this, where she turned away instead of coming over to talk to him. Had she been avoiding him since she got home? No. He'd just been busy working. She didn't want to interrupt. Right? Fuck. He didn't know. And it hurt. He was surprised by how much. But he shouldn't be. Brooke was...more important than he realized.

Fuck.

That night she came home late right before she was headed back to campus to start the new year of school came back to him. He'd confessed that he missed her. He'd wanted her to know that despite how busy and distracted he'd been, he cared and regretted not spending time with her.

The house wasn't the same without her here. Texts weren't the same as sitting atop their horses in the middle of the property, just the two of them, talking about everything and nothing.

He missed her spunk and the way she made him laugh.

He missed the way he was when he was with her. Relaxed. Unburdened.

Brooke laughed again, drawing his attention to her across the room.

Too damn far away.

Charlie was talking to her again.

Kristi put her palm to his cheek and made him look at her, instead of staring at Brooke. "Honey, you went to college. Don't tell me you spent all that time studying. I'm sure you haunted many a party on a Friday and Saturday night with at least one girl on your arm and a beer in your hand."

Cody reluctantly nodded, hating thinking about Brooke being the woman on some other guy's arm.

Back in the day, he'd taken them back to his dorm room for no-strings-attached sex. Just two people out for a good time. As long as they both had the same idea, the next day was business as usual—classes and friends and waiting for the next Friday-night party to begin.

The thought of Brooke laughing with some guy at a party and ending up a notch on his dorm room bedpost made Cody seethe. The thought of some guy touching her set his teeth to grinding. His hand clamped so forcefully around his tumbler, it was a wonder the glass didn't shatter like his self-control was about to.

"Look at you, so upset." Kristi tsked. "She's young and free. Of course she's having fun being on her own, no one watching her."

Cody gulped his bourbon, relishing the burn.

Brooke should be concentrating on her studies, not warming some guy's bed after a night of drinking. He wanted to go over and give her the talking-to of her life. She shouldn't be giving herself to every random guy she met at a party.

Wait.

He went still.

All of a sudden reason returned. He was being ridiculous.

That wasn't Brooke.

That wasn't the girl he knew.

But the girl he watched grow up wasn't the woman standing across the room. He had to accept she'd changed. How much, he didn't know.

Still, he had no idea if she was seeing anyone, let alone sleeping around. She wasn't that kind of girl. At least, he hoped she wasn't, because then...

What?

What are you going to do?

You love sex. Why shouldn't she?

I want it to be me.

Oh God. What was he thinking?

"Thank God your party days are over." Kristi interrupted his consuming thoughts. "I much prefer the upstanding lawyer you are now to the rowdy frat boy you used to be back on campus."

Kristi put her hand on his forearm. "You can't seriously think Brooke spends her weekends studying in the library. She's a pretty girl. I'm sure more than one college guy has noticed."

Anger flashed hot and swift through his system.

Kristi recognized it. "Oh, come on, Cody. Playing big brother now is a little like closing the barn door after the horse is already out. Wouldn't you say? I mean, she's all grown up. I have to say I prefer this mature version of her to the little girl who chased after you, unmercifully embarrassing you in front of friends and colleagues."

"We're friends," he said to explain the way Brooke behaved. She thought she loved him. It had been cute most of the time, and annoying some of the time. She had a way of looking at him and knowing just how he felt, and what he was thinking. She knew when he needed to bend her ear, and when he needed her to bulldoze her way past his temper and make him laugh.

He was an asshole for taking all her adoration and pretending he didn't see how he hurt her when he didn't reciprocate. He simply didn't know a better way to handle it.

So he let it go and took the easy way out to preserve their friendship.

So she wouldn't turn away from you. Like she is now.

His chest ached with that too-true thought.

Kristi's face turned red and her anger boiled over. She actually snapped at him. "Friends don't flirt." She took a deep sip of her wine and seemed to calm herself. "She's finally realized you love me. I like the way things have been the last few days that Brooke has been home. She's stopped being your shadow. She's backed off, and I appreciate it. You should, too."

"Don't be ridiculous, Kristi. Brooke is part of my life. She always will be."

Too busy watching Brooke say hello to some young guy, Cody ignored Kristi's scowl.

I'm jealous and I shouldn't be. I chose Kristi. I'm with her. But that doesn't mean I'll stop looking out for Brooke.

Kristi stepped into his line of sight and held his gaze, hers frosty. "Take a step back, Cody, like she has. Put the relationship on the level it should be now. Stop acting like you can't stand seeing her with those guys. They're her friends, too. She's known them for years, and here you are acting like they're going to take her away from you."

That would never happen. They were family. Sorta.

"I know you two are close, honey," Kristi said, echoing his thoughts. "But, please, let her loose. She has her own life. You have yours *with me*. I know you like being the only man in her life, but you can't expect that to always be the case."

"I don't." Something shook in his chest when the words left his lips.

Liar!

Fuck.

He did expect to be the only man in Brooke's life.

He liked being the man Brooke loved. He didn't want to see her pour out her affection for someone else. He didn't want to lose what they shared.

He didn't want to lose her. Ever.

She could be yours if you stepped up.

How would that work?

He couldn't take her away from school. Long distance would only make things harder.

He and Kristi were a good match. She was here and understood the demands on his time.

So would Brooke!

He tried not to let Kristi see how all this affected him, but her eyes narrowed and flared with anger again.

He had plans with Kristi. He needed someone present and connected to the people around him. Someone who could handle the high stress and very public role. Kristi was that person. Everyone loved her. They loved her with him.

Being with Brooke would be complicated. It would create gossip. He didn't care what people said about him, but he'd care if it hurt Brooke.

With Kristi, he didn't have to worry about that. She knew how to play the public game and she loved it.

Brooke was too private. She'd support him, of course. She'd do anything for him. He just didn't think she'd be comfortable in that role.

You sure about that?

Right now his thoughts and feelings were all over the place.

And Kristi wasn't helping. Probably because they hadn't seen much of each other lately. That was his fault because he'd taken on a very demanding case that needed his undivided attention.

If he was stalling her on the whole marriage thing, it was only because he wasn't ready to take that major step into the next part of his life.

He'd seen his father's marriage to Cody's mom break and how it hardened his father and made him bitter and distrustful. Cody wanted to be sure his marriage would withstand the tough times.

Kristi always supported him. She took upsets, date cancellations, and him either rushing through sex because he was tired or not showing up at all when she wanted him to stay at her place in favor of getting a good night's sleep at home. But lately she'd been passive-aggressively dropping comments about all of it, letting her unhappiness show.

Again, he took the blame. Work, the board, the ranch, other obligations kept him busy. None of that was going to change.

Was it too much for her to handle in the long run? He wondered about that all the time.

So he'd wait and see, because he really did want to get married and have a family.

When the time was right, he'd be happy to buy the ring and propose, knowing he was walking into the life he wanted.

Just not yet.

They had plenty of time.

Kristi kept a fake smile on her lips for everyone around them to see so no one knew they were fighting. Again. "You do expect her to adore you and only you forever, and you know it. What man wouldn't like to be worshipped by a beautiful young woman?" She put her hand to his cheek and made him look at her. "You have me, honey. I love you. We have a good thing and it'll only get better. Don't ruin it by trying to hold on to *her* when you really don't want her."

What if I do?

She softened her tone and stepped closer. "If it's more attention you need, I'm more than willing to give it to you." She pressed close and trailed her fingers down his neck to rest on his chest. She shifted slightly and rubbed her breasts against him. "Spend more time with me and less with your cases and the ranch and I will give you everything you need," she purred.

This was more like the Kristi he fell for in the beginning.

His hands went to her hips and he pulled her closer. He liked her this way. He wished she were like this more often. "Work has been crazy. Several of my cases are moving to court at almost the same time. I'm swamped. We'll have more time together soon." That was a lie. His career was taking off faster than even he expected. There would be more cases. He'd have less time.

Kristi didn't understand that. She didn't want to hear it. "Maybe step away from the ranch business and focus on being a lawyer."

"What? No. I've already given over most of the running of the place to the manager. But I like working the ranch when I have time. It gives me a physical outlet and time to not think but just be while I'm tending the animals or riding horseback through the fields."

She squeezed his arm. "I want more time with you."

"I want that, too."

She tilted her head and studied him. "Do you?"

"Yes. Absolutely." But he didn't want to give up the ranch.

Because it will give you an excuse to be with Brook?

Kristi let out a soft sigh and seemed to gather herself. "I understand how hard you're working to build a career, and a life, *for us*."

He already could more than support them.

He made good money as a lawyer and he loved the challenge and how he was building a name for himself. Not that he needed the money. His father had left him a wealthy man.

"After Brooke graduates, she'll help me with the ranch, and I'll have more time."

Another thing he and Kristi didn't see eye to eye on, because a piece of the ranch and his wealth had also gone to Susanne and Brooke. She thought it all should have gone to Cody. He didn't mind that his father left Susanne, his devoted, loving wife, a share. But it really irritated Kristi that Brooke got a share, too. It made Kristi jealous and angry that there would always be a permanent link between him and Brooke through the ranch, the home, that tied them together.

Cody didn't mind. His father had wanted to be sure that Brooke never had to rely on anyone to take care of her. After her own father left, she and Susanne struggled. Now Brooke would never have to rely on anyone for anything. It eased Cody's heart, just as much as it did his father's, to know that they'd provided that sense of safety and security to both of them.

It made him happy and secure to know Brooke would always call the ranch home.

Cody wanted to make Kristi happy, but he also wanted to make sure every guy in the room stopped hitting on Brooke.

Kristi grabbed his arm again, pulling him back because she didn't want to share him. "Don't do this. Don't leave me to go to her. She's fine. You'll see her tomorrow morning at breakfast."

He gave her a quick peck on the forehead and extricated his arm from her grasp. "I told you upstairs I wanted to catch up with Brooke tonight. I'll just be a minute."

She frowned and her eyes narrowed to a cold glare. By the look in her eyes, she was building up to an explosive argument. Another one.

He didn't want to fight with her. He wanted her to understand that Brooke was a part of his life. He shouldn't have to choose when Kristi knew he was with her and Brooke was just a friend.

Cody pointed to his left. "Look, there's your mom and dad with your boss. Maybe seeing you here will help him make up his mind about who gets the promotion at work."

"Maybe. He's traditional. He thinks young women aren't dedicated to their jobs and that their husbands want them at home. If you're with me and tell him how much you support me working, he'll see that I'm dedicated to my job."

"Okay. I can do that. Go say hi. I'll join you in a minute."

"Cody, please. Stop putting your stepsister before me. It's not fair, and I'm tired of feeling like you don't trust me and can't confide in me the way you do with her."

"You know that's not true." Another lie. The guilt soured his gut. Talking to Brooke was easy. He didn't have to carefully choose his words or rein in his emotions the way he did with Kristi, so as not to upset her or make things worse. "I'll catch up with you in a minute." He walked away before she argued even more.

He just wanted to talk to Brooke and make sure things were as they had always been between them. That's all he needed to know, then he'd be the doting boyfriend and talk up Kristi to her boss like she always did for him.

Chapter Fifteen

Standing alone in the corner of the room, he pulled out his phone and checked out Brooke's latest post. She must have sent it moments before walking down the stairs in that killer dress. Those legs! He could stare at them all day.

The picture she posted was of her up in her room standing in front of a full-length mirror. Hair and makeup making her even sexier.

@BrookeBanks: LBD and new shoes for our annual holiday party!

The strappy black heels sparkled with some sort of metallic thread. Her toenails were painted red. Her lipstick matched it. So did the rubies in her ears.

The perfect outfit for tonight. And she looked damn good in it.

Though he'd like to see her out of it, wearing just those heels and that I-look-sexy-as-hell smirk.

He sent her an appreciative reply.

@youseeme: Gorgeous! Wish I was your plus-one. That dress...

He added three fire emojis and sent the message.

She didn't have her phone on her. Where would she put it? That dress hugged her body, showcasing every curve. He'd like to map them with his hands, his tongue, his lips.

Fuck, he was hard and aching.

He hoped his two buddies didn't notice as they closed in and stood beside him, finishing up a conversation about which show they liked better, *Supernatural* or some new version of *Star Trek* that recently released.

You couldn't compare one to the other in his opinion. They were too different. So he kept his mouth shut and his gaze glued to his favorite person.

Brooke understood him. She was probably the only one who did.

She wound her way around the room. It seemed everyone wanted to be near her tonight. Him especially.

As she spoke to someone across the room, her gaze collided with his and a bright, beautiful smile bloomed on her red lips as she acknowledged him with a nod and held up a finger for him to wait. She'd be over soon.

His heart fluttered. Who knew he had one anymore? Any soft, happy, loving thoughts or feelings had been stamped out as a child with his parents' continued lack of interest and indifference.

Toe the line. Get with the program. Play your part.

That's all his parents wanted from him. They didn't care how he felt about any of it. He'd locked his uncontrollable feelings away until he didn't feel anything.

And then he met Brooke and something inside him sparked to life.

The spark grew to a flame, knowing she understood him, was interested in him. Not his father and what he could do for her. People often tried to use him for an introduction or to plead their case for whatever they wanted, thinking him an easy way into the inner circle.

They didn't know his father barely tolerated the prop that he'd brought to life but that didn't live up to family expectations. His parents expected him to put on a fake but convincingly genuine smile on his face in public to show the world they were a happy family, though they preferred to have him quietly tucked away at school, out of sight, out of mind.

No matter how much he tried to get their attention, another meeting, dinner party, or function they must attend always came first. Either their needs or someone else's had always come before his, leaving him forever in the background.

They refused to see or acknowledge how he struggled with loneliness and depression. *We don't talk about that* should be the family motto.

Brooke's sympathy and understanding this summer had comforted him, where in others he found it maddening. She saw *into* him, to the person shrouded inside the shell everyone saw on the outside—one that was the opposite of his larger-than-life father.

He'd always had a deeply entrenched feeling that something significant would happen to break him out of his supporting role, that someone would see him as important and worth loving.

It was her.

He knew it.

He felt it to his soul.

She was his. And he belonged to her.

Finally she broke away from the couple she'd been speaking with and headed his way, her steps determined, like she couldn't wait to be close to him, the way he wanted to be close to her.

One of his friends saw her coming. "Do you think she'll be mad about Marco breaking up with Mindy Sue and not want to speak to us?"

"She's cool. She's not like that," the other said, right as Brooke joined their little group.

Her gaze settled on him and her smile brightened.

He took in the warmth in her green eyes and the sultry message in her smile. She was happy to see him and wanted him. But she couldn't say or do anything about it with everyone watching.

Her gaze slid to his buddies, her smile still there but lacking the underlying message only he could see.

Brooke abandoned her barely touched plate on one of the veranda tables. "It's so good to see all of you. It's been a while. I'm so happy you came."

That last part was just for him, he was sure of it.

Chapter Sixteen

Brooke missed hanging out with Adam, Jeremiah, and Simon. They'd had some good times together. But like a lot of splits, Mindy Sue kept her friends, Marco his, and none of them wanted to make their friend think they were disloyal by mingling without them. Though Mindy Sue wouldn't mind her hanging out with these guys. Marco...you never knew what he'd find offensive and bash you for.

Adam, Jeremiah, and Simon were too shy and laid-back to really stand up to Marco. She sometimes wondered how the four of them became friends. Though Marco seemed to be the dominant personality and the other three were more alike to each other, so maybe Marco had used them to appear to have real friends, because he wasn't really that nice all the time and these guys wouldn't call him out on it.

"I hope your parents didn't drag you here and you actually wanted to come," she blurted out, nervous for some reason. They were all staring at her, probably hoping she'd address the elephant in the room.

Simon shook his head. "I wanted to come. You were always cool with us."

"Yeah," Jeremiah said. "And Marco got what he deserved. He should have treated your friend better. She was too nice to him for too long."

"We're guilty of that, too," Adam added. "But just because they're not together doesn't mean we can't hang out. Right?" His hopeful tone, along with the others' comments, made all her anxiety disappear.

They were probably all hoping she still wanted their friendship. "I don't blame the innocent for what others do."

"How did your finals go?" Simon asked.

She let out a dramatic sigh. "I'm so glad they're over. I spent a week studying late into the night and finishing a paper. I got all A's, so that's a relief. I don't want to slack off just because I know what I'm going to do after I graduate and my GPA won't matter to an employer."

"What are you going to do?" Jeremiah asked.

"I'm buying the local bookstore. Actually, a whole building. I'll open a café next to the bookstore, rent out the second-floor office space, and rent out the third-floor apartments. Well, all except the one I'll move into once I'm home." She hadn't told her mom or Cody about that part of her plans yet.

Adam gaped, his cheeks turning red with a blush. "You took my suggestion."

She grinned at him. "It was too tempting not to look into it. I'll be finalizing things this spring and will hopefully open at the start of summer. So thank you. You inspired me to believe in myself and that I didn't need to gain experience from working for someone else to take the leap to do this. I know what I want and what I'm doing." She let loose a self-deprecating laugh. "Well, I'm sure I'll make mistakes along the way, but I have my mom and Cody to back me up if I need it."

"You won't. You've got this," Jeremiah encouraged.

"You'll be amazing," Simon said, his gaze dipping away. "I wish I had my future as perfectly mapped out as you do."

"Sounds like your mom is supporting you." Adam looked like that was a novel idea.

Brooke understood that in his world, expectations were high. Adam, like Simon, didn't always meet them for his exacting parents and it took a toll on him. On both of them.

They stood and chatted for a few minutes about classes and life on campus. Jeremiah took the lead and seemed at ease, while Adam and Simon chimed in when they felt comfortable. Just like old times.

"We should meet up for coffee"—Adam rubbed the back of his neck—"or something," he blurted out when conversation waned.

Brooke nodded. "I'd love that. I bet Mindy Sue and Julie would love to join all of us."

Adam stuffed his hands in his pockets and stared at his feet. "Yeah. That'd be great."

"I can't wait," Simon put in.

Jeremiah bumped his shoulder to hers. "Just because Marco blew it doesn't mean we can't all be friends."

Adam and Simon's eyes both went wide and stared past her.

She wondered what had them spooked, until she turned and found Cody coming up behind her, his narrowed eyes glued to the three young men in front of her.

"Brooke. A word."

Adam, Jeremiah, and Simon all said, "Hey," at the same time to Cody.

"You guys having a good time?" Cody slipped his hand around her waist and pulled her to his side.

What the...what?

A whirl of butterflies took flight in her belly and her skin flushed with the heat of him sinking into her. He smelled delicious, like dark chocolate and spice. She stood still, trying to keep the placid look on her face and not let anyone know how deeply his nearness affected her. She stood as still as possible and forbade herself from leaning into him.

Be good. Don't do anything stupid. Again.

The guys stood staring, probably as curious as she was by Cody's not-so-subtle protective steak when it came to her.

Jeremiah took a big step back and said, "It was good to catch up. I'll text you about meeting up. I think I'll go check out the dessert table." All the sentences nearly ran together, he spoke so fast.

"Me, too," Adam said, turning to follow Jeremiah.

Simon gave Cody a long look before saying, "I really hope to see you soon."

Cody's embrace tightened.

Brooke subtly nudged him. He didn't move an inch.

Brooke gave Simon a big smile. "I'm looking forward to it."

Simon nodded. "And congratulations on the store and everything."

Her smile softened as her appreciation that he cared overcame her. "Thank you."

Cody waited for Simon to head off toward their other friends before raising a brow at her.

Chapter Seventeen

He didn't want dessert but picked up a piece of strawberry cheesecake and followed his buddies to one of the tables where he could still see Brooke with *him*.

Cody was her stepbrother. He shouldn't have his hands on her like that.

He seethed, a coiled rattler ready to strike.

Who was he kidding? He didn't have it in him to demand the guy take his damn hands off *his* woman.

Brooke didn't seem to mind.

She was being polite. Not making a scene in front of everyone. That's all it was.

He narrowed his eyes, wondering at Cody's game as much as Brooke appeared to be. Because the second he'd wrapped his arm around her, her eyes went wide with surprise, like this was something unexpected.

Why would Cody touch her like she belonged to him when the blonde in the gold dress, glaring from across the room, was his girlfriend?

Which meant all of this was for show. Cody was making sure every man in the room knew she was off-limits. He was being an overprotective stepbrother. That's all.

Not a problem. I'll see Brooke back at school. When she's alone.

He still had a shot with her.

Everything inside him centered on Brooke.

She was his future.

He stared at Brooke through the small crowd. She smiled and hit Cody on the chest as he kissed her on the head.

In that moment, he knew what he had to do.

He needed to be more like his father. Confident. Strong-willed. Take-charge.

How many times had his father said, "No one will hand you anything. You need to take what you want."

Maybe it was time he took his father's advice.

He'd let another guy take her away.

He shook his head, disgusted with himself.

He wouldn't let it happen again.

Thanks to Brooke, he had a purpose.

He'd transform himself into the man Brooke needed him to be.

And then, he would take what he wanted most. Brooke Banks.

Chapter Eighteen

B rooke focused on the man who always stole her attention. "Nice, Cody. The guys just wanted to catch up. You didn't have to intimidate them."

Cody glared at the three of them sitting on the veranda eating dessert. "They're not for you. You'd walk all over them and crush their poor soft hearts."

She smacked his chest. "I would not."

Cody captured her hand against his chest and held it there, his warmth seeping into her skin. The arm banded around her waist held her close. His familiar spicy aftershave made her inhale and savor this sweet moment. "No, you wouldn't. You'd never hurt anyone. You've got a soft heart, too."

She did. And she'd abused her poor heart enough by beating it against the locks on Cody's heart. He didn't want to let her in, and she was tired of making her heart bleed.

She slowly extricated herself from his side and stood next to him, a respectable distance from his hard, toned body.

She tried to hide her longing and forced herself to be an adult and respect his space and relationship with Kristi. Even if Kristi was all wrong for him.

It sucked being an adult and good.

Her mother had neglected to tell her that some growing pains were emotional as well as physical.

"It's a great party, Cody." She steered the conversation toward normal, everyday things.

"Yeah. It makes me miss my dad even more. I have you to thank for making me remember family, friends, and traditions matter."

"I miss him, too." She wanted to reach out and touch him but refrained.

He frowned, his gaze noting the distance between them.

She tried to cover. "Dad taught me how to dance. I'd stand on his feet, and he'd take me around the dance floor."

Cody's eyes filled with nostalgia. "You stood on my feet a time or two," he reminded her, taking her by the shoulders and kissing her on the head. He stared down at her for a long moment, then released her and stuffed his hands in his pockets.

She wondered about his odd behavior. Especially since Kristi seethed across the room.

It was a good thing she couldn't actually feel the daggers Kristi invisibly threw at her. But Kristi's murderous feelings were all too easy to read.

Cody pulled out one hand and brushed it down her arm. "You've been very popular tonight. Everyone looking at you. Several of the guys kissed and hugged you."

She caught the irritated tone and disapproval in his voice and ignored her first instinct that he might be jealous.

Yeah, right.

Like Cody would ever be jealous of another guy hanging out with her.

He'd more likely plant a hand on her back, shove her toward the guy, and say, "Here, you take her."

Instead of giving in to the fantasy that she was Cody's girl and he hated seeing her with other guys, she remembered all the years he'd made one thing clear to the men on the ranch: If they wanted to play with a woman's affections, they'd do it with any woman but Brooke. She was strictly off-limits.

They'd taken the warning to heart, even if they sometimes teased and flirted with her.

But they'd been different with her tonight and Cody noticed.

Apparently, he wanted to make things clear to them once more. No matter how old she was now, she was still off-limits to the guys who worked for them.

"Everyone's just happy to see me. I've been away longer than usual."

"You should come home more often. Your mom misses you."

It hurt that he didn't include himself in that sentiment. "I'll try. I've been busy with my classes."

"You've kept your grades up?"

"Of course." She inhaled, unable to help herself. God, he smelled good. He smelled like home. She'd missed him so much, but stayed away, so they both could grow. Her by easing into being completely independent and to get over him. And Cody focusing on his career and the first long-term relationship that seemed to be going the distance, with Kristi.

Cody held her gaze, his serious. "I hope you aren't spending your weekends partying with frat boys. All kinds of dangerous things can happen at one of those parties.

Least of which is some asshole slipping something into your drink and taking advantage of you."

Cody always looked out for her, but this was truly being overprotective.

Of course she called him on it. "Well, Dad, I swear I've never been to one of those parties or sipped a single beer in my whole life." Her words dripped sarcasm. She rolled her eyes. "Come on, Cody. You went to college. If memory serves, there were a great many parties you told me about."

"Then you should take the warning seriously. I want you to be careful. A house full of drunken assholes is no place for a girl like you."

She raised a brow. "And what kind of girl am I?" She truly wanted to know how he saw her.

"You'd better not be the girl at those parties going home with some random guy."

She laughed. She'd never gone home with a guy from a party—random or well known.

Okay, technically, there was that one time. But she didn't sleep with him.

Cody had been in her heart so long, she'd never had a serious relationship with a guy. She'd never allowed herself to look at another man and think what it would be like to have him touch her. When she thought about being with a man, it was always Cody in her arms.

She hoped he hadn't ruined her for other men. She wondered if she'd ever look at another man and not compare him to Cody.

"I knew every single one of them." She kept her tone completely serious despite joking with him.

Cody's whole body tensed for one split second before he whipped toward her and grabbed her shoulders again. "What the hell? Are you crazy?"

She wrapped her fingers around his forearms, holding on before he scrambled her brain again. Stunned by his abnormal behavior, it took her a second to think clearly.

His fingers bit into her skin, pressing muscle to bone. His pulse thundered at his throat. Furious with her, his mouth pulled into a disapproving frown.

She tried to soothe him with her soft voice. "Cody. I was only kidding."

He didn't let her go but hauled her up against his chest, let out a huge sigh of relief, and held her so tight she couldn't breathe.

What is going on with him?

He sucked in a breath and held her like he'd never let go. He pressed his cheek to her hair. "I'm so sorry, kid. You've got a good heart and guys can be assholes. I don't ever want to see you hurt. I don't want anyone to ever break your heart."

She leaned back in his arms and stared up at him, so he could see her annoyance. "I'm not a kid anymore. It can't have escaped your attention that I'm all grown up. You don't have to worry about me anymore. I can take care of myself."

"I will always protect you."

"Things have changed, Cody. I'm my own woman now."

"What does that mean?"

"I decide what I want and who I want to be with and when. And if I can't have the one I want, then I guess I'll have to find a dimmer version of happiness with someone else."

"No." The thought of her with someone else made him want to rage.

She belonged to him.

He wanted her to have everything her heart desired.

That's me.

He wanted her to be the happiest person on the planet.

God, I shouldn't want this, but I do.

She tilted her head. "No?"

"No." He got lost in her adoring eyes for a moment as he drew her in. She felt so right, so perfect in his arms and pressed along his body. The wave of heat and passion that swept through him didn't match up with the tameness of the embrace, telling him what they shared was something profound. Special. Raw. Too powerful to ignore or give up.

He forgot about everything and everyone—and maybe lost his mind a little bit—and kissed her.

The second his lips pressed to hers, it felt like everything out of line inside him clicked into place.

It felt like coming home.

It turned out to be so much more than he expected or anticipated.

He couldn't deny he'd thought about this. The reality was so much better.

His lips touched her pillow-soft ones and he was lost in her sweet flavor. Uniquely Brooke. His new favorite tempting treat.

The axis-tipping moment caught him off guard. So did the fact that he craved a deeper, more intimate kiss. And more. Much, much more.

What the fuck are you doing?

Thrown off-kilter, he needed to think before he did something that ruined everything.

You just did!

He hoped not. Reining in his desires, he covered his intense reaction to her with, "You're special, Brooke." He brushed a lock of hair behind her ear. "Don't ever settle for a guy that treats you otherwise."

He was just beginning to see how special she was to him.

After his father's death, he'd clung to the routine of his life to keep him on track and take care of all his father had left behind. Brooke had kept him sane. She was the constant in his life that grounded him.

Tonight showed him how much had changed since she went away to college and how much he hated it. This Brooke wasn't the one he remembered.

Yes, she is. But now she's more.

And you want her!

Brooke put her hands on his chest and pushed off of him. Or did she try to push him away? Hard to tell. She couldn't move him because he didn't want to be moved. He wanted to stay close to her. He wanted to get even closer.

She took another step back and suddenly stiffened as she stared past him. "Kristi," she whispered.

He turned just enough to see her across the room out of his peripheral vision.

The devastated look on Kristi's face disappeared with a plastered-on smile, hiding the betrayal she must feel.

I did that.

Fuck!

She went back to talking with her boss, but not before he and Brooke caught the promise of revenge in Kristi's glare.

I fucked up. I was supposed to talk her up and support her the way she always supports me.

Fuck. Fuck. Fuck.

Brooke met his gaze, hers serious and angry. "You should go to her and tell her it didn't mean anything."

I can't pull off that colossal lie anymore.

Brooke took another step back.

He hated the added distance and wanted to bring her back into his arms. He denied himself that pleasure. Reluctantly. Painfully.

He stuffed his hands in his pockets so he didn't reach for her again. "She knows we're friends. I wish I didn't have to keep explaining that plain and simple fact to everyone. Including her."

She lifted her hand but let it drop before it connected with his arm. "Yes. We are friends."

"But?" he asked, prompting her to speak her piece.

Remind me that we're more, like you always used to.

He hated to think that he'd killed her love for him when he pushed her away during the picnic.

"Being my friend isn't as easy as it used to be. Is it? If I was in her shoes, and you shared a close friendship with another woman, and kissed her the way you just kissed me, I'd be mad and jealous as hell."

Good. Because that's how I feel tonight watching every man in the room looking at you.

Cody brushed his fingers along her soft as silk cheek. "You've been jealous of every other woman in my life." He'd always known that, but never said anything. Now, he couldn't help the feelings exploding inside him.

And the new truth he couldn't deny. He wanted her to be jealous. He wanted her to want him the way she'd always wanted him.

She took another step back and his chest tightened with the loss.

He didn't like that at all. This time, he hooked his arm around her waist and pulled her back in.

Her eyes went wide. "You love Kristi."

Do I? Then why am I holding you like this?

"She deserves to have you completely."

That's not what I really want. Not anymore.

It blew his mind to think that.

Your hands are also dangerously close to sliding down over her lush ass.

He reluctantly released her and shoved his hands into his pockets once again, needing some space and room to breathe without taking in her breath and smelling her temptingly heady scent. "I see how different you are now. But there's something else. Something I don't like. There's this distance you've put between us. You've never been a fan of Kristi's. You made that clear. She's no fan of yours either. I wish it wasn't that way, but I get it. But tonight you're pushing me back to her, and the last few days, you've been outright avoiding me. Why, damnit?"

He just wanted things to go back to the way they used to be, when he and Brooke were simple. She was his friend, his confidant, his everything he needed her to be, and she was happy to be it.

Except she was right. He'd complicated things by kissing her and stirring up the feelings that sprouted when they shared that moment during the picnic and grew into what he felt tonight when he kissed her and meant it with every cell of his body.

"It's simple, Cody. I've finally grown up enough to see things from her side. I'm sorry that our friendship hurts her. It's not intentional, but it's real because she can see how much I care about you. She sees that you care for me. As a friend." A sad look came over her and he felt it in his chest. She wanted more from him.

He'd spent all these years trying to protect her heart for lots of different reasons—she was too young. It was inappropriate. He only cared for her as a friend—but things were different now. They could have something different than what they'd always shared. But she still had school. They lived apart. They were both extremely busy.

How exactly would this work?

"You know how I feel," she went on. "I don't think Kristi is good enough for you. Then again, we both know I think the only woman good enough for you is me."

He couldn't believe she'd put it all on the line like that even if she knew he knew how she felt. They'd never really discussed this part of their relationship.

Brooke grinned. "Don't start getting nervous, or thinking about how you're going to let me down easy like you always do. I appreciate that you always tried to spare my feelings. All I'm saying is our friendship hurts her, and if she leaves you because of it, that will hurt you. I never want to cause you pain."

With all the friction between him and Kristi lately, he wasn't so sure he'd be all that upset. It felt like as hard as he tried to be everything she wanted, he failed. Sometimes it felt like she liked who he was and what he did for a living and what it afforded her more than she truly liked him. If that even made sense.

He took Brooke's hand in his and stared down at her, truly, honestly looking at her.

God, she's beautiful. Inside and out. My friend. The person I need in my life the most.

His chest grew tight as his hand tensed around hers.

He wanted to hold on, but should he let her go?

Was he holding on because he needed her more than he needed Kristi, or was he just doing it because he didn't want things to change?

"I *won't* give you, and the friendship we share, up for her, or anyone else."

Brooke squeezed his hand, looking him in the eye with so much regret in hers he could barely breathe. "Then maybe you don't love her the way you think you do. If you did, changing the nature of our friendship wouldn't affect you like this."

She wants you out of my life and that can't happen.

Brooke released his hands and took a step away before he called her back. "Brooke." Just her name, that's all he could say for everything he felt. It was all a mess inside him, and he couldn't sort it out. He needed to before he lost the only person in his life he counted on to be there no matter what.

"Don't worry, Cody. We'll always be friends. Just not like it's been in the past. I grew up. I want more. You have your life with Kristi. Those two things don't go together."

Moving to him, she went up on tiptoe and pressed a kiss to his cheek.

He wanted to grab her and hold her and never let her go.

"I'm going in to spend some time with Mom. In a few days, I'll be back to school, and you'll have your life back in order, exactly as it was before I came home."

That's not what happened when you went back to school last time. All I do is miss you.

Would his life ever be the same again?

Brooke released him and walked away, leaving him standing there alone, his chest tight, his gut in a knot, and his heart cracked wide-open.

All he wanted to do was go after Brooke and kiss her again. He could still taste her.

Lost. Unbalanced. He walked back into the party and Kristi's cold glare bore into him.

He deserved her scorn.

He hadn't meant to hurt her.

Brooke's words rang in his head. She was right. He'd rather go after Brooke and solidify their relationship than go in and appease Kristi.

Leave it to Brooke to point out the bold truth he'd been avoiding since the picnic.

What did he expect?

What are friends for?

Chapter Nineteen

Cody said goodbye to the last of their guests and closed the front door. Susanne had already retired to her side of the house, leaving him, Kristi, and Brooke to lock up for the night.

This isn't awkward at all.

He wished he could call Brooke back as she ascended the stairs to his left with her sexy high heels dangling from her fingertips. Feeling him staring at her, she glanced back, lifted her chin toward his study, where Kristi waited for him, then hit the landing and disappeared down the hall.

He had to let Brooke go, so he could deal with Kristi.

She didn't wait for him to come to her and barreled out of his study looking for a fight. "I can't believe you kissed her in front of everyone!"

"I've kissed her a dozen times in your presence."

"Not like that!" Venom filled her words to go with the fury in her eyes.

He slipped his hands into his pockets and stood before her, ready for whatever she had to say. "You're right. Not like that." Their usual hello and goodbye pecks were a hell of a lot different than the kiss he planted on Brooke earlier. That one was...intoxicating. Addictive. Tame compared to how he really wanted to kiss her. "I don't know what came over me." That was the truth.

Whatever it was, it was still consuming him.

"Perky tits and a tight ass," she shot back.

"Don't talk about her like that." He tried to keep calm, but that irritated him.

"Fine. Then let's talk about how you left me to go to her because you were raging jealous that every man at the party was making eyes...at. Your. *Sister*."

He sucked in a breath and tried to hold back his temper. "I'm not doing this with you again. Brooke is my friend."

"You keep saying that, but the way you looked at her tonight... It looked like a hell of a lot more than friends and everyone saw it." Kristi always cared about what everyone else thought.

He got it. In their social circle, image mattered. He often curtailed a comment or toed the line to get ahead, even when he'd rather say or do something different.

Tonight, he hadn't thought about what anyone would think. He'd simply acted without thinking things through. He could have handled things better. He should have. But what was done was done.

And he didn't particularly feel like taking it back.

He wondered if what others thought bothered her more than him going after Brooke. "What exactly are you implying?"

"Are you fucking her?"

She meant to shock him and she did.

"No." And he hated that she'd think that of him.

"You kissed her," she pointed out, making her case.

"That's all I did."

She shook her head like he'd lied to her. "No. You take her side on everything. You'd rather talk to her about...everything than me. When she's not here, you miss her like you'll never see her again. Even when you're busy, you make sure to give her the few minutes you have, while I'm always made to wait."

True. All of it.

And he was beginning to see why none of his relationships went anywhere.

"I can barely get you to keep a dinner date lately." Also true.

He'd neglected her. All the fights they'd had lately proved that. "I've been working like crazy. You knew it would be like this when your father nominated me for the board position. You not only supported it, you talked him into it, didn't you?" Still, not a great defense. He rubbed his hand over the back of his neck and tight muscles.

She held her arms rigid at her sides. "Yes, I did, because I knew you'd be great at it. I wanted to help you reach your full potential." Her voice grew louder with each word.

He scoffed. "You wanted me to look even more appealing to all your friends you're trying to impress. And your parents." He gave her a *you know it and I know it* look.

Her blue eyes narrowed. "It's not like you're not benefiting from it, too," she snapped.

"You're right." He held his arms out, then let them fall, regret replacing his habit of pleading his case. "I've tried to be what you need me to be with the limited time we spend together."

She folded her arms over her chest. "We'd spend more time together if we lived together. If we were married." She dropped her arms. "But you don't want to have that conversation. So I'm left to wait. For you." She waved her arm at him, then touched her chest. "For what I want."

He wasn't ready to take that step with her. "I'm doing the best I can. I thought you knew at least that."

"What I know is that something has changed between you and *her*, and I don't like it." She pressed her hand over her heart. "You humiliated me tonight. You and she snuck away while I endured the stares and raised eyebrows. How could you?"

He felt bad about that. "I didn't know I was going to do anything like that. I didn't intend to hurt you. I didn't intend to kiss her like that."

"But you did."

It just happened, because in the moment he couldn't stop himself. He hadn't wanted to. "Yes. I did. And I'm sorry I hurt you."

It was like he hadn't even spoken as she spoke right over him.

"What's worse is you don't even seem sorry about it."

"I am sorry." Didn't he just say that? And he meant it. But he wouldn't take it back. He'd never forget that kiss. And as much of a bastard as it made him, he wanted another.

And another.

And another.

"You love me."

She and Brooke both told him how he felt about Kristi tonight.

Funny thing was, he'd never told Kristi he loved her. She assumed based on their relationship that he did. Up until tonight, even he thought he did.

Then why didn't you ever say it?

His silence set her off.

"You unbelievably arrogant asshole. You really think I'll dismiss this and just go on with you like nothing happened."

"No. Things have been strained between us for a while." Since he took the board position and got even busier. "I'm sorry that a lot of it is because of me. I'm not sure what I can do about it."

She studied him for a long moment, letting his statement stand like a wall between them. Then her eyes went wide. "I knew all along you cared about her. Loved her even. But it's not just her who's changed. Something changed for you, too, tonight. You're in love with her."

"That's ridiculous."

Is it?

"Is it?" she said, echoing his thought.

He didn't have an answer for her, because right now, in this moment, he didn't know if she was right.

"I'm done being the other woman in your life. Goodbye, Cody." She spun on her heels, walked right out the front door, and slammed it at her back.

He waited for the pain and urge to go after her to come over him and make this right. It never came. Because he had chosen Brooke over her and admittedly every woman he'd dated.

They'd left.

Brooke was always here.

She would always be here for him.

His heart beat fast and hard in his chest. His mind wanted to reveal what that truly meant, but he needed a minute to calm down before he started thinking things he'd never allowed himself to even contemplate.

Restless, wired, and unsettled, he walked into his study, hoping to find some peace and quiet and his misplaced sanity.

In a matter of hours, he'd managed to turn his very orderly world upside down.

But there was one thing in his life that was always consistent.

He turned on his heel and headed up the stairs to Brooke's room. He couldn't leave things between them the way they were, so he knocked on her door.

She opened it, still wearing her dress. "Hey."

He took her hand and tugged her out the door. "Come with me. We need to talk."

She scrambled to keep up with his longer strides. He slowed on the stairs. He didn't want her to trip and hurt herself. He led her through the living room and back to the kitchen. He released her long enough to grab two plates and the double-chocolate fudge cake from the fridge. "Your favorite."

"Everyone's favorite. It's chocolate. But let's share it. I don't want to eat so much sugar right before bed."

He liked that idea and cut one slab of cake, dumped it onto the plate, put the cake way, grabbed the forks, and headed back to his study. "Come on." He took her hand in his again, needing the contact and grounding effect it gave him.

He handed the cake off to her and went to the credenza where he kept a few glasses and decanters of liquor. He poured himself a bourbon and sat at his desk.

A lamp on his desk cast a soft glow, but left the rest of the large room in shadows. Brooke walked out of the dark and into the light like some ghostly dream materializing before his eyes, wearing that damn black dress, her feet bare. He found that endearing and sexy as hell.

"So what do you want to talk about?" Brooke asked.

Cody tried to ignore his tumultuous thoughts, but failed miserably when his gaze dropped to her cleavage bouncing above the edge of the dress as she walked around the desk toward him and his mind conjured one hot, naked image of her after the next. He shut that line of thinking down, but another part of his brain made him face a reality he'd been reluctant to see. She was a grown woman now.

She'd rocked his world earlier with the kiss and telling him their relationship had to change if he continued to date, or married, Kristi.

He didn't have to worry about that now.

Kristi had walked out.

Like always, Brooke was here for him.

"We never fight. We talk to each other. But things have been...strange lately." Cody raked his fingers through his hair and sighed. He tugged his tie loose and undid the two top buttons on his shirt, trying to relax and find the right words to fix this.

She watched his every move. He was used to her gaze on him, but tonight, it all seemed different. He felt the heat in her gaze touch every part of him. He flexed his forearms as her gaze swept up his arm, across his shoulder to the patch of skin he'd bared at his neck, then up to meet his gaze.

She had to see how much that sultry glance affected him.

She picked up his bourbon and took a sip, like she needed some liquid encouragement.

He scolded her. "You're not twenty-one yet." He needed that drink as much as she did. Or ten. Because this night had taken a turn and he didn't know how to right his world again. He didn't know if he wanted to.

She put the snifter down in front of him next to the plate of cake. Gently tugging the file out from under his hands, she quickly peeked at his burglary case, folded it carefully, and set it aside. She lifted her hip onto the desk, then settled into a sitting position, facing him, and stared down at him, looking past his tired eyes and straight to his soul. She always read him well and tonight she didn't disappoint.

"What's troubling you, Cody?"

"I'm not sorry about what happened between us tonight."

Her head tilted to the side, but her gaze never wavered. "You didn't fix things with Kristi."

Yep. She saw everything. "What makes you think that?"

"I heard the door slam."

He took a sip of the amber liquid, hoping it smoothed out his rough edges. He could smell her. Always roses and honey. Tipping the glass of bourbon to his nose, he inhaled deeply. He wanted to clear her out of his mind, his entire system. But all he could think about was her and the way his mouth fit to hers so perfectly he could still feel her lips against his. He thought about the way she tasted and his body rebelled against the command in his mind to not think of *her* in that way.

Rock hard, he ached for the one woman he shouldn't want, but couldn't let go.

"You're sitting here in the dark contemplating reading legal files on burglaries you know your client committed, instead of going after Kristi and having wild makeup sex."

"I don't want to talk about Kristi," he snapped, his frustration getting the better of him, because the woman he wanted was sitting in front of him driving him crazy.

And she was right that he'd have to go after Kristi if he wanted that, which he didn't, not with her, because he never slept with Kristi here. He never brought any woman here. Because Brooke lived here—with him.

What the hell does that tell you, idiot?

She took a bite of cake, chewing thoughtfully, waiting him out. Used to his quick temper when he was frustrated, she'd sit there all night until he decided to spit it out and unload his burden. When he continued to sit there sipping the bourbon, staring at nothing in particular, avoiding staring at her spectacular legs and holding back what he really wanted from her, her lips drew into a serious line.

"I'm sorry, Cody. I never meant to come between you two. Maybe I should have stayed at school. The last time I came home, the two of you had grown really close and my presence upset her."

"She's obviously upset about the kiss," he admitted.

He still couldn't believe Kristi accused him of having an affair with Brooke. He wasn't that kind of man. But he couldn't help himself right now and indulged in a little fantasy about what it would be like to have Brooke writhing under him.

Remembering Kristi's anger, even understanding that under it lay a hurt he'd caused, didn't stop him from thinking about the woman in front of him. Brooke had grown into a beautiful woman, sparking another erotic fantasy about him laying her out on top of his desk and taking her in the dim light on top of all his legal files.

She looked him dead in the eye. "So, why'd you do it? You knew it would set her off. Makes me think you wanted to make her mad."

"I wasn't using you to cause a fight between us. I didn't know she was watching us." He'd been too consumed by Brooke.

He stared up at her and watched the fork slide across her lips as she ate another bite of cake. His gut went tight. He shifted in his leather chair to accommodate his achingly hard cock. "How's the cake?"

"Decadent." She stuffed another bite of the rich concoction into her mouth. "You're avoiding answering me," she said around the cake. She swallowed and took the bourbon from him to wash it down. He didn't really like her drinking, but the hum of pleasure she made when she swallowed kept his mouth shut. Her happiness meant more than a silly scolding for something she didn't do often and never overindulged in.

She watched him with eyes clouded with confusion by the way he studied her. Obviously, the boys on her campus didn't look at her with the kind of hunger he felt, tried to contain, but failed at hiding from her.

"Look, Cody, if you're involved with Kristi, or any woman for that matter, our friendship needs to come second."

"Very noble of you." He snatched the bourbon back, turned the glass, and took a sip, fitting his lips over the very spot her lips had touched.

Brooke's gaze narrowed and her pretty lips drew into a tight line. His narrowed on her mouth. The too-tempting tension between them grew along with his desire to kiss her again. If she kept staring at his mouth, he'd give in and fulfill the yearning he saw in her eyes despite how hard she tried to hide it.

"I just want you to know I understand you love her, and that means I take a backseat in your life." That was Brooke; anything for him.

He dismissed the part about him loving Kristi. Maybe he had. Once. Until he'd had that moment with Brooke months ago at the picnic and something started to change inside him. And right now, he didn't feel anything but his aching need for Brooke. "She accused me of having an affair with you."

She set aside the cake, put her hands on the edge of the desk, and leaned in closer to him. "Which you denied without reservation."

"She also accused me of being in love with *you*."

She went perfectly still. It took her a long second to respond. "What's not to love?"

He'd spilled his guts, telling her the truth about the situation. Her flippant remark upped his frustration.

She slid from the desk and took several steps away, putting space between them. She'd never done that. Until tonight. She'd always wanted to draw closer, but something had changed these last months, and especially the last few days, with her putting increasing distance between them.

He hated it. He wouldn't stand for it.

Cody didn't let her get far. He wrapped his fingers around her wrist and tugged her back. Off-balance, just like he felt on the inside, she fell back and landed in his lap. Exactly where he wanted her. She stared at him over her shoulder, her green eyes wide with shock, her lips parted on a soft gasp.

He stared at her beautiful face and couldn't for the life of him deny how he felt in that moment.

He didn't exactly admit he loved her, but he definitely couldn't deny it.

"I've been thinking about what you said. You know...that I might not love her if I can't give you up. You're right. It's over. She ended it. And maybe I should be upset. But...I can't stop thinking about our kiss."

"It was memorable," she whispered, uncertainty in her bright green eyes.

He squeezed her hips between his big hands. "Stop being casual about something remarkable."

Her eyes went wide. "I thought you only wanted to be friends."

"You're not the only one who's changed."

Everything around them disappeared at the edge of the light cast by the single lamp, leaving them cocooned in its soft glow. The intimacy grew along with the silence.

He traced his finger over her forehead, drawing away a stray strand of dark hair, then brushed his nose against hers, and inhaled her sweetness. "Something changed when we stood in this very room in July and I put my hand on you and didn't want to let go. Then you walked down the stairs tonight looking so beautiful, I caught my breath. But instead of coming to me, you walked the other way, and it hurt. It felt like I was losing you."

"You were with your girlfriend. I didn't want to interrupt."

"You should have, because you matter to me, and I would never turn you away."

"I didn't turn away from you. I respected your relationship with her, because you matter to me. I didn't mean to upset you."

"It did. A lot. And it pissed me off to see all those guys at the party looking at you and touching you. Wanting you. Worse, I raged inside that you were looking at all of them. Talking to them. Smiling at them. You practically ignored me since the moment you got home. I kissed you because I couldn't stand how you were pulling away and I was holding back and I could lose you to someone else. They can't have you."

And still he couldn't bring himself to say the one thing she'd wanted to hear from him all her young life. She belonged to him.

She's mine.

The air held a thick tension as they crossed into uncharted territory.

The pulse at her throat fluttered, quick as hummingbird wings. He'd made her nervous, but still, she waited, not taking her eyes off him. Unmoving. Anticipation building. She waited. For him.

Cody took it as an invitation. His eyes locked with hers, he leaned into her, drawn by her enticing lips. His mouth fit over hers. He kept the kiss soft. Tempting.

Maybe it was the bourbon on her lips, or the soft light. Maybe it was the perfume she wore that insisted he draw closer, because he'd become addicted to her scent. Whatever it was, it set him off.

After the first nip at her bottom lip, he plunged, and then he plundered.

Like opening a window in a room and setting a fire free, the spark inside him ignited and consumed. His only thought: he had to have her. He had no idea why he'd taken so damn long to realize he wanted her when she'd made it so clear she wanted him.

He didn't care about the reasons or the whys, the past, or what this meant for their future. He needed her too badly to think of anything but her in his arms right now.

He wanted to feel her soft skin against his.

Now. Yesterday. Immediately.

Lost in her, Cody shut off his mind to everything but the feel of his mouth over hers and the taste of her tongue as they explored and found their unique rhythm. Stuck in the chair, unable to maneuver her closer, he stood with her in his arms and walked around the desk.

She wrapped her arms around his neck, turned into him, this time shyly taking the lead and sliding her tongue along his, finding her courage to give in to his gentle demand and her own curiosity. She took the kiss deeper and he let loose the groan building inside him from the moment his lips met hers.

So damn sweet. So damn good.

He released her legs, letting her body slide down the front of his until her feet hit the floor. No mistaking he wanted her. He blatantly showed her how much, pressing his hard cock to her soft belly. Desperate to touch more of her, he distracted her with another kiss and slid the zipper down on her dress. His fingertips trailed along her spine. Standing a mere inch away, he allowed the gown to fall and pool at her feet. He expertly unlatched her bra and let that drop, too, and never stopped kissing her, despite how much he wanted to see her beautiful body.

With her clothes out of his way, he let himself touch her lovely sun-kissed skin. She trembled at his fingertips.

He took her breasts into his hands and weighed them, molding the firm globes in his palms.

She fit perfectly in his hands, as perfectly as her mouth fit his.

Her sigh of pleasure shot through his system in a wave of heat. Every little sound she made expressed how much she liked everything he was doing to her. He sure as hell loved having her greedy hands moving over him.

He wanted to sheath himself deep in her warmth, knowing she'd match him in every way as they made love.

This wasn't just sex. This wasn't scratching an itch he never knew he had. This went deeper.

Every kiss, every caress, stoked the fire inside him and made something blaze in his heart and deep in his soul. No matter how close he held her, it wasn't close enough. He needed to be a part of her.

She's mine.

She'd always been his.

He wanted her. Now.

Kissing his way down her throat, he replaced his right hand on her breast with his mouth. He licked her taut pink nipple and her fingers contracted in his hair.

"Oh. That feels really good. More."

He gave it to her, swirling his tongue around the tight bud, then sucking it deep.

"Cody." She moaned his name.

Pressing her backwards, he held her around the waist as he laid her on the sofa. He slid his hand out from under her back, around her slim waist, and over her taut belly. He slipped his fingers into her lace panties and dragged them down her toned legs. He tossed that last barrier to her naked body on top of her discarded dress. When she was completely bared to him, he held himself inches above her and scanned her body from head to toe, taking in all her soft curves and creamy skin.

"God, you're beautiful. Why didn't I ever let myself see it?"

The hesitation and uncertainty just beneath the wild passion in her eyes disappeared. "You see me now."

He did. For the first time, he let himself really see her as more than his friend and as the woman he wanted more than he'd ever wanted anyone.

She'd done it. Cody saw her as the woman she'd become. A woman he desired. Her.

It seemed so amazing and surreal.

But did he love her the way she loved him?

It felt like it as he touched and kissed her so intimately. Passionately.

She knew sex and love didn't always go hand in hand, but between her and Cody, there'd always been love.

This could deepen it.

This could truly be the start of something new and wonderful between them. All she had to do was give herself over to it. To him.

Brooke had never been fully naked with a man. Cody's rapt attention made her feel vulnerable, but beautiful. The appreciation and hunger in his eyes told her how much he desired her. His gaze swept over her in a wave of heat that rippled over her skin. Then his gaze met hers again, filled with smoldering passion. He wanted her.

She'd tried so hard to tamp down the feelings she had for him. But right now, whatever he wanted, she was willing to give. Everything. Anything. It had always been this way, but now it went deeper.

His mouth came crashing down on hers, and he struggled to get his shirt off.

She wanted to look at him, touch him, so she went after the barriers with her own eager hands. Somewhere in the tussle of getting the shirt off his wrists, they landed hard on the floor. She gave a startled laugh, but let loose a ragged gasp when his mouth clamped onto her breast again. All she could think to do was arch up to him and hope he never stopped touching her. To make sure he didn't, she dug her fingers through his thick, golden hair and held on to him.

She let herself feel everything. His lips were soft, then strong against her breast. His tongue laved a wet trail over and around her nipple and the underside of her breast before he took her into his mouth again and sucked hard, making her moan. That soft sound drove him on and he took her other breast into his mouth.

He lay cradled between her thighs. His hard cock pressed to her center. She rocked against him and made him growl low in his throat.

Oh, I like that!

One big hand slid down her side and settled on her hip, stopping her movements, but all she wanted to do was rub against him and ease the ache building between her thighs.

"Cody. Please."

It was a lovely feeling to have his weight pressed down on her, but she wanted the release his body promised her. "I want to feel you fill me and move inside me."

"Fuck, yes!"

She loved touching him without having to hold anything back. Pressing her hands to the strong, taut muscles in his back, she slid her fingers down his spine to his hips. She splayed her fingers over his ass and squeezed.

He had a great ass. She'd always thought so. She pulled his hips to hers. His hard length rubbed against her sensitive folds and clit, setting off an eruption of pure pleasure.

She tried to take it all in, let herself feel everything, and didn't hesitate to fully participate and love him the way she'd always wanted to love him.

She tried to imprint it all on her heart and mind so she'd remember every little thing he did and made her feel.

His hot, wet mouth pressed openmouthed kisses down her belly. The last he pressed to her hip. His hands gripped her bottom and lifted her. She caught his eye a second before he pressed his flat tongue to her aching folds. She dropped her head back to the floor and sighed out the overwhelming pleasure building inside her along with the searing heat that raced through her veins. She let out a ragged breath and settled into this new adventure. Every kiss and lap of his tongue sent hot ripples through her system, building toward something she wanted to both prolong and welcome all at the same time.

And then it happened. Something amazing exploded inside her. Flashes of light went off behind her eyelids, and she felt like her whole body had been drawn tight and let loose in wave upon wave of pleasure. Wonderful and amazing and transformative all at the same time. She let the passion crash over her, making her shimmer on the inside.

Like a thrilling roller coaster ride that ended far too soon, she wanted to do it all over again.

But first she needed to get him out of the rest of his clothes. She took advantage of him sitting back on his heels as he stared at her splayed out in front of him.

"God, look at you." The amazement and appreciation in his gaze and words made her feel powerful.

Her inhibitions evaporated. "I want to see you." She reached out her hand.

He took it and pulled her up.

She used the momentum to rise up and straddle his lap as she wound her arms around his neck and pulled him into another searing kiss. She tasted herself on his lips.

"Did you know how fucking good you taste?"

"I do now." She kissed him again as he growled his approval and his hands went to her ass and squeezed, separating her cheeks and making her want his fingers to slide over her slick folds and thrust into her.

Like he read her mind, one of his big hands smoothed down over her ass. He slid one finger, then two into her tight channel, stretching her sensitive flesh.

She moaned and tackled his belt buckle, button, and zipper, dipping her hand into his slacks and sliding her palm over his rigid length. He was hard, thick, and long, the head round as she swept her palm over it.

"Fuck, Brooke. Do that again," he pleaded.

Oh, she liked that, too.

As she rode his fingers, she slipped her hand inside his boxer briefs, clamped her hand around his rigid shaft, and worked him up and down, hoping she was pleasing him as much as he was her. "Tell me how you like it."

"Harder."

She squeezed her hand tighter and saw the bead of precum pearl on the head. She rubbed her thumb over it.

"That's it. Fuck. That feels so good." He took her mouth in another mind-blowing kiss. Her heavy breasts pressed to his hard chest.

She wanted to map all his rippling muscles with her hands and mouth. Later.

He tugged her hair back and took the kiss deeper, holding her just where he wanted her.

She loved it and wanted more.

She rubbed her thumb over the damp head of his cock. "I want you in my mouth," she said against his lips.

"Fuck. I'm so close already. You do that and it's over. And I want inside you. Now." He pulled his fingers from her dripping sex, swept his wet fingers over her clit, making her moan again, then gently slid her off his lap and back onto the soft carpet.

Cody vibrated with need for this amazing woman who gave everything and held nothing back. He loved that she asked how he liked to be touched and let him know how much she liked what he was doing to her.

He wanted more. So much more.

As she lay before him, waiting for him, he quickly discarded the rest of his clothes under her steady and appreciative gaze.

"You are so gorgeous."

He grinned, feeling lighter and desperate all at the same time. "You always make me feel that way."

He kissed his way up her thigh, feeling her anticipation as his built anew. He stopped at her pretty pink pussy and gave her another lick and kiss on her clit before trailing kisses up her belly. He detoured to one peaked nipple, and then the other, sucking and laving them as she arched beneath him. Only his lips and tongue touched her. He couldn't wait to press his body to hers, but for right now he contented himself with teasing them both.

He finally made it to her lush lips and kissed her deeply. Passionately. He settled on top of her, a relief and torture because he still wasn't close enough, even though he was cradled between her long, gorgeous legs.

She shuddered at the contact of their two naked bodies pressed together and her arms draped around his neck. She pulled him in for a kiss, nothing but complete trust in her green eyes. The head of his cock nudged her wet folds and sank in an inch deep. She sighed his name, spread her legs wider to accommodate him. He sank in another inch deeper, kissing her, loving how her tight little pussy surrounded his aching cock, then thrust his way home.

The second she gasped and tensed, he went still, knowing exactly what he'd done.

She's mine and only mine!

He felt the possessiveness wash through him. He would never let her go again.

Why hadn't she told him? He'd get that answer later.

Right now, he needed to take care of her and make this good for her.

"God, baby, I'm sorry. I didn't know. It'll stop hurting in a minute. Just give it a minute." He clenched his jaw and reined in his need for her, giving her time for the pain to subside and to adjust to his thick length filling her.

Sweat broke out on his skin. So tight. He struggled not to pull out and thrust into her again and again to find the release riding him hard.

He pressed his forehead to hers and stared into her bright green eyes, so filled with awe and trust with a hint of pain. He kissed her softly on the lips, her cheek, her forehead, trying to distract her, feeling his heart soften more and more the longer he reveled in being part of her.

She rocked her hips forward and let out a moan he wasn't quite sure meant pleasure or pain.

"Honey, please don't move. Give it a second."

She took his face into her hands and made him look at her. Her soft smile melted his heart. Her sweet voice whispered what she'd always wanted, but never asked him for until now. Something he'd held back from her. Right now, he was ready to give her everything.

"Love me, Cody." She shifted her knees and he sank deeper. The second she realized she could bring him closer, feel every inch of him, she did it again, then rolled her hips against his.

Both of them moaned in satisfaction.

The sheer pleasure of it washed over them.

He let her try out the movements and find her way as he backed out a few inches, then sank back into her. Slow and easy.

She didn't disappoint by lying there passive. No, not his Brooke. She wanted him and gave herself over to him in a way he'd never felt with any other woman.

"Love me the way you want to." She unleashed him with those words.

His pleasure to give her what she wanted. He pulled out and sank into her again. She rocked her hips and met him, taking him deep and grinding against him. Her fingers dug into his back, pulling him closer. He lost control, knowing, feeling she wanted him that much. He'd never felt this deep connection, or need to possess so completely. He was her first. The only man who'd ever touched her like this, and it was a powerful feeling. She was only his, and it drove him to new heights of ecstasy.

He gave in to her demand and his desire. He thrust into her again and again with furious motions that were more reckless with each downward thrust. She clutched at him, grabbed on tight, and demanded more with her hands and those groans of pleasure he pulled from her. He rose up on his hands and gazed down at their joined bodies before looking back into her passion-hazed eyes. He thrust deep. "I can't get enough of you." He pulled out and pumped back into her sweet heat. "I'll never get enough of you."

Her fingers dug into his hips as her body tightened around his, wave upon wave of pleasure rolling through her and into him. He bit back his own release hard and watched her gorgeous body contract around his hard cock. She arched into him and gasped out his name.

Fucking music to my ears.

Cody had never watched his partner before. He'd never felt like he could. It made the experience so much more intimate and erotic.

She reached the crest in a beautiful display of passion, sparking his own release. Out of control and his mind, he thrust into her beautiful body, hard and fast, and followed her over the edge as his body contracted above hers. He spilled himself deep inside her, holding his body locked with hers as he pulsed with spent passion and the connection they shared.

Watching her, them moving together, it was like nothing he'd ever experienced, and it made for one hell of a climax. The best he'd ever had. He could barely catch his breath as his heart thrashed against Brooke's. He hadn't been the only one to reach that earth-shattering orgasm.

He collapsed on top of her, reveling in the feel of her soft body beneath his, heavy on hers. It felt so good to have her arms wrapped around him, holding him close. He didn't want to move, but stay wrapped in her love.

He gave himself a minute to gain his senses and strength before he rose onto his forearms, easing off crushing her into the rug, and took most of his weight on his arms. He should get off her. He just wasn't ready to let her go. He liked the feel of her around him. Still hard and held tightly between her thighs, he kissed her neck. He regretted hurting her, but he was right where he wanted to be.

"Are you okay?"

With her eyes closed, she let her hands roam over his skin, up his arms, and over his shoulders. She never stopped touching him. He liked it so damn much he didn't know what to say or do, but hope she never stopped.

"Mmmm. Perfect," she purred.

"I'm sorry I had to hurt you."

Now that the pleasure had faded, she was probably a little sore. He regretted that, but nothing else.

"I'm fine." Her eyelids lifted, but didn't open all the way.

He narrowed his gaze and studied her flushed face and drowsy eyes.

"I'm fine. Just a sharp pinch, then it was gone." To prove it, she hooked her hand behind his neck and drew him down for a soft, sweet kiss.

He let her kiss him, meaning to keep the sultry atmosphere wrapped around them. One taste made both of them fall into it deeper. He held her close, let his mouth show her all he couldn't say. He tried to pull back, but her tongue swept over his bottom lip. He growled deep in his throat, pressed his lips hard over hers, and kissed her until they both lost themselves in the moment.

Not wanting to strain her newly awakened body, he broke the kiss and stared down at her, watching for any sign of discomfort as he slowly separated their bodies. She let out a grumble as his dick fell out of her, letting him know she very much wanted him back inside her. He rolled to his side, pulling her into him, keeping her close to his chest, so she still felt their connection. "Why didn't you tell me it was your first time?"

"I didn't think it mattered. It's what I wanted."

"If I'd known..."

"What? You'd have stopped."

"No. I'd have taken my time, made sure you were ready."

"You did all of that. I knew what to expect. From some of the stories I've heard from friends, it actually wasn't as bad as I thought it would be."

"But your first time should be—"

"With someone I trust. Someone who is my best friend and would never hurt me if he could help it."

She humbled him. He'd taken her virginity—on the floor, for God's sake—and she spoke of trust and friendship like it was the most natural thing in the world for him to make love to her.

Maybe it had been inevitable.

It certainly felt right.

He'd never regret it. He'd never forget how she made him feel.

"I wanted it to be you, Cody. I waited all this time, *for you*."

His heart swelled and he hugged her tighter. "I'm so damn happy you chose me. I'm sorry I pushed you away." He kissed her on the forehead and combed his fingers through her hair, still needing the contact and closeness he'd only ever felt with her.

"We weren't ready for all of this."

He held her beautiful green-eyed gaze. "You were always so sure."

"You always saw me a certain way, and I wanted you to see me like this. But I had to get here first."

He understood exactly what she meant. She'd tried to grow up way too fast, trying to catch up to him. Now, they were on more equal footing.

He traced his finger across her forehead, drawing her hair from her face and tucking it behind her ear, and told her the truth about how he felt about this experience. Because for all her waiting, she deserved to know how he felt about being with her. "You were the most amazing lover ever."

"Sure. Right." She let loose a nervous chuckle, and her gaze fell away.

Catching her chin in his fingers, he turned her face back and made her look at him. "That's the truth. You were so free and giving and beautiful. I couldn't take my eyes off you. I wanted you more than I've ever wanted anyone."

She caught her breath and stared wide-eyed at him. "I didn't know it would be like that."

He kissed her softly. "That's what it's like for us. It's never been like that for me with anyone else." He needed her to know that what they shared was special.

She pressed her hand to his chest over his heart. "I'll never forget this, Cody. You made it so perfect." She raised her hand and pressed her palm to his cheek.

He loved the soft caress, but not the pinch of pain on her face as she moved. He gently nudged her arm over her chest so he could see her back and hissed at the raw spot on her shoulder blade. He released her arm and kissed her soft, silky skin above her collarbone. "I could have done better. I should have at least taken you upstairs to my bed." He kissed her again. He loved the way she felt, and with each kiss, she pressed closer to him.

The way she kept touching him drove him crazy. He was still half-hard just lying next to her.

Sore and tender, she wasn't up for an all-night lovefest. The thought held a lot of appeal, but he had to think of her, even if he wanted to feel Brooke moving under him again. He wanted to hear her say his name as the breath sighed out of her as he drove into her. He wanted to feel her need for him and the way she tried to get as close to him as possible.

"I don't know how you could have done better, but I'm willing to give you a million chances to prove it." She pressed her mouth to his, urging him on.

Lost to her, he gave in to her sweet demand and his need for her.

He kissed her with long, deep strokes of his tongue. Her swollen lips pressed to his as he pushed her back into the carpet. She grimaced and shifted to ease whatever hurt. He'd left more than one rug burn on her back. He felt like a prick as he bowed his head and rested his forehead on her pretty breast. The dusky pink nipple puckered, hard against his chin. He took it into his mouth, pressing his tongue over the tight bud. When she moaned and held his head to her, he knew he had to stop, or he wouldn't be able to in a minute. She needed to rest, recover from her first time. He wouldn't push his need on her and hurt her more.

It took every ounce of effort and self-control he possessed to release her. He stood and pulled her up by the hands with him. They needed to dress and go upstairs. Sleep.

Not that he would. He'd be thinking about her and what this meant for them.

One realization hit him like a swift kick to the gut. "Damn. I wasn't thinking clearly. At all, really. We didn't use a condom." He ran a hand through his messy hair. He hadn't even thought about it until this moment, and that wasn't like him. He was always careful and used a condom. Every time.

Guilt rode him hard. He should have protected her. He should have done better by her all the way around. He'd taken her on the floor, for God's sake. "Are you on the pill?"

Brow furrowed, she bit her lip. "No. I, uh, didn't need to until tonight." Concern clouded her expressive eyes. "I don't think the timing is quite right...but..."

He drew her close and rubbed his hands up and down her arms. "Don't worry. We won't borrow trouble. It'll probably be fine. If not, we'll deal with it."

Her gaze narrowed. "What does that mean? If you think I'll go to some clinic... No." She shook her head.

He loved her strength and conviction. She'd never give up a baby. He'd never want her to. He slipped his hands under her hair and held her head, sweeping his thumbs over her soft cheeks. "I mean, I'll take care of you and the baby. You know I will." He ran his hands through her dark hair and rested his hands on her shoulders. "I know you'd never get rid of *our* baby. You're too much of a nurturer to do anything like that."

"Nurturer, huh. That's how you see me."

"Honey, you took good care of me a minute ago."

A blush rose from her pretty breasts up to her forehead. So beautiful. She rested her hands on his waist and stood nude in front of him, not a touch of self-consciousness in her body or face.

The door to his study stood wide-open to the rest of the house, concerning him. Her mother could have come in and seen them. Brooke didn't seem concerned that they weren't alone in the house, but he could have, and should have, done things a lot better.

Next time.

He bent to pick up her gown.

"Thanks." She slid the pretty dress up her legs and over her body.

He missed the gorgeous view. Cody pulled on his pants while she snatched her underwear and bra from the floor and handed him his shirt, boxers, socks, and tie. She held the dress over her breasts. He dragged on his shirt but didn't button it, stuffed his tie in his pants pocket, wadded up his remaining clothes, and hooked his fingers in his shoes.

He held his free hand out to her.

She stared down at the carpet where they'd made love, then took his hand.

He'd never come into this office and not think of making love to her. He pulled her close, draped his arm around her shoulder, and turned them to the door. "Come on. It's late."

Leaning into him, she glanced up and gave him a shy, inquisitive smile, but she didn't ask any questions.

He could only guess at what was going through her mind.

She probably wanted assurances and to know what this meant.

He was still working that out in his mind.

But something made him want to make a million promises, because it seemed nothing and everything had changed between them.

They were still friends. But they were also so much more.

Cody stopped outside Brooke's bedroom door. Thankfully, her mom's room was on the other side of the house. They didn't have to worry about being caught half-naked in the hallway. His room was a couple doors down the hall, but he was reluctant to release her and let her go to her bed alone.

He wanted to go into Brooke's room, lie with her, and hold her for the rest of the night.

Cupping her cheek in his hand, he looked into her beautiful green eyes, the color of grass in spring. "Are you sure you're okay? You aren't terribly sore, are you? I could draw you a warm bath to soak."

She grabbed his belt loops and pulled him into the room with her. As she backed up toward the bed, a mischievous smile graced her face to match the light in her eyes. "I do have this ache. Maybe you could make it better." She went up on tiptoe and took him back into the fire.

Cody went willingly, slamming the door shut at the last second before she got him too far into the room and to the bed and no return. She smiled sweetly, even though this probably wasn't a good idea. He needed to be the voice of reason, even though reason quickly left him every time she smiled at him like that. "I don't want to hurt you, Brooke."

"You won't." She let go of her dress, dropping it to the ground along with the lingerie in her hands. She took his hand, pulled him into her, and pressed her breasts to his bare chest. "Stay. I don't want this to end. Not yet."

"God, help me," he said against her lips, dropped his shoes and the clothes he had in his hand, and grabbed her hips, drawing them to his pulsing erection. Her clever fingers slid down his belly and released his pants. They slid down his legs, and he kicked them off. She shoved his shirt over his shoulders and down his arms. Free of his clothes, he surprised her and picked her up under her arms and tossed her on the bed. She laughed heartily until he landed on top of her and silenced her giggles with a searing kiss. She shifted, and he remembered the raw spots he'd seen on her back. With his arms circled around her, he rolled them both over the bed until she was on top of him.

She rocked her hips over his hard length and he groaned. He thought he'd take his time and make sure they went slow. She had other ideas. The second she felt him at her opening, she pressed down in a slow, steady motion, sheathing him like a glove. She rose above him and rocked her body over his. Soft light filtered through the window sheers, allowing him to watch the pleasure come over her in a beautifully erotic display.

He guided her with his hands gripped on her slender hips, then reached up and cupped her breasts in his hands, tugging on her nipples with his fingers, bringing out a soft moan as she arched into him. "That's it, baby, do whatever feels good."

With her head tilted up, her dark hair spilling down her back, she was lovely riding him.

The longer he watched, the more turned on he got. Her passion spilled over into his as they moved together, and waves of pleasure crashed over them until her body tensed and convulsed around his hard cock. He spilled himself deep inside her. She collapsed onto his chest, breathing heavily. Her lips pressed to his throat as his heart thundered. He hadn't thought they could reach the heights they'd reached the first time they'd made love.

He was so wrong.

Wrapped in her arms, Cody held Brooke close, and they both settled into sleep locked together.

Nearly out, he heard her softly whisper. "Don't let go."

His last thought was his only thought as he held her tighter.

Never.

Chapter Twenty

Brooke scrunched her nose, then swiped her finger against the tip where it tickled and snuggled back into her pillow. Something tickled her nose again and a husky, masculine chuckle made her eyes fly open.

It wasn't a dream!

Cody dropped the lock of hair he'd been using to tickle her and kissed the tip of her nose this time. "Good morning, sweetheart."

He was lying on the pillow beside her, still naked, at least to his hips, where the sheet hid the rest of his gloriously muscled body. Hair tousled, golden scruff covering his chin and jaw, his eyes were alight with the same joy filling her up to bursting.

She put her hand on his face and brushed her thumb over his full bottom lip. "You're here."

He kissed her thumb. "No place I'd rather be." His hand slid under the covers and landed on her hip, where he squeezed her tight. "Are you sore?"

"A little," she confessed. "But in a really good way."

"Then we won't go riding today. So what should we do?"

She beamed, so excited and just...elated. "First, breakfast. I'm starving."

"Me, too. You gave me a good workout last night."

Said the man who woke her up in the early morning before the sun had even hinted at dawn to make love to her again. Slow and sweet, he'd been so tender it brought tears to her eyes from the sheer joy of being with him, lying in his arms as he kissed her hair and settled her beside him again. She'd fallen back to sleep with her head over his heart and his strong arms wrapped around her.

She still felt safe and protected and cared for with him beside her.

"I want to spend the day with you. Whatever you want, it's yours," he promised. "Think about it while you shower, then meet me downstairs for breakfast." His lips pressed to hers in a soft caress, just the barest hint of the passion they'd shared last night, but a new tenderness that made her ache for more. "Today is for us. Tomorrow we'll talk about the future. *Our* future." His smile, the open, excited one she hadn't seen often, warmed her heart and brushed away any and all fears and doubts.

She nodded, liking that he wanted to spend the day wallowing in the bright and happy emotions they were both feeling this morning.

He kissed her one more time, then slipped out of bed, standing there naked, not a care in the world.

She sat up, letting the sheet fall to her lap, baring her breasts. "God, you're gorgeous."

His heated gaze swept over her and his impressive cock swelled.

She couldn't help the grin or her excitement. "Is that for me?"

"Yes, damnit. Looks like a cold shower for me." He bit out those words. Then his voice and eyes softened. "You need time to recover today."

Regretfully, she did. And she needed time to process all of this. Everything was different now. Better. Amazing. But different. What did that mean for the two of them going forward?

Cody leaned over and kissed her again. "Not today. Today we enjoy it. Tomorrow we work it out."

With that, he snatched up his clothes, held them in front of him, and went to the door, giving her a really nice view of his perfect ass. He peeked out to be sure the hall was empty, then stepped out and closed the door behind him.

She wondered what her mother would think of Cody sneaking out of her room.

She'd be happy for them. She knew how much Brooke loved Cody.

But did he love her?

Yes, in a way. But maybe more now.

They'd talk about it tomorrow.

Today, she got to have Cody all to herself.

At least that's what she thought until she'd showered, dressed, and reached the bottom of the stairs and heard Cody's deep voice coming from his study. "I got your texts. All nine of them. What's so urgent? I thought we ended things last night."

"Cody, please, hear me out."

Kristi.

Brooke's insides went cold.

She should have known Kristi wouldn't give up Cody without a fight.

The cleaning crew was tidying the living room and patio out back from the party last night. She walked past them and stood just outside the study doors, listening and hoping Kristi didn't tear her and Cody apart.

Cody didn't notice her by the door and continued to stare at Kristi, looking mildly perturbed. "What are you doing here? You made it perfectly clear last night how you felt and that we were over."

Kristi sank onto the edge of the sofa and stared up at him. "I'm sorry. I said some things I didn't mean in the heat of the moment."

Cody folded his arms over his chest. "You accused me of having an affair."

"I was hurt about the attention you paid Brooke. It's no secret I'm jealous of your relationship with her."

Everything had changed when Cody kissed Brooke.

"Until last night, I never gave you a reason to think Brooke and I were anything but friends. I tried to apologize to you about the kiss, but you didn't want to hear it."

Wait. What? Cody was sorry he kissed me?

No. He wouldn't have made love to me all night if he regretted it.

"I was furious. I let my emotions get away from me. I hate that we left things unsettled last night."

"You settled everything when you said you were *done* and walked out the door. That was pretty damn clear."

She leaned toward him. "That's not what I want." The plea in her eyes begged him to understand.

Cody looked impenetrable, and Brooke hoped that meant he didn't want to get back together with Kristi.

"I love you, Cody. So much. We are so good together." Her whole body leaned toward him, imploring him to understand and accept her back.

Cody's arms dropped. "For a long time, we were. But lately...we fight more than anything else."

Kristi's eyes glassed over and her lips trembled. "We can't end this, Cody." The desperate way she said it made Brooke's stomach knot.

She felt something bigger coming.

Cody sighed and dropped his arms. "There's something you need to know about me and—"

"I'm late. I took a test this morning. I'm pregnant," Kristi blurted out, then burst into tears. She covered her face and cried harder.

Brooke felt her whole world shatter into a million pieces.

All her hopes and dreams exploded into tiny little splinters.

The pain in her heart became so unbearable she could barely breathe.

Her gaze locked on Cody, shocked into silence even as his mind worked out what Kristi had just told him.

She saw everything he thought reflected in his eyes. Kristi was pregnant with his baby. She needed him. The baby needed him. He had to take care of them. There was no other choice.

His gaze shifted to the floor and she knew he was thinking of them making love in that very spot for the first time last night.

He glanced at Kristi and Brooke saw all the light go out of him.

All the broken pieces of her heart crumbled to dust.

"The broken condom last month," he whispered.

Kristi nodded, her gaze on her hands in her lap.

Cody did exactly what Brooke knew he would do. He kneeled on the floor in front of her, took her hand, and reassured her like the good man he'd always been and would always be. "It's okay."

No it's not. Nothing is okay.

She wondered if Cody thought the same thing.

The sadness and loss in his eyes said he did, but he quickly hid those feelings away. He was good at that. She'd always been good at getting him to show her how he really felt.

This can't be happening.

Tears streamed down Kristi's face. "Cody, you don't understand. My parents are going to be furious with me. This will disgrace them. They won't be able to show their faces at church. People will talk."

"Your parents will understand. These things happen."

"They taught me to be a responsible woman and look what I've done."

"You didn't do anything wrong. We are both responsible for this." He raked his hand through his hair. "This is our child. We will take care of him or her. We will give the baby the family it deserves."

Kristi went quiet and stared at Cody. "Do you mean that?"

"Yes. We'll get married like we talked about and you and the baby will have my name. Everything will be fine."

Brooke didn't think even for a second that he wanted to marry Kristi. He was doing this for his child.

Apparently Kristi heard the same resignation she did in his words. She sniffled and looked away for a moment before turning back to him, disappointment in her eyes.

This wasn't the proposal she'd hoped for. Kristi probably hoped to tell Cody she was pregnant, and he'd be so excited he'd pick her up and spin her around, kissing her and begging her to marry him.

This definitely wasn't how Cody expected his morning to go either.

They both looked shell-shocked.

But after a year together, it was clear to Brooke and now Kristi that her feelings ran far deeper than Cody's did for her.

He'd be happy with his child though. Cody would be a fantastic father.

Which made Brooke question the timing of all of this.

Kristi had to be reeling after seeing Cody kiss her. She obviously suspected something more was going on and that she might lose Cody for good, so she sprung this on him this morning, so she could hold on to him.

It didn't matter.

A baby was on the way no matter when Kristi told him.

Today...a week from now...Brooke still lost Cody.

"Do you mean it? We'll get married?" The tears dried up and she smiled expectantly at Cody.

"Right away," he assured her. "We can probably be married no later than next month. I've got a few cases to tie up. I'll handle them, giving you time to plan a small wedding. We'll keep things simple."

Kristi's gaze narrowed with confusion. "But I thought we'd have a proper ceremony. People will expect us to invite our friends, families, and your colleagues and other prominent members of the community. They'll want to share in our day."

Cody shrugged and stood. "Invite whomever you want, so long as you can get it done soon."

She frowned, frustration clouding her eyes.

Cody tilted his head. "I thought you wanted to do this quickly, before people discover you're pregnant."

"Well, I've only just realized how late I am." Her voice shook and held a tremble of unease. "It's only been a little more than two weeks."

"You waited that long to say something." Cody didn't look happy.

Brooke understood why. If he'd known, he'd never have been with Brooke. At all.

Kristi tried to explain why she held off telling him. "I thought I was late because of stress, or... I don't know. It was a surprise for me, too."

Cody nodded that he understood, but that didn't mean he wasn't upset she'd held this back from him.

Kristi took Cody's hand. "With it being so early in the pregnancy, we have time to plan a lovely ceremony that can include all the things we want for our big day." Kristi could plan the extravaganza of her dreams to show off to all her friends.

Kristi noticed her standing in the doorway. The look she sent Brooke said so many things. She suspected something happened between her and Cody last night. Her eyes lit with triumph that she'd been right to come first thing this morning and claim Cody for herself.

Brooke shoved aside the agony of losing Cody, recovered her senses enough to plaster on a fake smile, and walked into the room. "Congratulations." She took a deep breath and swore she would not cry. Tears clogged her throat, but she choked them back.

She stared at Cody.

His gaze dropped to the rug, then came back up and met hers, and the bleak look in his eyes destroyed her. His pain, hers, blocked out the light inside her and left her in a darkness so complete it swallowed her whole.

She loved him so much; she didn't want to lose him. But she saw it all too clearly in his eyes. He'd made his choice. He'd give her up to give his child what Cody lost when his mom left: a family that stayed together. A mom and a dad, who loved their child.

She tried to understand and not resent him or the situation. "A wedding and a baby. I hope you two will be very happy together." The words tasted vile, but she got them out. For him.

"We will be." Kristi stood and took Cody's arm in her hands. She held him and beamed a triumphant smile at Brooke.

She'd won.

Brooke conceded. What else could she do? "You're a lucky woman. Cody's the best."

"As his *friend*, you'd know just how lucky I am. I'd thought you might be reluctant to give him up after all these years. *We* appreciate your support."

Brooke got the message. Kristi was marrying Cody and having his baby. He'd chosen.

Brooke couldn't fight that. She wouldn't. She'd bow out gracefully and try to salvage the broken pieces of her heart. She didn't think it would ever mend, but maybe, someday, she'd find a way to stop loving him and move on. Right now, it didn't feel like that would ever happen. It probably wouldn't. She loved him so deeply, he'd become a part of who she was. She didn't want to lose that, but maybe she'd find a way to be happy again.

"And of course you'll attend the wedding." Cody pleaded with his eyes for her support, to understand he needed her to get through this.

Go to his wedding—watch him marry another woman—she couldn't do it.

Feeling as if she'd woken in an alternate universe, she screamed inside, *Wake up! This can't be real!*

Nothing happened. This was real. She'd lost him. Forever.

The shrapnel of her broken heart had shredded her soul and it bled, leaving her feeling hopeless and more alone than she'd ever felt in her life.

"Um, I'll be back at school." She turned to Kristi and caught the victorious look in her eyes. *Bitch!* "I'll be gone before you know it." Brooke stared back at Cody, seeing her pain reflected back from the deepest depths of his eyes.

"*We* understand. Your classes keep you quite busy." Kristi used that damn false cheery tone she used whenever she spoke to Brooke.

The tone and that "we" grated on Brooke's last nerve. "Yes, quite," she said lamely. The tears threatened. She needed to get away. "I was just coming to tell you, Cody, I'll be out the rest of the day." She couldn't look at him anymore and not beg him to choose her. She spun around, but only took one step before Cody's deep voice stopped her in her tracks.

"Brooke." Just her name. That's it.

She turned, chin up, facing him with all the strength and tenacity he'd always told her he admired about her. "Kristi and the baby are your future now." Tears filled her eyes, even as she blinked them away. She couldn't let them fall and make this any harder on Cody.

She wouldn't give Kristi the satisfaction of seeing her cry.

She glanced at Cody one last time. Took him in and let him go all at once.

She walked out of the room, devastated to her very soul, throbbing with a pain she'd carry with her the rest of her days.

She'd thought last night was a new beginning for them.

This morning proved it had just been a going-away party for their friendship.

She'd never watch him marry Kristi and have a family with her.

Just her luck she didn't get away clean. Her mom walked out of the dining room and called out to her. "Darling, come, join me for breakfast."

Brooke sucked back the tears and headed for the front door without stopping. She needed to get away before she fell apart right here in the foyer and crumpled into a ball of misery.

"Sorry, Mom. I've got plans with a friend in town. I'll be back late. Don't wait up." She snagged the keys to the ranch truck and her purse off the entry table where she'd left them and walked out without looking back.

She closed the door and came up short in front of an equally surprised delivery man carrying a gold box.

"Brooke Banks?"

"Yes." She reached for her purse, hoping she had some cash.

The delivery guy held out the flower box. "Don't worry about it. The tip's taken care of."

"Um, thank you." She had no idea who would send her flowers. Right now, she didn't care. She needed to get out of here.

She followed the delivery guy out to the driveway, opened the truck door, tossed the box on the seat next to her, gave in to curiosity, and opened it.

A dozen red roses. Gorgeous. Their heady scent quickly filled the truck cab.

She pulled out the card and read the note.

You made last night remarkable.

Had Cody sent these?

Who else would do it?

She burst into tears, tossed the card back in the box, smashed the lid down on top of it, started the truck. She tried to drive away from her memories and all the hurt but they just went with her.

Chapter Twenty-One

The front door closed with a clack, breaking Cody out of the trance he'd fallen into the second Brooke said Kristi was his future, which sounded too much like goodbye.

She had to understand. He wanted his baby to have a mom and a dad under the same roof, not a fractured family like he grew up in. Like Brooke had growing up, too.

His gaze found Susanne's confused one as she stared at him from the living room. Then her eyes and expression turned to one of understanding. She knew he'd never hurt Brooke on purpose. That didn't mean he hadn't inadvertently upset her over the years she'd chased after him.

Susanne gave him a *fix it* look, then turned and walked back to the dining room.

He didn't think he could ever repair Brooke's broken heart, or his own. Not after this.

He'd thought everything had changed last night. He'd woken up this morning thinking he'd started a new chapter in his life with a woman who had become so much more than his best friend and lover.

Brooke was perfect for him in so many ways, he couldn't count them all.

In one night he'd had her and lost her.

His throat clogged and his heart hurt with every beat against his tight ribs, demanding he not do this and lose the one good thing he'd had in his life. The one thing he'd had and swore he'd never let go.

He'd never felt anything close to what he felt for Brooke with Kristi, but Kristi was pregnant, and she and his child needed his promises now.

Kristi sat on the couch, her grin falling flat as she looked up at him. "I know this is a shock. We didn't plan it, but it's happening."

Right. They were having a baby. He couldn't quite wrap his head around everything that meant.

As much as he wanted to wallow in the memory of his night with Brooke, in the heat and passion and overwhelming pleasure, he couldn't hide from his responsibilities. But when he looked at Kristi, right now all he saw was the rest of his life without Brooke and that kind of love and passion.

He and Kristi would have something different. Something more subdued, yes, but they'd find a way to be happy. He'd been content with her up until last night, when he'd discovered in Brooke's arms just what kind of life he could share with a woman.

He and Kristi would find a way back to their rhythm, and he'd settle into the routine they shared this past year.

Kristi sat up straighter, her smile brightening. "Now that I've told you, I'm kind of excited for us."

The band around his chest tightened. The bright future with Brooke he'd gotten a glimpse of last night winked out, leaving him lost in the dark and lonely.

He'd never forget how much he loved her. He'd hold that inside his heart and soul like a secret.

Everyone deserved a few good memories to get them through the hard times in their lives. He'd have his memories of Brooke.

A baby really does change everything.

He choked back the raw emotions clogging his throat, walked to the window, and stared out at the rose garden. Fading in the winter-weak sun, the rose's spiky sticks stood as barren as his heart.

"We need to plan what comes next." Kristi couldn't hide her excitement. "When should we tell everyone? I'll move in. We'll make this place ours. My things. Yours. We'll set up a nursery. We'll be a family."

She'd moved on to planning.

He was still stuck on the bomb she'd detonated in his life and the fallout.

He couldn't stop thinking about Brooke. "You shouldn't have thrown it in her face that we're getting married and having a baby. You know how she feels about me."

I finally know how I feel about her.

One night hadn't been enough. He wanted more. He wanted a lifetime. But it wasn't meant to be. "You made it seem like she wasn't welcome in her own home anymore."

Brooke walked away. She left.

He wanted her back so bad.

Will this ache ever go away?

"I doubt she'll want to spend much time here once she graduates college and starts her own life. What with you and me and the baby in the house, she'll probably prefer a much younger crowd to us."

He didn't want to consider the fact that Kristi might be right.

Brooke walked out the door, and she might not come back. Not after what he'd done to her.

He didn't even want to think of her finding someone else to have a life with and love. She'd loved him practically her whole life. She'd loved him with her whole heart and body last night and into the morning.

He couldn't imagine her loving another man. It simply hurt too much to even contemplate.

He rubbed the heel of his hand over his aching chest, swallowing the lump in his throat, and tried to breathe through the pain.

But he still managed to make things crystal clear to Kristi. "Remember one thing. Brooke owns a quarter interest in this ranch. This will always be Brooke's home. Don't ever make her feel unwelcome here again." He let her interpret the threat in his words any way she liked because he wouldn't let her or anyone else hurt Brooke or keep her from coming home.

Kristi didn't back down. "Are you going to let me make this my home now too?"

He'd never slept with her under this roof. He'd never asked her to stay over with him. But everything had changed and he needed to catch up. "Of course. Once we're married, we'll live here together." He hoped a month or two would be enough time for him to accept that and move forward without this crushing loss weighing so heavily on him.

"Excellent. We can turn the room next to Brooke's into a nursery." Kristi's mouth drew into a tight line. "Of course, she'll probably want to move to her mother's side of the house so the baby isn't waking her up all the time. Plus, we'll need our privacy."

Cody clamped his jaw tight, stuffed his hands in his pockets, and wondered how this had happened.

Kristi swore she was on the pill. He was focused on a career and thought he'd have kids in the future, when he was settled, which was why he always used a condom. It was his responsibility to protect himself.

Except with Brooke last night, he'd been too obsessed with being as close as possible to her. Nothing between them. Just the two of them lost in each other.

Hours ago, he'd been the happiest man on the planet. Now he couldn't feel anything but loss and pain.

He was going to be a dad.

And Kristi's husband.

He should feel something for them, but if he did, it got drowned out by how much he missed Brooke already.

To stop Kristi from talking anymore about changes she wanted to make to the house that used to be his and Brooke's, he suggested something that would make Kristi happy and took him one more step down the path of his new future.

He turned away from the desolate garden and his thoughts of Brooke, and faced Kristi and his circumstances head-on. "Do you want to go pick out an engagement ring?"

Her smile went megawatt and she pressed her hands together at her chest and shouted, "Yes!"

Well, he'd made one woman happy today.

He wished he hadn't destroyed what he had with another in order to do it.

Kristi grabbed her purse and he followed her out of the house to his car. He noted the missing truck and wondered where Brooke went, when she'd be home, and if she'd actually come back. Ever.

He drove out of the long driveway, hit the main road into the city, and tried not to panic that he'd never see Brooke again.

His heart sped up the second he spotted the truck parked near a copse of trees down a dirt road that led to the creek. He knew the spot well. Brooke went there when she wanted to be alone. He imagined her hiding out and cursing the day she'd met him.

"What kind of wedding band do you want?" Kristi asked.

He'd nearly forgotten where they were going. "I don't know."

"We'll get something that matches mine."

He didn't know what to say, except, "Sounds good."

The only thing he really wanted to do was find Brooke by the creek and beg her to forgive him.

The rest of the day went by in a blur of picking out Kristi's engagement ring at a ridiculously expensive jewelry store. He'd set a limit with the jeweler. Of course, Kristi picked out the most expensive piece she was shown. He didn't care. If she was happy, that meant he could be quiet and sink into his own guilt and pain.

They drove to her parents' house and announced their engagement. Kristi's parents were exuberant in their excitement and he felt like an asshole for being so staid in his response, so he faked his enthusiasm for Kristi's sake, shaking Kirk's hand and promising he'd take care of Kristi. That was the best he could do right now.

When her mother asked about the proposal, Kristi lied and said they'd had a disagreement last night and he'd called her to the house this morning because he couldn't sleep, thinking about her and making things right. When she showed up this morning at his house, they'd talked and he confessed that he hated when they were apart and asked her to marry him.

Her mother thought his impromptu proposal was so romantic.

Kirk smirked and said, "You figured out you couldn't live without her."

He nodded his agreement.

They didn't say anything about the baby. Kristi convinced him to hold off on telling anyone until after the wedding. She didn't want to start any gossip. After a couple of hours of batting around wedding plans with her parents and holding up the plastered-on smile he'd kept in place for Kristi's benefit, he took Kristi back to her apartment.

They sat in his car out front and Kristi turned to him with a serious look in her eyes. "The proposal story I told my parents will be exactly what we tell our friends and family. Agreed?"

"Sure." As far as he was concerned, no one needed to know what really happened. He'd hold the truth about his night with Brooke in his heart and mind and hoard the joy it brought him to the end of his days.

"How about I come home with you? We could celebrate." The sultry look in her eyes told him how she wanted to do it.

He couldn't even think about taking her to bed right now. "I've got some work to finish up before Christmas in a few days. I'll plan a dinner. We'll celebrate then."

"Promise?"

"Yes. Do you need anything? Are you feeling well?" He didn't know anything about a woman being pregnant, except they got morning sickness sometimes.

Kristi seemed perfectly fine. "You're so sweet. I'm doing okay."

I'm not.

"Then I'll see you soon. Call if you need anything."

Kristi held up her hand, flashing the ring. "We're getting married!"

At least one of them was excited.

He smiled for her, because he didn't want to rain on her parade.

She slipped out of the car, leaving him in blissful quiet as he drove home. When he drove past the empty dirt road, he hoped he'd find Brooke at the house. He desperately needed to talk to her, to explain how he felt about her, and why he was marrying Kristi. He had to make her understand that after all these years, he'd finally realized how much he loved Brooke.

This situation with Kristi hurt him as much as it hurt her. But he had a duty and obligation to Kristi and his unborn child.

He never got the chance. When he finally drifted off to sleep on the couch in the living room near four in the morning, she still hadn't come home.

He spent the next two days calling, texting, worried sick because she wouldn't answer him, angry at himself for making this happen, and feeling the loss of her with every breath he took.

Four days and nothing from Brooke. He hoped to find her at home, sitting by the Christmas tree this morning. No such luck. The cheerful decorations in the house mocked him. The angel at the top of the tree stared down at him with contempt.

It was all he could do to sit beside Kristi on the couch, her body snug against his side, and not leap up and scour the earth for Brooke.

Even worse, Susanne sat across from them, patiently listening to Kristi's jubilant plans for their upcoming wedding, talking about the doctor appointment he had accompanied her to two days ago after she'd gotten lucky, taking someone else's canceled appointment. The ultrasound confirmed they were having a baby. He had the picture of his little bean to prove it. Kristi had given him a Baby's First Christmas ornament with the photo inside. It hung on the tree, front and center. They'd delivered the news to Susanne this morning when Kristi presented him with the gift. What else could they do?

They still hadn't told Kristi's parents and asked Susanne to keep the news to herself. But he saw it in her eyes. She knew Brooke had left because of this but congratulated them anyway. She didn't fool Cody. Her polite but distant mood had worn on him the last couple days. Susanne blamed him for Brooke's absence and ruining the holiday.

"Ah, the happy couple." Brooke walked into the room, an instant piercing pain stabbing her battered heart when the huge diamond ring on Kristi's finger sparkled in the firelight.

Knowing her mother had worried terribly, she went to her and kissed her cheek in greeting. "Hi, Mom. Sorry I'm late."

"You're *four days* late getting home," Cody barked.

He knew exactly why she'd left and stayed away and he was mad at her. No fucking way!

"Well, geez, *Dad*, I was shopping at the mall, and they had this killer sale, and I lost all track of time. Then Mindy Sue asked me to meet her in Vegas for a couple of days, and I just couldn't say no when she was so excited. I couldn't let her go all alone. Besides, I won a hundred bucks playing poker, met an honest-to-God card sharp, and spent a night working off my bar tab wrapped around a stripper pole." She put her hands up like a prayer and smiled snidely at him. "Please don't ground me."

"You aren't old enough to gamble," Kristi pointed out.

Brooke refused to look at Kristi. Apparently, the stripper pole was more plausible than her gambling.

She never took her eyes off Cody. He had no right to ask her where she'd been, or snarl at her about staying away.

"People here have been worried about you. The least you could do is call home."

She saw past the anger to the worry that made him snap at her like that. It did assuage her own anger and she felt guilty for ignoring his texts and calls.

"Yes, well, I checked in with Mom and told her I'd be back today." She refrained from using the word home. Soon, this house would belong to him, Kristi, and their children. They'd be a family. This would be their life.

She wouldn't be welcome, or feel comfortable here ever again.

He kept staring at her, and she wanted to tell him he had no right to sit there implying he was worried about her when he had his fiancée cuddled up beside him.

"Where have you been?" he asked in a softer tone but still demanded an answer.

She could go where she pleased, and he couldn't do a damn thing about it. Her mother apparently kept the information about her calling and checking in to herself. Her way of letting Cody know he should be the one to suffer for whatever he'd done to Brooke. She hadn't explained anything to her mom, only that she couldn't be around Cody and Kristi right now. The engagement was enough of an explanation for her mother to understand Brooke needed time alone.

Brooke refused to tell him she'd gotten a hotel room and stayed in bed crying for the last few days. She wasn't going to tell him how she'd wallowed in her misery, not eating, and barely sleeping. She'd taken the time she needed to grieve for him and a dream that would never come true.

She'd grieved the death of a wish and the death of their friendship because nothing would ever be the same again. He'd never be a part of her life like he'd been for all these years.

He had someone else. He belonged to Kristi and their baby. Nothing would change that now.

Instead of answering him, she turned to go to the kitchen, but stopped short when she spotted the picture frame ornament on the tree with their ultrasound photo.

There it was in black-and-white.

Tears threatened to gush once again, but she choked them back as the ache in her chest consumed her.

"Brooke." Cody's soft voice nearly broke her.

She couldn't look at him. She couldn't seem to pull her gaze from that picture hanging on the tree. "Smells like Janie has been cooking up a storm. I'm starved." She really wasn't. "I'll go see about dinner."

"Don't you want to open your gifts?" Kristi's voice had become nails on a chalkboard. Every time she spoke to Brooke in that perky, *everything is wonderful* voice, Brooke wanted to cover her ears and scream.

"Come on, darling, open your gifts." Her mom nudged her toward the tree.

All the gifts had been opened, except for Brooke's.

The briefcase she bought Cody sat next to the tree, along with several other things he'd received from her mom, friends, and no doubt Kristi. She'd spent a small fortune to replace his old battered and scuffed one. His career had taken off and he needed something that showed his success.

"You'll love what Cody got you," Kristi said. "It'll keep you warm at school."

She couldn't help but glance over at Cody and yearn for him to be the one who always kept her safe and warm.

She couldn't sit through opening the gifts and pretending to be happy and appreciative for all she'd received when the only thing she wanted, she couldn't have.

"I don't want to hold up the dinner Janie spent so much time preparing. I'll open them later." She turned for the kitchen.

"Who gave you flowers?"

She stopped in her tracks, and looked down at the gold box filled with dead roses and the card she thought came from Cody that she'd totally forgotten was still tucked under her arm. She'd completely forgotten about them in the truck until she finally found the strength to get out of bed, shower, put on the clothes she'd worn for four days, and come home to a reality she didn't want to face. A life without Cody in it.

Why would he ask her who sent them when it only made sense that he ordered them for her?

A cold shiver raced up her spine.

She turned and faced him, looking for any sign that he had and was just trying to get her to acknowledge it. But all she saw in his eyes was a genuine question and maybe jealousy that someone else sent them to her.

"Actually, I don't know." Could it have been @youseeme? No.

How would he know where she lived?

How had she made his night remarkable?

Was he at the party?

In her house?

She thought about the silhouette of a man in her bedroom window the night of the picnic as the fireworks went off.

The chill inside her froze her bones.

"Brooke. Everything okay?" Cody's concern touched her, but she wasn't his responsibility anymore.

She shook off her dark thoughts. They were just flowers.

She didn't answer him and turned to leave yet again.

Her mom's voice faded as she made her way to the kitchen, but she caught every word. "Whatever happened between the two of you, fix it. We're a family. This is *our* home. You two have been friends since the day we moved in. She's leaving tomorrow to go back to school."

"What? So soon?" Panic filled his voice.

"Yes," her mom snapped. "Don't let it be the last time she walks out that door."

Cody hadn't known she planned to cut her holiday vacation short and return to her dorm. Better that than have to spend any more time watching Kristi touch Cody and command his attention when Brooke would never get to do that again.

It hurt too much to look at him and know it was over. If she couldn't be with him now, after what they shared, then she simply couldn't be here at all.

Her mom followed her into the kitchen. "Are you going to tell me what's really going on here?"

Their housekeeper and cook, Janie, read the tone and the shift in energy in the room and carried a platter laden with roasted leg of lamb and a bowl of mashed potatoes out to the dining room.

Brooke tossed the flower box on the counter next to the garbage can and slowly turned to her mom. "Cody and I... There's never going to be... He's not mine. He's marrying Kristi. They'll have a beautiful baby soon. And I have to start my own life." Tears spilled down her cheeks.

Her mom cupped her face and stared into her eyes with sympathy. "I'm sorry."

"I love him," she confessed. It was the only part of what happened she could really tell her mom. "I know you think it's silly. A crush. Whatever."

Her mom shook her head. "No, Brooke. Those feelings are real and they run deep. I understand that seeing him with Kristi hurts."

"I can't love him and not have him. Not anymore."

Her mom wrapped her in a hug. Brooke wanted to run away again. But she'd promised her mom Christmas dinner and wouldn't back out now after spending days away and cutting her winter break short.

"It will all work out the way it's supposed to, Brooke. You'll see. You will love again."

She didn't think so. Not right now. Because she couldn't imagine not loving Cody because she'd always loved him.

"Come. Let's get through dinner, then we'll go up to my room, crawl into my bed, and we'll drink hot chocolate and watch *Elf* together. You love that movie."

She wouldn't be on Cody's side of the house. She wouldn't have to see him pass her room with Kristi and go to his, because of course Kristi would never leave Cody alone now. Not when she suspected something happened between Brooke and Cody. Not until she had a wedding band on his hand.

"Sounds great, but I'll need to pack first."

Her mom held her by the shoulders. "I hate that you're leaving."

"It's time I grew up, finished college, and started my own life away from here." She had plans already in place without even knowing she'd not only want to live on her own, but would need to as Kristi slowly pushed her out. Well, with the baby coming, *shoved* was more like it.

Her mom frowned, put her arm around Brooke's shoulders, and they walked out into the dining room. Her mom hugged her close as they approached the table where Cody and Kristi were already seated. "Maybe your secret admirer will contact you again."

Brooke hoped not. Because now the messages had a stalker vibe to them that worried her.

Cody's eyes filled with fury.

Brooke loved her mom for poking at Cody and trying to make her feel better. "I don't have a clue who sent the flowers or what they meant in the card. Or why they didn't sign it." She scrunched her lips and thought about all the messages she'd been receiving since she returned to school after summer break.

Kristi gave her one of her famous not-so-nice smiles. "Well, you certainly got a lot of attention at the party. You've got your pick of those guys to choose from."

Yes, so many suspects.

You've watched too many crime shows.

Someone likes you but isn't sure how to approach you and is taking the long way around. That doesn't have to be a bad thing. Right?

The only man Brooke wanted was seated at the head of the table, looking anything but happy about Kristi pointing that out.

And was that some sort of compliment? That Brooke could get anyone she wanted.

Except Cody.

Kristi made sure of that.

She didn't have anything else to say about anything, so she took a seat at the table. Not the seat on Cody's right where she normally sat, but the one her mom usually sat in. She didn't want to be that close to him. She didn't want to look up and stare across at the triumphant look in Kristi's eyes that she didn't even bother to hide. Instead, she put the scrumptious food Janie had spent more than an hour cooking for them on her plate, and managed to get a few bites down before Kristi launched into a whole bunch of chatter about wedding dresses and baby clothes and if it would be a boy or a girl and what color they should paint the baby's room upstairs.

Brooke sat silently enduring it for her mom's sake, but she couldn't eat past the lump in her throat or fill her tight stomach. She found herself staring out across the living room and right into Cody's office. The lights were out. She couldn't see anything past the edge of the rug on the hardwood floor. All she saw was what they'd had and what they'd never share again.

"Brooke. Do you want dessert?" Cody's deep voice brought her out of her stupor.

Dessert? She didn't think she'd ever eat cake again.

Her mom touched her shoulder. "It's your favorite."

Brooke hadn't even realized dinner had been cleared from the table. "Um. I'm not hungry. I think I'll go upstairs and pack before we..." She tore her gaze from the study and looked at her mom.

"I'll get the hot chocolate. We'll have dessert later."

Brooke nodded, stood, and walked away from the table and Cody's gaze that she could feel on her back.

"Cody, honey, where are you going?" Kristi demanded.

Brooke was at the top of the stairs when she heard the study door close and Cody throw the lock.

"Cody, let me in," Kristi pleaded.

Brooke knew exactly what Cody was doing. She'd found him in his office many times, bourbon in hand, worrying about a problem or situation that upset him. He'd never locked her out.

Apparently Kristi wasn't welcome to join his brooding party.

Or maybe Cody just wanted to get drunk and forget what happened between them.

She really didn't know anymore.

Not her problem, even if it put a heavy stone in her gut.

Packing didn't take very long. She basically just tossed everything into her backpack and suitcase haphazardly and called it done.

She walked back toward the stairs and her mother's side of the house. Just as she crossed the landing over the foyer, Kristi turned from the study door she'd been knocking on and asked, "How do you get him out of there?"

She didn't miss a step or even look at Kristi and just said, "That's your job now."

She kept on walking when Kristi pounded a fist on the door and demanded, "You can't ignore me like this, Cody."

Apparently he could, because Brooke didn't hear the door open. But she did hear the front door slam when Kristi left.

She wanted to go to Cody. She wanted to prove to herself and Kristi that he wouldn't shut her out of his life. But that was petty.

And for the first time in her life, she wasn't sure Cody would open the door for her. And if he did, what did that mean? That he loved her, too?

Knowing that would only make things worse.

Him opening the door would only complicate matters more.

She was right to leave. She was right to never come back.

She just hoped she could live with her decision and that somehow her mom would understand.

Maybe, in time, years from now, she'd be able to see Cody and not hurt like this.

Right now, she needed as much distance as she could put between them.

Chapter Twenty-Two

Cody spent a very lonely and anguished night in his study while Brooke hid away with her mom upstairs. He couldn't bust in on that, not without explaining things to Susanne. When he finally emerged early the next morning, hung over and surly because he'd barely slept three hours, he headed straight upstairs to Brooke's room, hoping to have a private conversation and clear the air.

He didn't know if it would help or make things worse, but he really needed to know where they stood. He needed to know that she'd always be his friend if they couldn't be more.

He didn't want to lose her forever. He couldn't imagine his life without her in it in some way. He didn't want his child growing up without Brooke there to spoil him, the way she'd always spoiled him.

It was easier to imagine his life with his child right now than it was to think of his marriage to Kristi. She'd been right last night when she pounded on the door to his study. He couldn't ignore her. He needed to find a way to focus on the baby, the impending wedding, and the birth of his child. But he'd needed Christmas night to himself, so he could drink away his feelings and find that blissful numbness he needed desperately after seeing Brooke with those damn flowers, wondering who sent them to her, and if that guy would make her happy after Cody had crushed her heart.

He couldn't stand that she could barely look at him.

Watching her staring from the dinner table at his study killed him. He'd sat there, wishing he could go back in time and live in the moment where he and Brooke were in each other's arms, happy and in love, a world of possibilities in front of them.

But that wasn't his reality now. It wasn't that he didn't care about Kristi. He just loved Brooke on a whole other level he never even knew existed.

Kristi was pissed. He owed her an apology and to get on board with the plans for their future. He had the rest of his life to make things up to her.

He'd spend that same lifetime regretting losing Brooke.

But he couldn't let her leave without them talking things out the way they always did.

He stopped in her open doorway and found her dressed and standing next to her suitcase with her backpack at her feet. "You're already ready to go?" He thought he'd have more time.

She tapped something on her phone and said without looking at him, "The bus leaves in an hour."

He stared, dumbstruck that this was happening so fast. "I'll drive you back." They'd have a couple hours in the car to talk.

"I've already got my ticket. Mom will be ready in a minute to drive me to the bus stop."

"Seriously, Brooke, this is how you want to leave things?"

She finally met his gaze, hers sad and resigned. "I need to leave. You need me to leave. You know that."

It gutted him. "That doesn't mean it's what I want."

"Yeah, well, we don't always get what we want. You made your choice. I've made mine." She picked up her backpack and slung it over one shoulder, then took the suitcase handle and walked past him and out of the room.

He went after her. "I'll drive you."

Susanne looked up the stairs at them coming down. "I'm taking her, Cody."

He couldn't let her go. Not like this. "Susanne, please, I need to do this."

"No. You don't." Brooke headed for the door.

Susanne frowned at Brooke, then looked at him and read everything he couldn't bring himself to say to explain to her that losing Brooke was killing him. But she turned for the door, too.

"Brooke, please," he begged. "Please don't leave like this."

Brooke stood with her back to him and sighed so hard her shoulders went up and down. "Nothing we say to each other will change anything."

"I know. But I still need to say it to you anyway. Please."

Brooke's shoulders went slack. "Fine."

Susanne went to Brooke, hugged her from behind with her chin on Brooke's shoulder. "I love you. I'm here for you. Always."

Brooke turned and hugged her mom for a long moment, then stepped back. "Love you, too. I'll call you when I get to school." Brooke's eyes glassed over.

Cody's chest went tight. He hated that he was the reason for this early goodbye and that it felt much heavier and more sorrowful than any other time Brooke went back to school, because it felt like a last goodbye, even if he knew Brooke would always stay in touch with her mom.

Brooke walked out the door with her stuff.

Susanne touched his shoulder just before he walked out after her. The simple gesture meant a lot because Susanne knew he caused this, but she hadn't turned away from him. He appreciated that so much because she was the only mother he'd ever known even if he was grown when she came into his life. He never wanted to disappoint or hurt her. He'd done both.

Brooke stowed her things in the backseat and slipped into the front.

Cody took his seat behind the wheel of his car and drove them off the ranch and onto the main road.

Wholly aware of her and how close they were to each other, he tried not to notice the pair of silky white legs tucked into an impossibly tight, and short, jean skirt beside him. Tried and failed. The memory of those legs wrapped around him just days ago set his heart to racing and his body swelling. He tried equally hard not to notice the distant look in her green eyes.

He tried to think of what to say to make this right, but now that he had her all to himself, he couldn't think of any words that would fix this.

I don't want you to go!

She had to know at least that.

Distracted by her, this aching distance between them, he missed a yellow light, slammed on the brakes, and skidded to a stop just over the crosswalk line.

Someone honked their horn, and he swore under his breath and tried to slow his racing heart with a deep breath.

She glared at him as she fell back into her seat after being thrown forward, the seatbelt locking tightly against her breast and shoulder. "Pay attention to the road," she snapped. "I'd like to get there in one piece."

Brooke crossed her arms under her breasts and went back to ignoring him.

He wished he had the hours it would take to drive her all the way back to school instead of the twenty-minute drive that was almost over. He needed more time to thaw things out between them, so they could have an honest talk.

But that wasn't going to happen with his phone going off every twenty seconds with a text from Kristi. The woman he'd chosen instead of the one beside him.

His life was royally fucked.

"Say something. Say anything," he demanded, hoping she'd start and he'd know how to make her forgive him before he had to put her on a bus and watch her leave.

She didn't say a word and went back to staring out the window, so still and controlled.

He hated that their close friendship had turned into this crushing distance and silence between them.

She loved him. She had since she was ten years old. She was the one person he could talk to who really listened. She was the one person he could count on to keep a secret. He trusted her without reservation. She told him the truth, even if he didn't want to hear it. She had a way of getting past his sometimes volatile temper with her quiet demands that he stop acting like a jerk and talk to her about what really bothered him. He hadn't realized until this moment how much he depended on her constant nurturing spirit in his life.

The light turned green, and he continued through the intersection and thought about the night they'd made love. Everything had been perfect. If he couldn't have that back, he wanted what he'd always thought would remain. Their friendship.

He'd spent the better part of last night knocking back four doubles, trying to convince himself he wasn't in love with her. It was just lust. That's all it was, he lied to himself. What they'd shared wasn't special. He'd reduced their night together down to the bare basics of sex enjoyed by two people.

He wasn't feeling reluctant to let her go back to school. He wasn't feeling possessive and hating the idea she might find someone at college to take to her bed. He absolutely didn't have any tender feelings toward her other than friendship.

What a fucking crock of shit!

He wondered how long he could lie to himself and everyone else. He wondered if one day he'd wake up and believe the lie so he could get through one second of the day without thinking about her.

The headache pounding behind his eyes had more to do with the situation than the hangover from the whiskey he'd drowned in last night, trying to forget he'd ever laid a hand on Brooke.

Blocks from the bus stop, he only had a few minutes to say what he wanted to say. "Brooke. I know you're upset. I'm sorry I hurt you. Please give me a chance to explain."

She let out a soft sigh and stared at her lap. "I understand. You thought things with Kristi were over until she showed up the morning after you and I had sex and told you she's pregnant. You put a diamond skating rink on her finger, so that she can show it off to her snotty friends. She's got the invitations already on order, a catalogue full of dresses to choose from, ideas for the flowers, the cake, the food, the tux, everything. You'll stand beside her and promise to love, honor, and cherish her for the rest of your life." She turned to him. "I will be at school."

He stopped the car in front of the local hardware store. The bus was already waiting at the curb. "You won't come. Even as my friend. You can't put aside one night after all the years we've had together and come and be by my side on my wedding day?" He was a jerk for asking it of her, but he couldn't help himself. He needed her there. By his side. Like always.

She stared blankly out the window at the bus ready to take her back to school and away from him. "Do you love her?"

He didn't want to talk about Kristi. He wanted to talk about them. "We're going to be a family."

"Do you love her?"

Cody tried to rein in his frustration. "You just don't like her." He couldn't blame her. He'd slipped that ring on Kristi's finger and she acted like she owned him. She'd made Brooke feel uncomfortable in her own home.

She should have told him sooner that she was pregnant instead of ignoring it for two fucking weeks. If she'd taken the test sooner, none of this would be happening right now.

But then I wouldn't have discovered a love so sweet and perfect like I found in Brook's arms.

And then I lost it.

We lost it.

Brooke hurt just as much as he did, and he hated it, because it was his fault.

Brooke continued to stare out the window and not look at him. "I won't tell you I like her and come to the wedding and smile for my friend when he's making the biggest mistake of his life. Don't you think I'd be there if I could look at you with her and see you happy for the rest of your life? Maybe before we made love all night, I'd have stood there and smiled and wished you well, and then been there to pick up the pieces with you when it all turns to shit."

He believed that one hundred percent.

She finally met his gaze. "I can't do that when I look at you and see that night and know you chose her after what we shared. It might have been my first time, but even I could feel how special it was between us."

So, so special.

Remarkable.

"She's having my baby." He couldn't help the misery in his voice when he said that because it meant losing her. Happiness would come eventually, but right now, he hurt too much to find the joy in his impending fatherhood.

He'd grown up without his mother. She'd left when he was six. He barely remembered her. She'd been a young bride to his older father, and she'd hated ranch life and his father's oftentimes cold heart. She had a new family. He had a brother and sister he'd never met. They'd be about Brooke's age now.

He'd never abandon his child or let him grow up passed between two parents.

Brooke had been raised by her mother after her father abandoned her and left Susanne for a younger woman and never looked back.

They had that in common.

Brooke sighed. "And because there's a baby on the way, I'm trying to be an adult about this. That's why I congratulated you both and wished you well, despite the fact you don't have to marry her to have a happy kid. But I get it. You want your child to have what we only had when your dad married my mom. You're right, for a little while, we were a happy family, and your child deserves that. That's why I'm getting on that bus." She turned her whole body, facing him head-on. "Be happy, Cody. It's all I've ever wanted for you. I just thought I'd be the person who made you happy.

"You've shared a year of your life with Kristi. You share friends and interests and lifestyles. If the circumstances were different—well, they're not. I'm just a college student, and there are years that separate our life experiences. When you were in college, I was worrying about how to put on makeup to cover my pimples and if the boys would make fun of my braces and flat chest."

The corner of his mouth turned up. There wasn't much to dispute about their past. They'd always been in different places in their lives.

But it was different now. She was all grown up. She was starting to spread her wings, and he'd thought he'd be a part of that.

Not anymore.

Cody stared out the window, wishing this wasn't his life. She was right. Kristi and he had a lot in common and shared a common life. If he hadn't lost his head, they probably would have continued their relationship and maybe he'd have finally decided to ask her to marry him.

If you excluded Brooke, he and Kristi had only sped up the timeframe for what seemed inevitable. That's if you excluded Brooke, and he hated that the circumstances called for him to do that now that he knew how much she meant to him.

Only one thing would make him exclude Brooke from his life. "You're right. I want my child raised by both his parents."

"I know. It's one of the reasons I love you the way I do."

Her words sank deep into his heart. She'd never actually said she loved him. He just knew it by her actions. No one would ever love him the way she did.

Without another word, without him telling her he loved her, too, she slid out of the car without their usual kiss goodbye, retrieved her bags from the backseat, and walked to the bus with her bag rolling behind her, and her backpack on her back. She left her Christmas gifts, the ranch, and Cody behind, and it hurt like hell to know this might be the last time he ever saw her.

He watched her through the windshield as she stepped onto the bus. The last things he saw were her lovely legs.

Her words rang in his ears.

She still loved him, but she was leaving because he couldn't act on his love. He had to bury that deep. He had a child to think about, and she loved him enough to walk away.

He wanted to run to the bus and beg her to stay.

He wanted to keep her and take care of Kristi and his baby, too.

That was the kind of asshole he was.

He sat in his car with the engine idling until the bus pulled away. He watched it go down the street and turn the corner. He stayed there until the bus was out of sight and the tightness in his chest subsided and the unshed tears in his eyes cleared.

He missed her desperately. She'd taken a piece of him with her. He'd spend the rest of his days feeling incomplete.

Cody drove home slowly, reluctantly. He took the turnoff down the dirt road and parked where he'd seen the truck the other day. He stepped out of the car and walked, not caring as the dew from the tall grass clung to his slacks and wet his legs up to his knees.

The creek's song called to him. He followed the narrow path through the trees until they gave way to the water. He found the flat rock next to a huge oak. Brooke's favorite spot. He sat down with his back against the tree and looked out over the water as it rushed by. This was as close as he'd get to Brooke again. Everything inside him told him she wasn't coming back. It had been in her eyes and the way she'd said she loved him.

He sat for more than an hour, knowing Kristi was at the house, waiting for him to come home and go over the guest list. He couldn't muster up the energy to decide if her third cousin on her mother's side, who'd married her uncle's best friend and caused a scandal, should be invited. He didn't care if her great-aunt Beth couldn't sit with her cousin Monica because of the fruitcake with nuts, or was it without, incident three years ago. He didn't care about any of it. He wanted her to send the invitations, make the arrangements, and tell him when to show up.

In fact, that's what he was going to tell her. As far as he was concerned, she could have the wedding of her dreams. She didn't need him to help her plan it.

Unable to avoid his life and reality forever, he stood and took a moment to look out over the water.

Brooke had herself a pretty spot. Peaceful. The birds chirped in the trees, the water rushed over the rocks and made a pleasant sound that smoothed out his rough edges as much as that was possible right now.

This was a spot you could sit with yourself and really think.

The only problem, he could only think of Brooke, memories of her flipping through his mind like a slideshow.

Here, he could sit in the quiet and be with her.

He'd come back.

Maybe he'd find a way not to make this his permanent home.

Turning to leave, his gaze locked on the tree behind the rock he'd been sitting on. Carved into the bark were his and Brooke's initials. CJ + BB. Cody Jansen plus Brooke Banks. His initials were over hers and he wondered how long ago she'd carved them into the tree with a heart around them. It was the freshly carved teardrop coming out of the heart that hurt the most. He knew she'd done it days ago. He wondered if her heart was crying, or bleeding. Maybe, probably, both. He traced his finger over their initials. Then, he took out his keys and carved his own message to her.

FF. Friends Forever.

Chapter Twenty-Three

He loved having Brooke back at school where he could see her and show her how much he cared. How much he wanted her. He hoped she liked today's gift.

He balanced Brooke's box of donuts in his hands and made his way up the stairs to the third floor. He checked the corridor, grateful the hall was empty. He didn't have to explain his presence or worry about anyone seeing him deliver his present. He'd left her several others, hoping she appreciated all the effort he put into the secret admirer routine.

He'd never had a girlfriend.

He had bungled several false starts with girls in high school when he was too shy to truly pursue them and ended up in the friend zone because he didn't go in for the kiss, or missed some other opportunity to make it clear he wanted more. Once that happened, the girls looked for someone else who liked them and wanted to fool around.

From the outside watching others with girls, they seemed easy.

They were not. You had to read things right. And he'd gotten it wrong so many times.

Brooke was different. No one spoke to him the way she did. No one drew him in the way she did. It was all he could do to attend classes and keep up his grades when all he wanted to do was be with her.

Soon.

He stood in front of her door, wishing she discovered him standing outside. He imagined she'd throw her arms around his neck, kiss him, and say, "I'm so glad it's you," when she discovered the gifts came from him.

She'd be so happy. She'd know how much he loved her.

They'd finally be together.

But first, he wanted to romance her and show her how much he wanted her.

She deserved that.

He wanted to give her everything her heart desired.

He'd make her fall in love with him a little at a time, until he was all she thought about and wanted.

Chapter Twenty-Four

B rooke stopped short in the middle of the dorm's hallway, staring down the long corridor at the box outside her door. She approached it cautiously and froze when she spotted the picture on top of it of a couple sitting at an outside café table. A man had his face buried in a woman's neck as he kissed her, but the woman's face had been replaced with Brooke's face. Her stalker had written *This will be you and me soon!* in what had to be Brooke's favorite red lipstick.

She'd lost a tube of it from her purse. She'd left it unattended for like two minutes in the library while she returned a book to the stacks a week ago.

The fear built in her gut and rose up to her throat, choking off her air. Scared, she sucked in a slow breath and let it out to calm her racing heart and the anxiety she'd developed since returning to school after Christmas a month ago.

"I can do this."

"Do what?"

Brooke jumped, spun around, and gasped out her fright when her friend Mindy Sue surprised her. "Don't do that."

Mindy Sue held her hands up in front of her. "Sorry. What are you doing?"

Brooke stepped to the side, unable to put into words what had been happening to her these last few weeks. @youseeme had gone from leaving her online messages to leaving her pictures of her he'd taken without her knowing around campus and in town with gifts. He liked to leave them on the bulletin board attached to her dorm room door.

Mindy Sue stared down the hall. "Shit. Another one."

"My favorite morning treat from the Donut Hole. And a message in my lipstick."

"What the actual fuck!" Mindy Sue folded her arms over her chest like she wanted to protect herself from this madness. "Maybe you should go home. Fix things with him. Tell him and your mom—"

"No. I can handle this. I'm a grown-up. Cody made his choice, and I have to live with it."

"Then it's time you talked to campus security and the police and let them know someone is stalking you."

She didn't want to believe that, but the evidence had been mounting for months. This person hadn't just been commenting online, he'd been in her life, at her home, following her at school.

They walked all the way down the hall to their door. The box of donuts seemed innocuous, except that it came from the shop she loved. Put that together with the creepy photo/note and other items left at her door—the scarf she'd tried on in a boutique downtown, the earrings she admired in a shop window after picking up a coffee at the local Starbucks, and the margarita pizza someone had delivered to her dorm room from her favorite pizza place while she studied for a test—all that equaled stalker.

Even creepier, someone had covered the bulletin board hanging on her door with a collage of photos of her on campus with friends, at the café where she loved to grab a snack, standing by the bike rack, talking on the phone. In the center was a picture of her sitting on the lawn, her back to a tree, and her face turned up to the sun, tears streaming down her face. Whoever was watching her wrote on the back, *I miss you more.*

Mindy Sue opened the box and stared at the half dozen each of chocolate glazed and sugar donuts. Brooke's favorites. "That's seriously creepy. Are you sure you have no idea who is doing this?"

"None. As far as I can tell, the pictures of me all over campus and town span the last month."

Mindy Sue pointed to one of the photos on the board. "That's us outside the movie theater two days ago. And at the library about ten days ago."

She'd taken the first pics down, but whoever took the photos put them all back up again. Now she just left them there. Whoever was doing this to her wanted her to see them every time she came back to her room. They wanted to remind her of them.

It freaked her out.

Someone was out there, watching her, waiting, pursuing her, and doing it all behind her back. And it needed to stop before it got worse.

Mindy Sue picked up the photo. "Does the guy look familiar?"

She shook her head. "I'm guessing it's a photo of some random couple he, or she, saw while following me and this is his fantasy for us." That sent a cold shiver down her spine.

Mindy Sue scrunched her lips and nose with revulsion. "I just...who the fuck thinks this is any kind of way to try to be with someone?"

"I'd prefer a silly pickup line over this."

Mindy Sue put her hand on Brooke's shoulder. "Call Cody. He's got connections. Maybe he can help."

"No. I need to do this on my own." She couldn't rely on Cody anymore. She needed to stand on her own two feet and build a new life for herself without him in it. "It's not like this person is threatening me."

"Not yet. But he keeps coming to our room. Sure, right now he's dropping stuff at the door. What happens when he wants in?"

Brooke's stomach dropped. "You're right. It's just...I don't need this right now."

Mindy Sue put her hand on Brooke's shoulder and stared at her in sympathy. "I know. But you have to go to campus security and file a report."

A tingle of fear danced up her spine, like someone walked over her grave. "Will you come with me?"

"Of course. What kind of friend would I be if I didn't hold your hair while you puked, or go with you to report a stalker?" Mindy Sue put her hands on her hips. "I mean really."

Despite the fear still tightening her gut, she laughed. "You're the bestest friend ever."

"Damn right. Now let's collect everything the psycho left you and take them with us. From now on, you don't go anywhere alone. Keep your eye out when you're on campus and in town. Don't drink or eat anything someone else gives you."

"What?"

"You never know if he'll roofie you or something," Mindy Sue said, staring down at the seemingly innocuous donuts. "What does this guy want?"

"I don't know, but I wish he'd just leave me alone." Her shoulders sagged.

Mindy Sue put her hands on Brooke's shoulders. "You've got a lot on your plate. This is the last thing you need. Stress is not good for you."

No, but it had become her constant companion, along with the bone-deep sadness she carried with her. That picture of her crying beneath the tree showed the depth of the sorrow she felt every second of the day. How many other times had this bastard spied on her when she couldn't stop the tears or pain from sucking her under and leaving her raw?

Why did he care about anything she did?

Why wouldn't he leave her alone to grieve in peace?

She wanted it to stop. She wanted the pain and sadness to stop. She wanted everything to go back to the way it used to be, when Cody was her best friend and a box of donuts didn't freak her out.

Chapter Twenty-Five

Brooke met Mindy Sue and Julie at their favorite café just as Adam, Jeremiah, and Simon walked in. "Come and join us."

"Are you sure?" Jeremiah asked.

"We can get another table," Adam said.

"No. Don't be silly." Brooke smiled at Adam, hoping he saw the sincerity she put into her gaze and relaxed.

Julie held her hand out to the empty seats at their table, encouraging the guys more. "We haven't gotten together in a while."

"We saw Brooke at her Christmas party last month." Simon took a seat at the table.

Jeremiah and Adam followed suit.

This was the first time Brooke had been out with anyone other than Mindy Sue after returning to school. She'd been too lost in her grief to want to do anything more than drag her ass to her classes each day, then back to her dorm room to wallow in her nest of blankets and pillows, avoiding her feelings about Cody and her stalker.

This morning she hadn't felt well, but whatever bug caught her didn't last, and she was feeling better this evening. Well enough to go out at Mindy Sue's insistence that she couldn't spend her senior year as a hermit.

"What brought you guys here tonight?" Mindy Sue had a strange look in her eyes when she studied the three guys.

Jeremiah answered for them. "Adam and I were studying in the library when Simon texted that he was hungry."

"I'm always hungry."

Jeremiah rolled his eyes. "We know. Anyway, we met up at the quad and headed over here."

"Do you guys eat here often?" Mindy Sue asked.

"It's one of my favorites," Jeremiah said.

"Me, too," Brooke agreed. "They have the best fried chicken salad."

Jeremiah scrunched his nose. "I like the French dip sandwich. They also have the best fries in town."

"Totally," Adam and Simon said at the same time.

The waitress arrived and took their drink and food order.

"How are all your classes going?" she asked the guys, trying to keep the conversation going.

They all took a turn complaining about their classes, sprinkled with a few things they liked about them, too. All of them were as anxious as her to graduate.

She couldn't wait to be on her own and be her own boss. She was excited to get started on the building. In just a couple of months, she'd own it.

And since Cody and Kristi would be living in the ranch house, she'd set herself up in one of the apartments on the third floor. She'd decorate it with bright colors and soft furnishings.

It would be a new start.

"Did you guys hear about the dude on campus who's running around flashing girls?" Julie scrunched her lips.

"Yuck. Like we want to see a dude's junk while walking to class."

Adam cringed. "That's weird."

Simon leaned in. "I have a friend who goes to UT Austin. Three girls have been attacked by some guy while they're walking home from local bars."

"That's so fucked up." Mindy Sue shook her head. "Did any of the women ID him?"

"Nope. Dude hits them on the head, knocks them out, then does stuff to them." Simon cringed.

Brooke shivered with revulsion and the same chill that ran up her spine every time she thought about her stalker. She didn't say anything to the group about him, because all of these guys had been to her house multiple times. They'd hung out on campus while Mindy Sue was seeing Marco even before the picnic. "Let's talk about something else."

Mindy Sue must have been thinking along the lines Brooke's mind had gone because she stared at the three guys, wondering like her.

No. No way.

It couldn't be one of them. They were so nice. And they spent time together. They had plenty of opportunity to ask her out.

The waitress brought their food and distributed it to the table and everyone eagerly dug in. Brooke was the last to be served. The second the smell of the fried chicken in her salad hit her nose, her mouth watered and her stomach turned.

She leaped up and ran to the bathroom, barely making it to the toilet before she threw up what little she had in her stomach.

Someone rubbed their hand up and down her back. "Hey. You okay? That's the second time you threw up today." Mindy Sue pulled her hair back into a ponytail and used her free hand to touch Brooke's forehead. "You don't have a fever."

"I must have some bug." She pulled a bunch of toilet paper from the dispenser and wiped her mouth.

Mindy Sue hooked her hand under Brooke's arm and helped her up. "Maybe. But I've noticed you've seemed...off for a couple weeks. We should stop at the drugstore on the way home."

Brooke went utterly still. "No." She shook her head, but that night with Cody came back in vivid detail. The way they'd been so consumed with being together they'd forgotten all about using protection. "No. I can't be..." She tried to take in a calming breath. "She's already... No. This can't be happening."

"I think it is." Mindy Sue pulled her into a hug. "No matter what, it's going to be okay."

She held her amazing friend even tighter. "I'm not so sure."

Am I pregnant?
Am I going to be a mom?
How will I tell Cody?
What will he do?

"Oh God. This is bad."

Mindy Sue leaned back and shook her head. "No. It's not. This is Cody's baby. You wanted him in your life forever. Now you've got it."

Her heart pounded in her chest. "Not this way. Not like this."

"I know. But if this is the only way, then take it, Brooke. Be happy with this little piece of him you get to keep. Enjoy the moments you'll get to share with him watching your child grow up together, even if he is with her. Let it be enough."

"It's better than nothing," she reluctantly admitted.

Mindy Sue put her hand on Brooke's shoulder. "When you tell him, maybe he'll choose you."

"He already chose her." She couldn't even hope for a different outcome.

Cody wouldn't go back on the promise he made to Kristi.

"She's wearing his ring. He'll remind me we're friends and that we can raise the child together in that way."

Mindy Sue pressed her lips tight. "I think he'd choose you. Give him a chance to make that decision."

Tears welled in her eyes. "I can't take the chance he still chooses her and it breaks my heart all over again."

Mindy Sue cupped her face and brushed the tears away with her thumbs. "Then he doesn't deserve you, because you're awesomer than all the rest of us."

"Not true. I have the most awesomest friend ever!"

"Okay. Then let's get our food to go and hit the drugstore. You need to know, so you can plan what comes next."

Brooke washed her hands and rinsed her mouth in the bathroom sink while Mindy Sue went out to deal with their food and tell their friends they had to leave because she wasn't feeling well. She'd keep the why of it to herself for now.

She took a deep breath, then went out to face everyone.

"Are you okay?" Jeremiah asked.

"You look pale," Adam added.

"I think it's just a bug. I wasn't feeling well this morning, but thought it had passed. Guess not. Sorry to spoil the evening. You guys stay and have a good time."

Julie stood and hugged her. "I'm going to hang out. Jeremiah and I are going to play video games after dinner."

"Have fun. Mindy Sue and I will see you tomorrow."

Her friend arrived with the food bagged up and they headed out. Within twenty minutes they'd gone to the drugstore, purchased a test, and made their way into their dorm. They went to the bathroom and Mindy Sue waited outside the stall while Brooke peed on the stick. Since it needed several minutes to do its thing, they took it back to their dorm room and waited, neither of them saying a thing as the timer on Brooke's phone counted down.

When it chimed, they both leaned over the desk and stared at the double pink lines on the test.

Mindy Sue grinned.

She found herself grinning back, despite how scared she was about how she was going to do this mostly on her own. "Oh my God."

"You're having a baby." Mindy Sue's glee was infectious.

"I don't...I don't know what to even say or do."

"Now that you know for sure," Mindy Sue began and left a pregnant pause. "What are you going to do?"

It didn't even enter her mind that she wouldn't keep it. Mindy Sue had been right. This was a piece of Cody. Maybe the only one she'd ever get to truly hold close. "I'm going to love them with everything I am. I think I already do." She pressed her hands over her belly, a smile blooming on her face that made her cheeks hurt.

Mindy Sue leaned down and said, "Hello in there! I'm your Auntie Mindy Sue."

Brooke laughed with her friend and they hugged each other tight. "Thank you for being here with me."

Mindy Sue hugged her harder. "I wish he could be here with you."

"Me, too." What else was there to say?

She'd have to tell him. Soon. After the wedding. She didn't want to put him in a tough spot. She wanted him to enjoy his happy day, even if it was killing her to keep it to herself and not share this wonderful news with him.

Chapter Twenty-Six

He went through all the trouble of getting the guys to go with him to the café where he'd overheard Brooke was going when she made plans on the phone with Mindy Sue and didn't even see him standing near her while she walked to her last class. And Brooke didn't even stay to eat with them.

He wanted to be the one who took her back to her dorm and tucked her into bed. Maybe she'd let him lie with her and comfort her while she got some rest.

Damnit, he'd been so close to getting her to see that he was the one who loved her. He was the one who made sure she got everything she needed and wanted.

He spoiled her.

He made her happy.

All he wanted was for tonight to finally be the night she threw her arms around him and told him that she loved him, too.

Well, he'd just have to get her attention another way.

He obviously wasn't being romantic enough. He needed to up his game even more.

He'd show her she belonged to him.

I'll show her she's mine!

Chapter Twenty-Seven

C ody dreamed about Brooke again, same as he did every night. There she was waiting for him, arms open wide to pull him in close and love him. Her body the safe haven he sank into and craved with every breath and heartbeat.

He worked like a demon all day just so he could collapse from exhaustion and find relief in Brooke's loving embrace. Every breath without her hurt and every moment he spent with her in sleep was a pleasure and pain, because when he opened his eyes, she'd be gone all over again.

But not right now. Brooke's lips pressed to his, and he was so hungry for her, it seemed so real. He could actually feel her body pressed against his. Reaching for her, he found that in between his dream and being almost awake, he wasn't alone.

He didn't want to wake up. He tried to sink back into the dream, but reality pulled him from Brooke and he found himself looking up into Kristi's bright blue eyes, not the green ones he loved so much.

Disappointment washed over him, and he closed his eyes as her lips coaxed him to continue kissing her. Brooke's image and the way they'd made love came back to him.

He hated that he did it, but he pretended Kristi was Brooke and dug his fingers into Kristi's hair, turned her head so he could fit his mouth to hers for a deep, penetrating kiss, and pulled her down to him.

"Mmm. Honey, if this is what I have to look forward to every morning, I'd have insisted on waking up with you every day since we met."

"Shh." He pulled her mouth back to his. He wanted to block out Kristi and be with Brooke, if only in his fantasy.

You're a special kind of bastard.

He ignored that inner voice and kissed Kristi again.

The wedding was fast approaching. Between his caseload, the ranch, and the wedding plans, he and Kristi hadn't had sex, despite how often she pushed for it. He'd used work and exhaustion as an excuse.

She'd been preoccupied with wedding plans on top of her job. Plus the pregnancy made her tired, too.

It gave him the time he needed to mentally switch gears and recommit to her.

And right now, his body ached for release and she felt good in his arms. He palmed her ass and rubbed his achingly hard cock against her softness.

He didn't need to analyze the obvious reasons why he hadn't made the time for this kind of intimacy before now.

But he couldn't hold on to Brooke and have Kristi and look at himself in the mirror later, so he pushed all thoughts of Brooke out of his mind and concentrated on the woman in his arms as he kissed her, clamped both hands on her ass, and squeezed, making her moan.

Kristi was here. She was his life now.

He'd made his choice, even after it had been made for him. It took a while, but he'd finally settled into becoming Kristi's husband.

It took the better part of the last two months to get there. Despite his rigorous work schedule, the ranch, and his sour moods, they'd actually grown closer. Their routine and interactions went back to the way things had been before Christmas. He still enjoyed her company. Though they were still struggling to find their balance again. She still hated his work schedule. He couldn't seem to find enough hours in the day to meet all his obligations. She stopped arguing with him about it and seemed to accept this was how things were right now.

He promised her when the baby arrived, he'd take family leave and be here to help and support her. He didn't expect her to do everything on her own. He wanted to be a hands-on dad.

The wedding got pushed out by a month, so he could take care of a few important cases. She hadn't liked that at all, but her father had intervened, calming her down by saying they'd have more time for their honeymoon if Cody took care of the cases now. Exactly what Cody had said to her, but apparently it sounded better coming from Kirk.

For him, acceptance came slowly that Brooke couldn't be a part of his future, but a very real, important, and precious part of his past.

Grief had overwhelmed him.

Once that waned to reluctant acceptance, it had been easier to be with Kristi and spend time with her without wishing she was someone else.

Most of the time.

Okay, not every second he was with her.

He slid one hand over her rump and pressed his fingers to her soft folds, rubbing her though her pants and underwear. He wanted skin. Heat. Mind-blowing fucking.

Brooke had stopped all contact with him. No late-night texts to check on him. No funny memes or jokes to make him smile. Not a single phone call, so he could hear her voice and know that she was okay.

Nothing but her absence. Silence.

After what he'd done...well, he deserved it.

But it was a constant ache in his heart and a deafening roar of silence in the back of his mind.

They'd never be the kind of friends they were before all this happened.

Except for in his dreams, he'd let her go.

It hurt. But it had to be done.

He wanted to enjoy making love to Kristi, his focus on her alone. She was warm and sweet, and even though she didn't make love as ardently as he'd like, she was his.

He rolled her under him and kissed his way down her throat and found her pulse. It beat fast against his lips, even if it wasn't hammering. He needed to step up his game if he expected her to respond with unleashed passion.

She was so reserved in her responses; he wanted to find a way to break through that restraint and have her panting in his arms. It was a challenge, but one he accepted.

He cupped her breast in his palm over her blouse and bra and rubbed his thumb over her nipple. Her hands lay softly on his head, her fingers threaded through his hair. She didn't moan or sigh as he kissed her neck and plucked at her nipple, hoping to get the reaction he wanted.

"Honey, we need to talk about something," she said, seemingly unaffected by his attention.

What the hell? She'd been begging him to spend more time with her and be more attentive. Well, here he was. She had him all to herself and she wanted to talk?

He wanted to get her naked. "Not now. After."

He wanted her to grip his hair and hold him to her breast.

He wanted her to roll her hips against his.

Something.

He kissed the soft skin just beneath her ear, his body heavy between her legs.

He wished she'd do something with her hands. Slide them over his shoulders and down his bare back. He wanted to feel the bite of her nails in his skin as he took her up to the peak.

He rose up on his hands and reached for the buttons down her shirt, greedy to get his hands on her warm skin.

She pressed her hands to his chest and stopped him. "Wait."

What?

He didn't move, just stared down at her as he held himself above her. "What's wrong?" He glanced down at her flat belly and thought of the baby. "Am I too heavy to be on top of you?"

"No." She bit her lip and stared at his chin, unable to look him in the eye. "Um, we need to use a condom."

Cody went completely still. Everything inside him went taut. His mind ground to a biting halt. "I know I'm sometimes a dumbshit when it comes to women, but I'm very sure I can't get you *more* pregnant."

Kristi turned her head to the side and stared at the wall. "I'm not pregnant anymore."

Cody's heart sank. He gently touched her face with his fingertips and turned her to look at him. "You lost the baby?"

She nodded.

Cody's heart clenched. He couldn't breathe. *We lost the baby.* "When?"

Her eyes clouded with sadness and her bottom lip trembled. "A week after I told you."

His mind went blank. He couldn't have heard her right.

She reached up, held his face in her hands, and made him look at her. "I know you're upset. I was, too. But I was only a few weeks along at best. These things happen early in a pregnancy for all sorts of reasons. My doctor assured me everything is fine. It just wasn't meant to be. Not this time. Not now. But that doesn't mean we can't try again after we're married."

She lost the baby. We aren't pregnant anymore.
What?

It simply didn't make sense. "You've known this for weeks and you didn't say anything." Anger replaced his sadness. He untangled himself from her and the sheets and stood with his back to her, trying to understand why she hadn't told him.

"Let me explain," she pleaded, a hitch in her voice.

He tried to think clearly and turned to her as she sat up on the edge of the bed. "Are you all right?"

She seemed so calm while he was a whirlwind of contained emotions.

Of course, she'd had time to process what happened.

He was still reeling from the loss.

She bit her bottom lip. "I'm fine. I woke up one morning with terrible cramps. It happened quickly, just my body's way of saying something was wrong." Her gaze fell to the floor, then met his again. "I told myself it was for the best. We could take a little time to settle into marriage before we tried again."

"And you didn't feel the need to contact me, to call me to come over and help you, to come to me at all?"

"You were in court that day. One of your big cases. I took the day off work and was back in the office the next day."

Like nothing happened. Like it didn't change anything.

Her shoulders sank and her eyes pleaded with him. "I tried to tell you so many times. The only time we've truly had together, we've either been in a crowd, or we've only had a few minutes to talk about the wedding."

Was that more important than talking about their baby?

"You've been so busy with your cases, the trouble here at the ranch with that bull, or whatever…"

"And you couldn't take two seconds to say, 'Hey, Cody, guess what? I lost the baby.'" He couldn't believe she'd kept this from him. He didn't want to admit how much it hurt that not only did he lose a child, but she hadn't even thought it mattered enough for him to be with her to see her through the ordeal.

"I know how much you were looking forward to being a father."

It was the one thing that made losing Brooke bearable.

It was the reason he and Kristi were getting married.

She lost the baby and just kept on going with those plans without telling him that his baby was gone.

He didn't know what to say or feel right now. Everything inside him felt numb.

"There's no reason to think we can't still have kids. We'll just wait until after the wedding. That's how it should be anyway."

He'd lost his best friend and now he wasn't going to be a father. "I really don't know what to do right now. Maybe we need to take a step back and figure this out."

Her head tilted and her eyes narrowed. "Are you talking about calling off the wedding? Because I lost the baby?"

"It was the reason I asked you to marry me." His blunt words made her cringe.

"Yes," she admitted, her eyes filled with anger now. "Because that's the kind of man you are, and the man I love."

That sounded too much like what Brooke had said to him, and it hurt. Deeply.

She stood before him. "We talked about getting married long before I told you I was pregnant. The pregnancy was a catalyst for our engagement, but it isn't the only reason we're getting married."

"I know that, but you should have told me immediately that you lost the baby. It was *ours*."

"I know. I'm sorry. I've just been...overwhelmed by everything."

"You and me both. That's why I think we need to take a moment and think about the future."

"Don't do this, Cody. We've built a solid relationship for more than a year. We've grown closer with each passing day. I love you." Tears gathered in her pleading eyes.

She pressed her overlapping hands to her belly. "You love me. I know you do. What's between us isn't just an obligation because of a baby. We love each other, and we have a good life together." She placed her hand on his chest over his heart. "We have a bright future ahead of us and children will be a part of it. Please, Cody. I love you. Marry me." A tear slipped down her cheek, followed by another, though she held it together and didn't completely fall apart.

He had to admit, he hadn't made it easy for her to talk to him lately about anything. He'd cut her off a dozen times when she'd tried to talk to him, imploring him that it was important. As much as he wanted to blame her, part of the blame rested on his shoulders.

He pulled her up and into his arms and held her.

"I know the last two months have been hard. I've been difficult. You've tried to talk to me and I either ignored you or told you it had to wait."

She leaned back and looked up at him. "And let me guess, you're late, so we'll have to finish this later, too." She sounded so dejected.

He took the verbal slap. It was nothing less than what he deserved. "What? No."

Her eyes filled with skepticism. "Aren't you supposed to be down at the stables helping Charlie this morning? That's why I came so early."

Right. With the blow she'd dealt him, he'd completely forgotten about helping Charlie and never questioned why she was here, in his room, when they never stayed here.

"Charlie can wait. We need to resolve this." He glanced at the clock and figured he could spare half an hour. He'd been letting things between him and Kristi move along without his really thinking beyond the fact that they were expecting a child and the wedding needed to get done.

"Cody," she said softly. "I understand you're upset I didn't tell you right away. The truth is, things between us were rocky at best at the time, and I was afraid I'd lose you. Things are better now. I knew we'd find our way back to each other and we have. But I also thought you might need some time once I told you about the baby, so I didn't send out the invitations. In fact, I moved the wedding date altogether. Again."

What? "You did?" He read the sincerity in her eyes.

She was sorry things had gotten so crazy in their lives, and she hadn't told him sooner.

And she was right, there was more between them than just the baby they'd lost.

"I had the engraver change the date on the wedding invitations to the third weekend in June. I booked the church for that weekend and changed the caterers and the band and everything else." She took him by the arms and looked him right in the eyes. "I really want this, Cody. I hope you do, too. I know it isn't how we might have done things originally, but that doesn't mean we shouldn't do it at all."

He understood what she wasn't saying. She wanted him to take the next few months to make sure she was really who he wanted to marry. He appreciated the fact that she understood something had happened before Christmas with Brooke, but she didn't ask about it. She didn't put it front and center and in between them.

Probably because if she did, it would hang there forever.

With Brooke away at school, Kristi had given him the time he needed to put it behind him and try to make a life with her.

"I know your first instinct is to run to Brooke because that's what you've always done. But she cut you out of her life because of our relationship. That's not a friend."

Ouch!

It's not like Kristi made an effort with Brooke.

"Please consider that I'm here, while she's away at school, living her life with a future she's just starting to plan. By this summer, she'll have her degree. After, she'll build a career. It will be a fresh start for her with a world of possibilities in front of her."

This was as close as she'd come to saying outright that she knew he wanted a relationship with Brooke.

Kristi tapped her fingers on his arms to get his attention back. "You and me, we run in the same circles and have so much in common. We're the same age, which makes it easy for us to relate to each other. I have my own career. I'm ready to settle down and have a family with you. That's where *we* are in *our* life together."

All true. She made a good case.

Where did he fit in Brooke's life?

He couldn't very well give everything up here and go and be with her in San Antonio. How would they repair their broken friendship with a long-distance relationship?

How would they be together when they lived such separate lives?

He didn't even know if he could get her to talk to him.

What if she'd already moved on and found someone new?

What if they tried and things didn't work out between them and he lost her again?

He didn't know if he could live through that kind of pain a second time.

You'll never know unless you try.

This is your chance to have everything you really want. Take it!

He glanced at his watch. "Do you have plans for today?"

"Just some errands, nothing that can't wait."

"Okay. Good. I...I need a little time to think about all of this, but I don't want to leave you hanging. Let me run down to the barn and take care of what I need to do. Can you meet me back here at noon? We'll finish this talk and decide what to do next."

"Sure." All her trepidation came out with that single syllable.

"Thank you."

"You don't have to thank me, Cody. You need time. You can have it. I want you to be sure." With that, she kissed his cheek and walked out of his room.

He quickly showered and dressed, then snapped up his phone.

CODY: Can we talk?

She didn't respond right away, so he headed downstairs and to the stables. Halfway across the pasture, his phone chimed.

BROOKE: We said everything we needed to say.

CODY: Maybe there's still a chance for us to have a relationship.

BROOKE: I'm having enough trouble with someone else. I can't handle any more Kristi drama too.

Cody stopped in his tracks and stared at the message for God knew how long.

She'd moved on. She had someone new.

He was too late.

"Was that him?" Mindy Sue asked, as they both stared at the Polaroid she'd just found stuck in her textbook. She'd left it on the library table yesterday while she combed the stacks for another text. When she got back, she hadn't noticed any of her things disturbed. She really shouldn't leave her stuff unattended, but she'd only been gone a couple of minutes.

The picture showed her sitting with a classmate. Billy had asked her to tutor him for an upcoming test.

He'd left and she'd stayed to finish some other schoolwork.

"No. That was Cody." Distracted by the latest picture from her stalker, she hadn't really had her head on straight when she answered Cody.

He wanted to talk about them being friends while he lived in bliss with Kristi. She had a guy who wouldn't leave her alone.

One problem at a time.

Anyway, he must have gotten busy, because he hadn't said anything after her text.

She needed to figure out who was doing this to her.

"That's a threat, Brooke."

The stalker had written her a very clear message. *You're mine! Not his!*

She barely knew Billy. They saw each other in class. They had a couple of group projects together. That was it.

"You know what you need to do."

"I'll take this over to campus security. They'll contact and update the police." For all the good it would do. They never found any prints or figured out who was doing this to her.

Still, she'd add this to the trail of evidence. Maybe one day it would be useful.

Hopefully before this guy did something worse to her.

Cody dealt with the ranch business, then met Kristi up at the house.

"Hey," he said when he found her in the living room waiting, her hands clenched tight in front of her, showing her nerves. "I'm glad you're here." He hoped to put her at ease. "Let's go in my study and talk privately before we eat."

She followed him inside and took a seat on the sofa, right where she'd sat when he found out she was pregnant.

He'd spent the last couple of hours thinking about her and their relationship. Kristi was right. Their relationship stood on solid footing because they shared the same friends, interests, and were in the same place in life. They wanted the same things and were ready to embark on the future they'd talked about.

He sat next to her and took her hand. "We'll keep the wedding date in June."

She gasped and stared wide-eyed at him. "Really? You mean it? You're sure?"

"Yes."

She beamed, her smile filled with excitement.

Good. He didn't like seeing her upset or anxious when it came to them. "My schedule is just starting to lighten up at the law practice. All the critical agenda items for the children's hospital have been voted on and initiated, too, so I'll have more time for us this summer."

"I would really like that."

"Me, too. I'll make a bigger effort to listen to you when you want to talk to me. We'll go out more often. I'll even help you with the seating chart. We'll sit your great-aunt Beth next to my uncle Sirus. He spent half his life as a bartender. He has about a hundred recipes that use rum as the main ingredient. They'll get along great. We'll take the next few months to settle in and move forward with both of us on the same page."

Her smile went up two notches. "We'll build something better."

He smiled back, catching some of her enthusiasm. "Yes. Better."

And different. Because it wouldn't be what he'd hoped for with Brooke.

June was a good length of time for them to reconnect and focus on all the good things they had between them. They'd wait at least another year before trying to get pregnant again. Time enough to settle into being married. He liked that idea, warmed to it.

Kristi kissed him with noticeably more enthusiasm.

This would be a new beginning for them. They'd hit a bump in the road, but they were back on track. "Let's go have lunch and really catch up," he suggested.

Kristi kissed him again, then practically floated out of the living room, she was so happy.

He felt better, too, but there was one thing he still needed to do...

Alone in his office that night, he poured a shot of whiskey, sat at his desk, and pulled out his cell. Nerves knotted his stomach. He hit the speed dial for Brooke like he'd done a thousand times the last two months, but this time he put the call through, hoping he found the right words to tell her everything.

"Hey, it's Brooke. Sorry I missed your call. You know what to do. Text me."

Just hearing her voice made his heart throb with pain and regret. He missed her with every breath he took.

At the beep, he spilled the truth he wasn't sure she'd understand after all that had happened between them. "Hi Brooke. It's me. I hate to leave this as a message, but I get it, you're busy with school and your...friends."

Yeah, some guy who better be treating you right.

"Listen, I wanted you to know that Kristi and I postponed the wedding until the end of June." He sighed and spit out the truth she deserved to hear from him. "She lost the baby." He got choked up on the words. "We're taking some time to get things back on track before we get married. We'll have a family later. I hope you're happy. I hope you're doing well. Please come to the wedding. You said you would if you knew it's what I really want. It is. Please. You can bring whoever you're with if you want. Please come. We'll always be friends, right?" Choked up, he ended the call, knowing she wasn't going to call him back. Not now. Maybe not ever. Not when he'd chosen Kristi again.

If the sound of Brooke's voice telling him to text her a message made him want her again that badly, he couldn't help it.

Just like he couldn't help walking into her room that night, stretching out on her bed, pulling her pillow to his face, inhaling her scent, and falling into a restless sleep full of dreams about her.

Chapter Twenty-Eight

B rooke listened to the message for the fourth time, tears running down her cheeks, her heart broken all over again as Cody's deep, rich voice told her yet again everything she didn't want to hear.

He picked her again!

Mindy Sue unlocked the new deadbolts on their door and walked into their dorm room with a huge smile on her face. She kicked the door closed behind her, executed a perfect pirouette on tiptoe, and did a rockin' booty dance, shaking her butt with her hands in the air. She stopped abruptly with her right hip cocked out to the side when she spotted Brooke lying on her back in bed. "What happened?"

Brooke pressed her phone to her chest and let the tears fall in a torrent. Mindy Sue sat beside her, pulled her up by the shoulders, and wrapped her in a hug. Brooke held on for dear life.

"What is it, sweetie? Tell me. Is it the stalker? Did he send you that bracelet with the heart charm?"

Brooke grabbed the silver box off the desk beside her and threw it against the wall. "It's not that."

"Okay. Definitely pissed at the stalker, but that's not what's making you cry." Mindy Sue leaned back and met her gaze. "Is it the baby?"

"No." Brooke put her hand to her slightly swollen belly and sobbed harder. "Cod-dy."

"Has something happened? Is he hurt? What about Cody, Brooke?"

She sucked in a deep, shuddering breath. "He left me a message."

"Finally. One of you needed to make the first move. What did he say? Does he want to talk about what happened?" Mindy Sue leaned back again. "Did you finally tell him you're pregnant?" Mindy Sue thought Brooke should have called him the second she found out she was carrying his child.

Cody deserved to know he was going to be a father—twice over. But Brooke had made up her mind when she found out she was having his baby that she'd wait until after the wedding so she didn't spoil his day. It was just a month.

But now...June!

She didn't want to wait that long.

"I missed the call because I was on the phone with campus security about the damn bracelet." Brooke released Mindy Sue and flopped back on her pillow. "He called to tell me they moved the wedding to the end of June. June! He wants me to come to the wedding. He says he and Kristi are in the same place in their lives and they want the same things."

"Well, you expected this right? She's pregnant."

"She lost the baby." Brooke wrapped her arms around the baby she carried like she could protect it from nature.

Mindy Sue shot up to her feet. "What!" She sat down heavily and made Brooke bounce on the mattress. She took Brooke's hand and held it in hers. "Oh my God, Brooke. This changes everything."

Brooke wished that were true, but that wasn't the message Cody left her.

"Not in Cody's mind. They're still getting married and plan to have a family later. He said I have school and my life here. Obviously, he loves *her*."

Brooke's heart broke over that yet again. "He said I could bring whoever I'm with to the wedding. He thinks I've simply moved on." She was too upset to even process or understand why he'd think that he was so easy for her to replace.

"Asshole." Mindy Sue held tight to Brooke's hand. She leaned down and kissed her on the belly and said to her slightly swollen stomach, "I'm sorry, baby. But your daddy isn't being nice to your mommy."

Brooke smiled despite how upset she felt about the call.

She couldn't wait to be a mom. The pregnancy was going well. She tried to find joy in it despite not being able to share it with Cody.

Mindy Sue teased her about her middle-of-the-night cravings for ice cream and oranges.

Though she still had seven months to go, she'd already started working on lists of things to buy for the baby, what she needed to bring to the hospital, pediatricians' names back home, and daycare centers near her new apartment. She wanted to be a good mom and have everything set up and perfect by the time the baby arrived.

Brooke hated the idea of leaving the baby in daycare, but she'd have to at least a few hours of the day if she was going to work in the bookstore and expand her business into other ventures over time.

Of course Cody would be a part of their child's life. From the beginning, she planned to tell him about the baby— after he got married.

Now, she'd have to wait until she was only a few months from her September due date.

Mindy Sue took the cell phone and held it in front of her. "Call him. Tell him you're pregnant. He'll dump her. You and he can raise the baby together."

Brooke took the phone and wiped more tears away. She held her finger over the call button, but didn't tap it.

Instead, she let the fantasy play out in her mind. She'd call him. He'd come immediately. He'd be happy about the baby, especially after losing the one with Kristi. They'd get married and raise their child together on the ranch. She'd spend the rest of her life making him happy. He'd never regret marrying her. They'd be happy together. Forever.

That's what she'd always wanted. A life with him.

But not this way.

She didn't want him to marry her out of obligation. He must love Kristi. He'd chosen to make a life with her. She wouldn't take that away from him. They could be good parents to their child without being married. She'd even find a way to forge a cordial relationship with Kristi, so her child would know he or she was loved by all their parents.

She'd had a great relationship with her stepfather. Cody adored her mother.

Stepparents could be just as important and special as a biological parent, and she would give Kristi that chance to prove it.

Holding the phone to her forehead, she tried not to cry again.

"Why aren't you calling him? Tell him about the baby. You know he'll do the right thing."

"Kristi lost their baby. There's no obligation now for him to marry her. But he is still going to marry her because it's what he wants."

"But *you* are pregnant. He has an obligation to you. He'll do the right thing because as you said about Kristi and her baby, he doesn't want his child to grow up without both his parents."

True. But now that Cody had a chance to ask her to work things out and see if they could be together, that's not what he did. "I don't want him to marry me because he feels obligated. We had one night together. She's been with him for over a year. Hours after we had sex, he said he'd marry her. He didn't hesitate. He didn't take some time to think it over. He loves her and a life with her and his child was what he wanted. It's what he still wants."

She put her hands over her belly where her baby lay sleeping and growing. Her pants were a little tight, but you couldn't tell she was pregnant yet. She kind of couldn't wait until her belly popped.

"If that night meant as much to him as it did to me, if I meant that much to him, he'd have called tonight to tell me he and Kristi are over and he wants to be with me. But he didn't."

The tears ran down her cheeks again.

"I love him. I want him to be happy. And, apparently, that's with her. I'll tell him about the baby later. He can come to the delivery. He'd probably like to be there for that. They'll already be married. He can be a father to the baby. We just won't do it together. Lots of kids grow up without both parents living together."

"Yes, but you could go back to the ranch and live there with him."

"And her." Brooke rolled her eyes. "It's bad enough she'll be a stepmother to my child and living in my house. I can't live under the same roof with them."

"It's a big roof. You could move to your mother's side of the house."

"I'd be miserable seeing him with her every day, and you know it. I don't want my child to see me like that. I don't want my child to ever think my unhappiness has anything to do with him."

Mindy Sue squeezed her hand. "If Cody can't see what a great woman you are, then he doesn't deserve you. I'm sorry, sweetie. You've been best friends for years. If that isn't a foundation to build a marriage and a family on, I don't know what is. I wish he could see that." She put her hand over Brooke's on her belly. "I wish that for you and the baby."

"Some wishes just don't come true. I've had to learn that the hard way. He won't be mine, but he'll be a good father to our baby. It's all I can wish for now."

They sat in silence for a moment, both wishing things could be different.

Brooke had faced reality the second she'd gotten on the bus to return to school. She'd desperately wanted to beg Cody to choose her. And in that moment, she'd realized she'd spent her whole childhood chasing after him, trying to make him love her.

It didn't work.

Their night together hadn't changed anything.

She couldn't make Cody love her.

She wouldn't use their baby to get what she wanted.

That was selfish and no way to start a marriage and expect it to last.

Cody made his decision.

Brooke had to learn to live with it and the consequences of her actions.

She needed a distraction. "Tell me why you did your ballerina-slash-booty-dance when you came in."

Mindy Sue looked up and softly smiled. "It was nothing. It's late. I bet you're tired. You've barely been able to keep your eyes open lately."

Brooke pointed to the book on pregnancy beside her bed. "First trimester is the hardest. The second is supposed to be better."

"I bet you can't wait until next month."

"You bet. Now, tell me about your date with Tony, and why you came in smiling like a maniac and dancing."

"You don't want to hear about my date." Mindy Sue stood to get ready for bed.

"Tell me. I want details." Brooke sat up and caught Mindy Sue's hand to turn her back. "Did he kiss you?" Brooke smiled mischievously.

"Did he kiss me? I thought my hair was going to catch fire." She sat beside Brooke again and they laughed.

They spent the next hour devouring a pint of vanilla bean ice cream and talking about Tony, his kissing ability, and what Mindy Sue would wear on her next date. For an hour, Brooke managed to put her stalker who wouldn't quit, being pregnant, and Cody's message on the back burner.

Tonight was about being a college coed and sitting with her friend and talking about boys and clothes.

Life was too short to spend worrying about what might have been, and what could never be. She'd take ice cream and girl talk over thinking about her obsessed stalker and a man who didn't want her.

Chapter Twenty-Nine

BROOKE: Thank you for completing the purchase of the building and working with Danny at Quinn Construction to get a project manager in place immediately.

CODY: Hi

CODY: How are you?

CODY: I'm excited the building is yours and renovations are starting. You're on your way!

She ignored the first two texts and stuck to business.

BROOKE: I need the project manager's number so I can make some priority changes.

CODY: You signed off on the project, including completion dates for each stage of the renovation.

BROOKE: I know. But I need one of the apartments upstairs completed by May instead of the end of July.

CODY: Why?

Why do you think? She wanted to scream at him.

BROOKE: Because I need a place to live when school ends and I want to have time to furnish and decorate before I officially move in, come June.

CODY: You have a place. Here. On the ranch you own.

BROOKE: I don't belong there anymore.

CODY: You will always belong here.

CODY: Please Brooke. Don't do this.

BROOKE: It's already done. I own the building. I want the three-bedroom place.

CODY: You'd get more rent for it than the two-bed-room units.

BROOKE: I need an office, so I can work from home, and a guest room so my friends can visit.

Lie. She needed the spare room for the baby.

Mindy Sue would happily bunk on the couch or even with her. They'd done it a lot over the years.

CODY: Is that what you really want?

I can't have what I really want.

BROOKE: Yes.

CODY: I will make it happen.

BROOKE: Just give me the guy's number and I'll call him and do all the follow up.

CODY: I'll take care of it.

She knew what he was doing. He wanted her to go through him for updates and changes and whatever came up on the project. He was still protecting and taking care of her.

She appreciated it, but at some point, he needed to let her fly on her own, because he had someone else who depended on him now.

BROOKE: I can take care of myself.

CODY: I know. Just let me do this.

BROOKE: Don't you have enough to do?

CODY: I always have time for you. That hasn't changed. It never will.

CODY: I wish you'd come home so we can figure this out.

BROOKE: You already did and put a ring on it.

CODY: It doesn't have to be like this.

BROOKE: For now, it does. But I'll be back in town in June and it will be different again.

CODY: What do you mean?

BROOKE: We can't be what we were, so we'll have to be different.

BROOKE: See you later

She wondered if he'd remember that he'd said goodbye to her in August and she'd reminded him that they were friends, so it was never goodbye, only see you later.

Cody stared at the final message from Brooke as he sat in his office downtown and a tear slipped down his cheek. This was the first real conversation they'd had since she left after Christmas.

She wanted him to know though things looked dire, they were still friends.

Those simple three words meant so much to him. His heart ached with longing for her and what they'd shared in the past.

Was she still seeing whoever she was having the relationship with?

None of his business. Even if it killed him to think of her with someone else.

He didn't want to think about how different things would be going forward, both of them with someone else.

That was too heartbreaking to imagine. He could only hope that one day soon they'd find their way and things would be okay again between them.

Chapter Thirty

*S**he's perfect.*

He hid behind a large bush and watched her walk down the darkened path. He'd busted three of the overhead lights, providing him the perfect cover.

The other two girls had given him a taste of what he wanted. They had a similar look to Brooke, but this one...she could be Brooke's sister. She had the same long dark hair and green eyes. And that mouth. The perfect balance between a full bottom lip and bowed upper.

His heart hammered in his chest as she drew closer, her gait unsteady thanks to the three drinks she usually had when she met her friends at the bar and grill across from campus. Like the other two, he'd picked her because she liked to get plastered and walk home alone.

Stupid girl.

Lucky me.

Brooke would never be that dumb.

She was perfect in every way.

And soon, he'd be her perfect lover.

He just needed some practice.

The second the girl walked past, he rushed her, bashing her on the head with the knife handle. She fell hard to the ground, her palms sliding on the pavement. She screamed, so he hit her again. Hard. Her cheek smacked the pavement and her limbs went limp.

"Gotcha."

He moved fast, hoping no one spotted him dragging her into the bushes. He'd chosen this spot well. Staked it out for days. Watched his pretty target walk this way a few times a week for the past three weeks between eight and nine.

She'd walked right into his trap.

The first two drunk girls he'd let go after some heavy petting and kissing. He'd gotten pretty good at that now, though the girls weren't as cooperative as he'd hoped.

Brooke wouldn't act like she didn't enjoy it.

She wanted him.

She loved the gifts he sent her. She knew he was watching over her, making sure she had everything her heart desired. Like the bracelet she saw when she stopped outside the jewelry store window and stared at. He knew she wanted it, so he ordered it using a stolen credit card and had it delivered to her.

He'd wanted to leave them at her door, but then he risked Brooke discovering his identity too soon.

Those first two girls complained about him to campus security. Like they didn't want his hands all over them, just like the guys in the bar had done while they drank and danced, showing off their bodies in their skimpy outfits. They couldn't ID him, and even if they could, they'd been drunk off their asses, eyes blurry, minds foggy.

College girls. Not too smart.

Like the one he dragged into the concealed nook in the bushes now. He dropped her upper body. Her head thumped on the ground and fell sideways. The scrapes on her cheek bled. He didn't like that, but he'd work with the inferior girl, knowing it would get him what he really wanted.

Brooke. His perfect, beautiful soulmate.

He cut the strap on her purse and tossed it aside. Thanks to the warmer spring temps, she only wore a simple white T-shirt, which he slit up the middle, exposing her pink and black polka dot bra. Her breasts swelled over the edge. Smaller than Brooke, but she'd do for his training purposes.

He closed his eyes, thought of Brooke, the nights he wanted to share with her, and sank down on top of the girl, straddling her hips. He molded his hands to her breasts and squeezed the soft mounds. His need for her grew until he couldn't control himself and he grabbed her hard into his hands.

She moaned, driving him on.

He wanted her so bad, his dick pressed hard against his fly. He used one hand on her breast and the other on his dick, rubbing both, feeling the softness of her and the contrasting hardness in him.

That's what he wanted. Brooke's soft beauty to balance the darkness inside him.

"Please…"

"That's right. Beg for it. You want me." He undid his pants, freed his aching flesh, and pushed up her skirt.

"Don't do this."

He pressed the knife to her throat.

She whimpered and went limp beneath him, half-naked, his to have just like Brooke would be soon.

Brooke would moan his name.

He tried to close his eyes and picture Brooke; she came to mind so easily.

"Please stop."

The whispered words overflowed with fear and a desperate plea.

They weren't in the right voice. They said the wrong thing.

And when he looked down all he saw was the wrong woman.

"You're not Brooke!" Rage exploded through his system, then he punched her in the head with the knife handle again to shut her up. Her whimpering was ruining this for him. Blood ran down her face, mixing with her tears. The rush washed through him again seeing her bleed. She screamed in pain.

He liked that. A lot.

"Hey, what are you doing?"

He hadn't heard the jogger run up on them. She stumbled through the bushes and stopped short.

"Help me," the girl beneath him rasped.

Fuck!

He had to get out of there. He jumped up, grabbed his open pants together, and ran.

No one else was around. He kept to the shadows, fumbling the zipper up on his jeans as he rushed to get away. He pulled the black mask off his head as he rounded the corner of one of the buildings. His heart raced with fear. He slowed his pace to match that of the few students walking the path from the rec center building to the quad and tried to settle his rampaging thoughts. He'd almost had her. Frustrated, he smacked his fist into the side of his thigh.

Since things didn't work out with his date tonight and he needed something to soothe him, he'd swing by Brooke's place, see if he could catch a glimpse of her returning to her dorm from the library she studied at nearly every night.

He missed her.

He was almost ready to have her.

Chapter Thirty-One

B rooke answered her cell phone without looking at the caller ID. "Hello."

"Miss Banks, this is Detective Radnor. San Antonio police. We've spoken a few times about your case."

"Yes, Detective. How can I help you?"

Brooke stood on her dorm steps. A wave of fear shot through her. She turned, looking behind her, searching the faces for anyone watching her. She couldn't help the reaction anymore. When not in her room, she always felt like someone was watching now. Even though no one walking past or sitting on the lawn beyond seemed to take any special interest in her—but he was out there. Watching. Waiting. Biding his time. For what, she didn't know. And the not knowing was making her crazy paranoid.

"There's been a series of attacks on campus. The first two girls, though drunk, got away after a minor assault and brief struggle with their attacker. Last night, the girl wasn't so lucky. The assailant had a knife. There's no other way to say this—"

"He raped her." The words came out as a whisper but they were no less ominous.

"No. But only because a jogger interrupted him right before..."

She filled in the blank in her mind.

"He said something interesting to her."

"What?" She didn't really want to know.

"You're not Brooke."

"What?" she gasped. Stunned and a little sick, she pressed her hand to her stomach. "Oh my God." She swallowed back the bile rising in her throat. "I can't believe..." She choked back the words. Of course she knew this was about her. She couldn't deny it. Especially now. "It's him, isn't it? My stalker is the same person attacking these women."

"Yes. It seems that way. Though he didn't go after you. He's using surrogates. That's a hunch, because of the pattern we've found in these three attacks."

She made an educated-by-*Dateline* guess. "They all look like me."

"Smart girl. Yes."

A chill ran down her spine. "What does it mean?"

"This guy is dangerous. He's not going to stop. His attacks are more aggressive with each victim. Be vigilant. Don't go anywhere alone. Keep your dorm room locked at all times. If a stranger approaches you, be careful."

"Right." Sound advice, but useless. If this guy was determined to hurt her, nothing would stop him. And from what she could tell by his online messages and notes, she knew him.

He'd been in her house. That still disturbed her on a deep level.

"We have a vague description. The guy's about five-nine, five-ten with a slight but strong build. He wears latex gloves and a black knit ski mask."

"So absolutely no help." And it was so vague she couldn't eliminate enough of her friends, classmates, and acquaintances to point the finger at anyone. "Well, thank you for notifying me. I'll let you know if anything else happens." Like that had done her any good so far, but at least she had it all on record. If it was the same guy, he hadn't done anything more disturbing than following her around and taking pictures of her. The gifts were all things she loved. Creepy, but not menacing.

But if it was the same guy, he'd attacked three women and nearly raped one of them.

She felt terrible for those poor students.

"Maybe you should think about going home for a few weeks while we investigate this latest attack."

Not an option. And it would probably only make things worse. Her stalker could just follow her home. "I'll think about it, but I'm not safe there either. He knows where I live. He's been in my house."

"Being on campus gives him more opportunity. At home, you could be safer, more easily protected."

At this point, she didn't think anyplace was safe enough. "Maybe. I'll let you know what I decide." Brooke hung up and sank down on the step, trying to ignore the desperate and overwhelming urge to run up to her room and lock herself inside. Forever. If her stalker came for her, she wasn't safe there. She wasn't safe anywhere. The bastard left her notes and gifts at her room, in her classrooms, and had them delivered to her in the library and out in the quad by unsuspecting delivery services. He used burner phones to place the orders. He paid cash or used gift cards to pay for everything, so nothing could be traced back to him.

The whole thing was frustrating and maddening.

She refused to give in to this guy's terror campaign and move back home. Besides, she couldn't do that when Cody was getting ready to marry Kristi. She didn't want to ruin that for him.

But she should tell her mom. Just in case something happened.

She closed her eyes, took a deep breath, opened her eyes again, and dialed her mom. Cody should be at work, but she still prayed he wasn't there. Her mom answered on the fourth ring. It had been months since she'd been to the ranch, or returned her mother's phone calls without leaving a message when she knew her mom was busy.

"Brooke." The relief in her mother's voice squeezed her heart with regret. She should have spoken to her mom sooner.

"Hi, Mom. How are you?"

"I'm fine, honey. How's my girl?"

"I'm okay." She was, too. The morning sickness had subsided now that she was in her fourth month. She hardly ever woke up only to throw up.

"We missed you during your spring break. I'd hoped you'd come home."

"I've been trying to get some things done here at school. I have term papers due at the end of the semester, and I want to get a head start on them."

Lame excuses, but the truth. She'd spent spring break doing research for two classes that she had papers due for in June before finals. She'd also had a doctor's appointment for a check-up that she didn't want to cancel or move. The baby was more important than going home.

"You mean you didn't want to come home and see Cody."

"He has his own life, and I have mine. Here. At school. For now, anyway." Just like he'd said in his message to her.

"Well, maybe it's for the best, honey. They've grown very close. Closer than I've ever seen them."

For the best.

First Cody tells her that and now her mom. She didn't want to hear it. She didn't believe it. She'd never believe anyone would be good enough for Cody. No one would love him more than she did.

But he didn't care. Neither did her mom.

"You're so young. You've got plenty of time to find the right person and fall in love."

She supposed that love and friendship just wasn't enough for some people. Not her. She'd have jumped at the chance to marry Cody. But she wouldn't use her pregnancy to get something that her mother and Cody thought wasn't enough.

"Then you understand my absence. I've moved on, and I'm letting him do the same."

"Come home the weekend after next for a visit. He won't be here. They'll be in San Antonio for a benefit Cody has to attend. Come to the ranch and let your mom spoil you for a few days. We'll go horseback riding."

"You hate horseback riding." Not that it mattered, because she shouldn't be on a horse in her condition and she wasn't going home.

"But you like it, and I'd go with you just to spend some time alone with you. I'm worried about you, honey."

"I'm fine, Mom. In fact, there's something I need to talk to you about."

"Have you decided to come to the wedding? I would love to see you two being friends again. But I understand if it hurts too much."

Watch the man she loved marry another woman. Never going to happen. "I'm not coming to the wedding, Mom. That isn't what I wanted to talk to you about."

"Then perhaps you can find another way to mend this rift between you two, so you can at least be in the same house together at some point."

"I'm not punishing him."

"I didn't say you were. I hate seeing what's happened between you. I want my girl to come home when she wants to and not have to step lightly because Cody is here, too."

"Not just Cody, Mom. Kristi. His soon-to-be *wife*."

"Yes, they'll be married, and you'll have to live with it."

Her mother didn't mean to sound so harsh. She missed Brooke and wanted her to come home. Brooke's absence and silence had pushed her too far, and Brooke was sorry for it.

She didn't pile on with her troubles.

"I have to go, Mom. I'm meeting some friends at the café for a study group. I'll call again soon." She couldn't tell her mom. Not right now. Not when things were strained like this. If she told her about the stalker, she'd insist Brooke come home. If she told her about the baby, she'd go straight to Cody. She'd expect Cody to do the honorable thing, and Brooke wanted more than honor. She wanted love. For her and the baby.

Chapter Thirty-Two

"Tonight at six on KNTB News, three recent attacks on women at the University of Texas at San Antonio have prompted school officials to ask all women on campus, especially those with long dark hair, to use the buddy system. Join us at six for the full story."

Cody caught the news update just as he walked into the living room and found Susanne sitting on the sofa watching TV. He immediately thought of Brooke as the threat sparked endless nightmares of what could happen to her. Was she being careful? Did she know about the attacks?

Campus security would step up patrols. He hoped they caught the guy soon.

Brooke had lots of friends. She would follow the advice of the police and security on campus. She was smart. She wouldn't do anything to put herself in jeopardy.

Suzanne noticed him standing there. "Did you hear about the trouble up at the university? Someone is attacking women with long dark hair. Three girls have been assaulted."

"When is the last time you spoke to Brooke?"

"Nearly two weeks ago." Susanne frowned. "It seems the longer she's gone, the less I hear from her."

"Call her. Make sure she's okay."

Susanne pulled out her cell and made the call. "She hardly ever answers her phone anymore."

His fault. She didn't want to talk to him or her mom or have anything to do with home right now.

Maybe she was too busy being with her boyfriend.

"She's probably in her three o'clock class," Susanne murmured.

Cody tried to hold it together. "Try her anyway."

Susanne already had the phone to her ear. "Damnit. Voicemail."

Cody silently swore.

"Brooke, honey, it's Mom. Listen, I just saw on the news there's been some trouble on campus. I know you're being safe and staying with your friends. Please be careful, honey. I love you. Miss you, honey. Call me. I'm worried about you."

Cody stepped closer. "What if something happened to her?" He didn't want to even think it.

"Someone would have called if Brooke were hurt. She would call."

Cody hoped so, but couldn't hide his skepticism. "She hasn't exactly kept in touch."

"Did you try to call her?"

"I left her a message about the wedding. She never called me back." That had been in February. "We started exchanging texts in March about the building renovations. They're moving along. The last text exchange was last week about bathroom tiles for her apartment." It was almost May.

He folded his arms across his chest and tried not to show how much it hurt that they couldn't even talk to each other anymore. Everything was a text. And she kept it all about business. Every time he asked how she was, or about what she was doing at school, she ignored him.

"Look, Cody. You're both adults and you should work things out between you."

"But?"

Susanne had blessedly been quiet about the whole thing up until now. Cody wished she'd keep it that way. But how could she when he was the reason her daughter refused to call or come home?

"Are you prepared for her to never set foot on this ranch again?"

No. "I don't like that she and I...had a falling out. I tried to talk to her...It's complicated."

"Love is complicated. You might think about why you end up in her room whenever you've had a particularly hard day."

He went to her room at some point every day. "How did you know I go into her room?"

"Just like you, some nights, I can't sleep. I'm so worried about her. I sometimes get up and go into her room to be close to her. I can smell her there and touch her things and remember her. The house isn't the same without her here. It's been too long since she came home. Every time I offer to drive to campus and see her, she has some excuse. Classes. Homework. A programming project. Study group. She's busy with friends." Susanne let out a frustrated sigh. "She's hurting and she doesn't want me to see it."

The guilt sucked him under; it was a wonder he could still stand. "I don't know how to fix things with her," he admitted, raking his fingers through his hair.

"You guys never used to have any trouble speaking to each other. I remember you two sitting for hours in the study laughing and talking."

"I tried talking to her."

"You left her a message telling her what you'd decided. That isn't a conversation."

She was right. But he knew why Brooke had pulled away from him and Susanne didn't. "Brooke and I will have to work things out our way. So far, both of us seem inclined to give each other some space. It's for the best. I hope she'll come home for her birthday and again after the semester ends. If she's waiting until after the wedding, I can't say I blame her, and maybe that's for the best, too." It didn't feel that way. At this point, he'd just like to set eyes on her so he could see for himself that she was okay.

"Maybe," Susanne said, sounding unsure.

"I have to go and get ready for dinner tonight. I've got to pick up Kristi in half an hour."

"Enjoy yourself."

"You'll let me know if Brooke calls? I need to know that she's safe and okay."

Susanne nodded and gave him one of those smiles mothers give their children when they understand far more than what's been said.

He frowned as he left the room with his hands stuffed in his pockets. When he passed Brooke's room, he refused to look in. He didn't need to. Her memory was everywhere in this damn house and stamped on his mind and heart.

Chapter Thirty-Three

Cody spent the evening attending a dinner party and trying to stay in the moment and not think about Brooke and the trouble at her school. He had to live his very hectic life and keep the promises he'd made to Kristi, while working toward partner at his law firm and keeping on top of his board responsibilities.

Brooke had her own life, a life separate and different than the one he lived.

Shifting his focus to his fiancée, he took in how pretty she looked tonight. Beautiful in a navy-blue gown, her golden hair shone bright, and her eyes were blue as the sky. She spoke to a group of people and laughed. The sound made him feel a little lighter. He liked seeing her this way, relaxed and engaging with everyone in the room. She fit in perfectly.

Their lives would be like this from now on.

If he felt like something was missing all the time, he ignored it. He had to.

But...

This was the closest he'd been to Brooke in months. The university wasn't that far from tonight's party. He and Kristi would spend the night in the city. In the morning, he could let Kristi sleep in while he went to see Brooke. Check on her. Make sure she was doing okay. See her. Look at her. Talk to her. Hear her voice.

She doesn't want to see you. You closed that chapter, and Brooke burned the book.

Still, Susanne would appreciate it if he checked in with Brooke and made sure her studies were going well. He'd make sure she didn't need anything. Whatever trouble was happening on campus, he wanted to know it hadn't touched her.

He hoped it wasn't one of her friends who had been attacked.

He could swing by Brooke's dorm. Just for a minute. That's all he needed. He'd feel better if he saw her.

You made your choice, and it's what's best for everyone. Seeing her isn't going to change anything.

It would cause a fight between him and Kristi.

Most of the time when he thought back on all that happened, he wondered how it all turned to shit and realigned into this new life, where he didn't have his best friend anymore. Where the woman beside him was good enough, but not quite perfect.

He knew that wasn't fair to Kristi. She'd done nothing wrong.

Well, except somehow the pill didn't work, she'd waited weeks to find out she was pregnant, and she'd neglected to tell him about the miscarriage when it happened. He knew there were reasons, but sometimes he wondered if they mattered and if things could have been different if only...

Yeah. If only.

Kristi broke away from the group she was talking with and headed for him with a smile on her face. When she reached him, she gave him a quick kiss, and put her hands on his chest. "Enjoying yourself, honey?"

"It's a great party." Cody took a sip of his drink. He rubbed his hand up her arm to her shoulder just to touch her. Kristi was here. Brooke was living her own life. She didn't want to talk to him. She didn't want to see him. She had someone else. All he had with her was the possibility that he'd see her later.

"They're about to serve dinner. Let's take our seats."

Cody escorted her to their table.

Kristi smiled, pleased they were at the head table with the benefit organizers, one of whom served on the board at the children's hospital with him and made sure he and Kristi were at his table. It spoke to the position and standing Cody held within the community and state now.

Mrs. Ireson was the wife of a very prominent judge, and one of the ladies responsible for organizing tonight's dinner. She leaned into Kristi. "You're marrying one of the most eligible bachelors in the state."

Cody rolled his eyes at that flirtatious announcement.

Mrs. Ireson waved her hand at him. "You know it's true. Most of these people will either attend your wedding or wish they had been invited."

Kristi shone with the attention.

Cody couldn't care less.

Mrs. Ireson focused on Kristi, thank God. "How are the plans for the wedding coming, dear?"

"They're moving along nicely. I just can't wait for the big day."

"I heard you postponed the wedding until late June," Mrs. Ireson said.

Kristi glanced at him and he read the hesitation in her eyes. They never spoke about the baby. They didn't tell anyone besides Brooke and Susanne. Not even Kristi's parents knew about their loss.

And the extra time they'd taken had allowed them time to grow closer together and for Cody to see that they were a good match.

They fit. Several people had already commented on how great he and Kristi looked together. What a great couple they were.

"We put the wedding off a few months because of Cody's caseload. We wanted to wait until things slowed down, and we could take a nice honeymoon without him feeling guilty for taking time away from his clients."

"I'm sure he knows a thing or two about being guilty," Mrs. Ireson joked.

Kristi squeezed his hand, reading his darkening mood.

He tried to lighten things up. "Not all my clients are guilty," Cody said with lighthearted protest. "Some of them might actually have been framed," he quipped.

"Spoken like a true defense attorney. How many guests are you expecting at your wedding?" Mrs. Ireson asked with interest. "You two make such a lovely couple."

"Thank you." Kristi beamed. "Two hundred and fifty, give or take a dozen," Kristi said enthusiastically.

The waiters served dinner and conversation stilled.

Kristi leaned over as he picked up a bite of chicken with his fork and said, "I got the RSVP back from Brooke. She's officially *not* coming. I thought you should know."

His hand dropped to his plate, the fork clinking loudly. Dinner forgotten, he tried to breathe through the punch of pain.

He didn't blame Kristi for telling him this way. She probably thought it best done quickly and as matter-of-factly as possible, and in a place where he couldn't disappear to be alone for hours at a time.

Cody had tried very hard not to let Kristi see how much he missed Brooke these last few months, but she sometimes caught him in his office looking at the pictures on his desk and the walls. Pictures of him and Brooke.

He tried to show Kristi that he'd changed.

Without Brooke in his life, he confided in Kristi more. He talked to her about his work and things that were troubling him. Okay, maybe not unless she prodded, but still, he opened up to her about some of the things he used to share only with Brooke. Kristi's way of handling things was always about him schmoozing someone to get what he wanted, or cutting corners to make this happen faster. Brooke had always encouraged him to be the better man and lawyer, saying that taking the easy way wasn't always the right way. She always made him feel better about his final decision where Kristi sometimes made him feel like he wasn't getting where she wanted him to go fast enough.

They still had nearly two months until the wedding. "Maybe Brooke will change her mind. By then, she'll be home for the summer." Cody remained ever hopeful that one day soon she'd call and they'd talk and find a way to be friends again.

"Maybe it's for the best if she doesn't attend."

He was really tired of hearing that.

"You'll only be uptight and worried about her. It's *our* day. We want to be happy and carefree on the day."

He hoped he could pull that off.

"I'll move into *our* house after the honeymoon. We'll have the summer to settle in together as husband and wife. It wouldn't surprise me if she had a boyfriend and she'd rather spend the summer with him."

Cody downed the last of his bourbon, turned to Kristi, and in a low voice advised, "Maybe we should stick to how things have been the last few months and not talk about Brooke."

Kristi's eyes went wide at the anger in his voice, and she plastered on a smile for their audience at the table and asked in a cheerful voice, "How is that new bull working out at the ranch?"

Cody sucked it up. "He's ornery as hell. He's already gone through two fences. When we start breeding him, he'll be happier. He's going to make beautiful babies."

"And so will we someday." The minute the words left Kristi's mouth, she went still and her eyes turned somber, like she couldn't believe she'd said that after what happened.

Cody often thought about the baby they lost. He hadn't realized how much he wanted to be a father until he knew there was a baby on the way. He knew these things happened, especially early in the pregnancy. The tiny being had barely had time to develop before they lost it. Still. It stuck with him.

He took Kristi's hand and squeezed it. "We will have beautiful babies someday," he said and tried to smile, but he couldn't quite pull it off.

They'd have beautiful blonde-haired, blue-eyed babies. Not dark-haired, green-eyed ones.

He tossed that thought out of his mind and tried to eat his meal. It was no use. His appetite disappeared along with his good mood. Kristi seemed to sense it in him and made the rest of the evening easier by keeping things light-hearted. If he missed a beat in the conversation, she covered for him. He could rely on her in situations like this. She got him through the next hour by charming their friends and his colleagues. No one seemed to notice his distraction.

He took Kristi home the next morning after a quiet breakfast in the hotel's café.

He didn't stop by the university to check on Brooke, deciding instead to live with the choices he'd made and give Brooke the space she so obviously wanted.

He'd committed to Kristi and a life with her.

Chapter Thirty-Four

F ate brought him and Brooke together tonight of all nights. Her birthday. Twenty-one.

On his way to complete his next objective, he came around the corner on the way to the bar and there she was walking with Mindy Sue and some other friends headed in the same direction.

Why was she always wearing that baggy sweater?

Mindy Sue and Julie were with their boyfriends, Tony and Jeremiah, leaving Brooke still waiting on him to come to her and join their group.

Tonight had to be the night.

It felt right.

He'd wait until she had a drink or two, then approach her. Maybe when her friends were on the dance floor and Brooke was alone.

Yeah. They could share a private, intimate moment.

But Brooke and the others didn't continue on to the bar; instead they went into the packed ice cream parlor. On a hot night like tonight, the place was filled with families and university students.

It was bright and cheerful with no place for him to blend into the background without looking like he didn't quite belong.

He'd gotten good at watching Brooke and the others without being seen, mostly because no one ever really noticed him.

But this didn't feel right.

He had it all planned out in his mind. An intimate evening alone with her, so they could talk and be together.

This wasn't how he planned for it to happen. But it gave him an opportunity to leave Brooke the special gift he got for her very special birthday.

You could make tonight the night with her!

No. Mindy Sue would spend the whole night with her because it's her birthday.

If he hadn't been interrupted with the last girl, maybe he'd have been ready by tonight. With campus police upping their patrols after the last girl, he had to wait, so he didn't get caught.

It made him angry that he'd screwed this up.

Brooke is waiting for you and alone on her birthday and it's your fault.

He'd make it up to her. He'd finish tonight and be with her soon.

But first, if he couldn't be by her side, he could still be a part of her special day.

He delayed his plans at the bar, turned back the other way, and went to his car, where he had her gift ready in the trunk. A necklace to match the bracelet he'd already given her.

He drove to her dorm, pulled on his black hoodie, and walked in behind a group of students who'd used their security badge to get in.

Not so safe and secure.

He hardly ever delivered anything by himself anymore. Too dangerous. But it was her birthday and she deserved his personal touch.

He found all kinds of ways around security measures so he could make Brooke happy.

He kept his head down and walked with purpose up to the third floor and right to Brooke's door. He silently thanked Mindy Sue for decorating their door with balloons and streamers. He pulled on the pair of latex gloves he'd taken from his trunk along with Brooke's gift. He used one of the streamers to conceal and tie the small box to the doorknob, then walked back down the empty hall, down the stairs, and out the door without anyone paying him any attention.

The security cameras wouldn't catch even a glimpse of his face.

He was back in his car and at the ice cream shop again in less than half an hour, even with the difficulty of finding parking on the busy street. He peeked through the windows and found Brooke laughing and enjoying herself with her friends, an empty sundae glass in front of her.

She was having a good time.

He had some fun planned for tonight, too.

This would be the last time he went out without Brooke. He wouldn't disappoint her again.

He watched Brooke for another moment, then reluctantly left her to her evening, knowing she'd be so happy when she got back to her room and found his gift.

The music in the bar drew him down the street and right in the door, nearly deafening him when he walked into the crowded room. It took him a couple minutes to push his way through all the bodies to find the woman he knew would be here tonight. A woman who'd give him exactly what he wanted.

Luck had been on his side earlier tonight when he spotted Brooke with friends and getting her gift to her. It shone on him now when he followed the woman he'd picked to help him tonight right out of the bar without having to wait for her to finish partying with her friends and head home.

He knew her pattern and wasn't surprised when she stepped out of the bar, stood on the sidewalk, looked up at the sky, took in a breath, then glided down the street, carefree and light and buzzed, if not drunk. He hadn't been there to see how much she'd had to drink.

Didn't matter. She belonged to him tonight.

He wouldn't be stopped.

He needed to do this one last thing so he'd be prepared when he went to Brooke.

And when the woman turned down the alleyway that led to a little-used trail on the backside of one of the campus's parking lots, he caught up to her without her seeing him coming.

He pulled his knife from behind his back and bashed her in the temple with the heavy handle.

She went down hard, landing on her hands and knees, her palms skidding out from under her.

She instinctively rolled and tried to ward him off.

He snagged her by the wrist and dragged her behind some bushes that backed up to a cement block shed where they kept huge dumpsters.

She tried to scramble away, but he socked her in the face. Blinking to try to clear the blood from her eye from the wound on her temple, she fell back. "Take my bag. Take whatever you want, just leave me alone."

"I will have what I want." This time he'd get it right.

She suddenly bucked and tried to flip over and scramble free.

He knocked her in the head again, then put the knife to her throat. "Stop ruining this."

Tears streamed down the sides of her face. She whimpered. But she didn't move.

He did.

Blood pumping, adrenaline rocketing through him, his dick twitching with need, he didn't waste time and finally took what he wanted.

And when he was done, all he could think about was being with Brooke.

He left the other woman there to sleep it off and headed back to his car.

Brooke was just leaving the ice cream shop when he returned for one last glimpse of her, feeling like he finally knew everything he needed to know to make her happy.

She passed right by him. He turned and whispered, "Happy birthday, Brooke. You'll definitely get your wish. We'll be together soon."

Chapter Thirty-Five

B rooke walked out of the ice cream shop with her friends, all laughing at a funny story Mindy Sue told about them at summer camp when they were twelve, when Brooke had fallen off the dock and into the lake and got pecked a dozen times by a mama duck protecting her ducklings.

She rolled her eyes and stared up at the night sky, wishing she was on the ranch and could see the stars better. Wishing she was spending her birthday with Cody.

Her phone chimed with an incoming text just as she slid her hand over her baby bump and promised her daughter next year they'd eat ice cream together.

The notification on her phone surprised her.

CODY: Please answer your phone.

It rang in her hand. "Give me a sec, guys." She stepped away from the group and leaned against a large flowerpot next to the curb outside the ice cream parlor. "Hi."

Cody let out a huge sigh of relief. "Thank you for answering."

"Cody." That's all she could get out. She missed him so much.

"Happy birthday." Caution and wariness filled his voice. It shouldn't be like this.

"Thank you."

"I hope it's a good one."

Not without you.

"I'm out with friends."

"I hope you're being safe and not drinking too much."

Not at all, actually.

But she couldn't tell him that because then he'd ask why. This wasn't the time to tell him about their daughter, though she wanted to more than anything. So she lied to him again but gave him a partial truth, too. "We're looking out for each other and making it an early night. I'm headed back to the dorm now, actually."

"Oh, well, that's good." Silence for the next minute made things feel as strained as ever. Finally he said, "I'm so glad you liked your gift."

First thing this morning, a messenger had arrived outside her building, texting her that he had a special delivery. The peridot stud earrings were the same color as her green eyes and bigger than a pencil eraser. She was wearing them right now. A little piece of him with her today. "I love them." She'd texted him a thank-you before she went to class this morning.

"Brooke?"

"Yeah?"

"I miss you."

Her heart swelled with joy and sorrow.

Cody went on like that simple statement didn't gut her. "And I know now isn't the time to talk about...everything. I just wanted you to know that."

Choked up, she wanted to blame her hormones for the emotions clogging her throat, but the reality was that she loved him. She'd always love him. And this hurt like hell. "I miss you, too. And I'll be home soon. Just a few weeks. We can talk face-to-face." They'd figure out a way to go forward as co-parents. "And everything will be all right. Different, but all right." They wouldn't be the family she hoped they could be, but they could still be friends and love their daughter together.

"Promise?" It sounded like Cody choked out that word, as emotional as she was about him.

"I want to, but the truth is, we both have to figure out how to live with the choices we've made." And she vowed to herself that she'd let him marry the woman he loved and not interfere.

"I want you to be happy, Brooke."

He made her happy.

"I want the same for you." And if Kristi did that for him, then Brooke had to accept it.

She appreciated that he didn't dive into all that had torn them apart or mention Kristi, so she didn't either.

Cody let out a weary sigh. "Waiting to see you again is killing me."

I know how that feels.

"Cody." She couldn't keep her sadness and desperation to have him back out of her voice.

"I know. Not fair. I just...need you to know none of this is easy for me. I think about you all the time."

"I can't stop thinking about you either. But..." Everything standing between them hadn't changed.

"Yeah. I know." It felt like he silently ended that statement with, *It wasn't meant to be.* "I'm glad I got a chance to talk to you. I needed to hear your voice and know that you're okay."

Am I?

Not really. Not since the morning after they slept together.

Never again. Because a piece of her would always be with him.

"See you later, Brooke."

"See you later, Cody." She ended the call and burst into tears.

Mindy Sue wrapped her in a hug. "It's okay. You'll see him soon. You can tell him everything, and you'll work it out."

Their other friends had gone ahead back to the dorms.

Brooke met Mindy Sue's concerned gaze. "I know we'll figure it out. It just won't be what I hoped it would be."

"Call him back, tell him about the baby, and it could be what you want."

She huffed out her frustration. "I can't do that to him."

Mindy Sue raised a brow. "How about doing it for your daughter?"

She shook her head. "Pushing a marriage on him he doesn't want will only make things worse. I don't want him to resent me. I don't want our daughter to see that I make her father unhappy."

"You and Cody love each other. It won't be that way."

"He loves *her* more."

Mindy Sue dropped it and hooked her arm through Brooke's. They walked the busy sidewalk back toward the dorm in silence. What was there to say? They'd hashed this out a dozen different ways only to come to the same conclusion each time. Cody wanted to be with Kristi.

If he wanted Brooke back, he would have said so tonight.

That he didn't made her stomach clench and her heart break all over again.

But thoughts of Cody disappeared the second they got to their dorm room door and Brooke spotted the gift tied to the knob. "He was here."

Mindy Sue swore.

Of course *he'd* ruin her birthday.

Chapter Thirty-Six

B rooke tried not to panic about Mindy Sue and Tony being late picking her up. They probably got caught in traffic after the movie let out. She hated to interrupt their date, but even the thought of walking across campus alone sent her heart rate into overdrive.

Her stalker was still sending her gifts and leaving notes and pictures for her in her classes. He avoided her dorm room because of the added security.

Except the night of her birthday last week. That really freaked her out.

Twenty-one. It still hit her at odd times that she had finally reached that milestone.

Her birthday had been fun, even if she didn't get to experience what most college students did and drink herself silly. She'd loved the ice cream party with her closest friends.

It seemed like a great night right up until she arrived at her dorm and discovered yet another stalker gift and woke up the next morning to the news that he'd raped someone.

That poor woman.

Brook couldn't stop thinking about it.

The four attacks on campus left her feeling vulnerable and like she was inevitably going to be his ultimate target.

That's why she'd started wearing the big cardigan to hide her baby bump. Some small measure of protection, even if it didn't convince everyone she wasn't pregnant.

A shiver of cold dread raced up her spine. Constantly on guard and in a state of near panic every time she left the relative safety of her dorm room or one of her classrooms, she hated going out at all now.

Even being in the library made her feel like a sitting duck.

She smoothed her hand over her belly, trying to ease herself and the baby.

She always had someone with her when she went out. She and Mindy Sue had made it a habit now. Neither of them went anywhere alone. They had enough friends between them to make it possible to find someone who could go with them between classes, or out to eat.

Her friend Julie had walked her to the library tonight and stayed as long as she could before meeting Jeremiah. Mindy Sue and Tony promised to pick her up before closing.

If they didn't show soon, she'd contact campus security and request an escort home.

Brooke felt the baby roll and rubbed her growing belly again to soothe her daughter. She'd found out at the end of May she was having a girl. Excited beyond measure, she felt the awe of carrying a life inside her every time the baby kicked or rolled. She didn't even mind waking up in the night when the baby stretched her legs and did somersaults. Brooke felt so blessed.

It eased the sting of losing Cody and made it worse at the same time because he wasn't here to share it with her.

One of the library staff headed her way.

Brooke packed up her stuff. She had her term paper finished and even managed to get some studying done for her Business Management class. All she had to do now was get through finals and graduate.

June third had been her twenty-first birthday and the day she'd become financially independent. She finally had her own money. Until a week ago, Cody had controlled her trust and paid out her tuition and dorm fees. Her monthly allowance had come from her share of the ranch profits.

"Miss, the library is closing."

"Yes, thank you. I'll just call my friend to see if she's here to drive me back to the dorms."

"That's a good idea. Can't be too careful these days. If you'll head to the front of the library, I'd appreciate it."

"Sure." Brooke grabbed her cell phone, stood, and lifted her backpack onto her shoulder.

Brooke walked to the front doors of the library, but didn't see Mindy Sue. All the other students filed out. Just her luck, she didn't recognize anyone from her dorm, or any of her classes. Her cell phone beeped, indicating she had several missed calls. She scrolled through the list of numbers. Her mom had called. Again. Probably to complain she hadn't come home for her birthday last week.

Of the five calls she'd missed, four of them were from Mindy Sue. She listened to her voicemail and Mindy Sue telling her she was running late. "No kidding."

She hit the speed dial and didn't even hear the phone ring before Mindy Sue picked up.

"How far away are you?"

"Less than five minutes. Are you okay?"

"I'm hungry." Brooke laughed. She was always hungry these days.

Mindy Sue laughed with her, relief in her voice. "Sorry, I had this strange feeling something was wrong."

"I'm fine." Brooke said the words, but it had been a long time since she felt fine. The stress was getting to her.

Cody. The stalker. Finals coming up. Missing her mom and home. Planning for the arrival of her baby girl. The list went on.

It was a lot to handle mostly on her own.

"I think there might still be a pint of ice cream in the freezer."

"Are there any of those cheese curl chips left too?"

"You eat the strangest things. I don't know about the chips, but there's an apple and an orange on the desk. Eat those."

"You're right. I will. How about I meet you guys at the south parking lot. There's a covered bus stop with lights. I can sit and wait for you."

"Just wait in the library."

"They're about to lock the doors with me inside. I'll meet you at the parking lot. It'll only be two minutes at the most and there are a couple of other students headed that way. I'll tag along with them."

"Okay, but you stay put. We'll be there in a few minutes."

The librarian waved her arm, shooing everyone out. "Come on, I need to get home or my babysitter will quit because I'm late again."

Brooke tucked her cell in her back pocket. She wished she'd worn one of her dresses. They were less constricting than pants, even if they were maternity wear. She headed down the library steps, the click of the locks sounding behind her.

She kept the phone in her hand as she made her way down the path that led around the building to the parking lot in the rear. She followed three other students headed in the same direction. Nothing would happen with them so close.

A beautiful star-studded night, not too hot or humid. She gazed up at the bright stars and wished she were at the creek. She loved it there late at night with the water rushing by and the quiet of the night wrapped around her. She loved it when the breeze whispered through the leaves, making them whistle in the wind. She wondered if she'd ever see her perfect little getaway again.

Maybe when she took the baby to see her father.

Cody would teach her to ride when she got older, just like he'd taught Brooke. She hoped her daughter loved horses as much as she did.

The three other students she'd been following disappeared around the corner to the parking lot. She hurried to catch up. The two lights above this section of the path had burned out or something. She looked at her phone to turn on her light, but got distracted by a rustling noise coming from the nearby bushes. She looked into the shadows, but didn't see anything. Still, her heart jackhammered and her mind conjured one horror after the next.

She hurried to close the distance between her and the other students but stumbled on a crack in the pavement with her unsteady pregnancy bod and had to slow down again.

Suddenly she heard the scrape and thump of footsteps behind her. She tried to turn and face the threat she felt all the way to her bones, but an arm came around her neck and another wrapped around her chest and suddenly she was pulled up against a tall, thin body.

"Hi, Brooke."

She wanted to believe the guy was a friend or classmate just being overly affectionate with his surprise hello. Greg from her business class who was an outrageous flirt. Thomas, who worked at the campus bookstore and asked her out before he realized she was pregnant under the cardigan she usually wore.

But no. This felt off from an overly friendly, or even drunk and happy, guy snuggling up to her like they knew each other as more than passing acquaintances.

She couldn't shake the creepy feeling she got every time she felt like her stalker was watching her. But she didn't want to be wrong and offend someone she knew either, even though every internal alarm went off the second he touched her.

"Do I know you? Your voice. It sounds familiar, but I'm sorry, I can't place it." The man wasn't much bigger than her. Based on the skinny arm she could see and the frame of him pressed up behind her, she knew he wasn't that big of a guy.

His head pressed to the side of hers. "Of course you know me. You understand me better than anyone. You see me the way others don't," he said, excitement in every word.

The only man she knew like that was Cody, and it wasn't his tall, muscular frame pressed up against her. It wasn't his deep, familiar voice at her ear.

But God, she wished he were here right now.

She wished she'd stayed in the library and waited for Mindy Sue and Tony to come to her. They'd be here any second.

But it didn't matter, because she wasn't safe anywhere, because the man holding her wanted her, and he'd stop at nothing to have her.

She'd been warned by campus security and the police detective working the assault cases.

She tried to turn her head to see who had been terrorizing her for the last six months.

His arm drew tighter around her throat. "Don't. Not yet. I don't want to spoil the surprise. Just say you'll come with me. I've got my place all set up. It's perfect. Everything you like. I've seen to every detail, right down to the same blankets you have on your dorm bed, the food you like to eat, even the soap and shampoo you use."

An ominous chill went down her spine.

How did he know those things?

"You'll love it. And I'll love you tonight like I've wanted to for months. I know you've been waiting for me. I just needed time to make everything perfect, to be what you'd want me to be. I'll show you I'm the man you've always wanted. I've finally become the person no one else but you could see inside me."

She tried to stall. "My friends are waiting in the parking lot to pick me up. Let me just tell them I'm going with you."

"Mindy Sue will understand. She's your best friend. She'll want you to be happy. I will make you happy."

She prayed someone came along and found them. "I wish I could, but I'm tired, and I'd like to go home. Maybe we could do this another time."

"No." He shook her. "It has to be tonight. I've been practicing." He sounded manic as he shook her again. "I'm ready." His tone turned menacing and she shivered with fear.

"Please. Let me go. You're scaring me."

He rubbed his cheek against her head again. "I'm sorry." He sounded sincere. Then he didn't. "But you need to do what I say. I have this all planned out. Everything is ready. Now come with me." He dragged her several steps back toward the grass and bushes and away from the library parking lot. "My car is parked on the other side of the small grove of trees. Come on."

"Stop," she shouted, pushing against the arm around her throat to get him to stop pulling her backward and so she could get some much-needed air.

"Don't fight me, Brooke. You know you want this."

She struggled against his grip even more. "Stop. I don't want to go with you." She sucked in a breath to scream.

He suddenly stopped pulling her along with him and the scream lodged in her throat when he pressed the tip of a knife to her cheek. "Don't do it. You know I don't want to hurt you. The waiting is finally over. You don't have to keep looking for me everywhere you go. I'm here, Brooke. We can finally be together."

She froze, knowing this had gone to a whole other level of dangerous. Strong with a thin build, a knife he'd used in the other attacks to subdue his victims—he had the advantage, but she still wondered if she could fight him off.

She'd do anything to save herself and her baby.

She held perfectly still and tried to think of what to say to get herself out of this mess. The guy was insane and obviously delusional.

"Thank you for the gifts," she suddenly blurted out.

He rubbed his nose into her hair and she felt the mask she knew he wore when he attacked the other women. "I wanted you to know I was always with you, even though I couldn't be with you yet. I hadn't yet become the man you saw in me."

She finally remembered the phone in her hand. She swiped her thumb across the screen and though she could barely see the screen down by her thigh and out of his view, she managed to hit the speed dial she set up for 911. She hoped the call went through. She hoped they could hear and find her before anything else happened.

"If you really care about me, you'll let me go."

"I did all of this for you. You need to come with me so you can see your surprise and we can finally be together." He pulled her harder this time, dragging her along after him across the grass, into the bushes, headed straight for the trees and the street beyond. His erection rubbed against her bottom, grinding into her every time he took a step.

She didn't want to think about what he wanted to do to her. She only knew that she needed to protect her baby. She let her bag fall from her shoulder. It dropped near some bushes as they came into a relatively clear space inside the trees. This was her chance. If he took her any farther from the library building, she might not be found at all.

"Please. You don't want to do this. You don't want to hurt me. Put the knife down and we'll talk." She hoped 911 heard her, that they'd already sent help.

"Shut up. We'll be there soon."

Tears welled in her eyes. This couldn't be happening. Her voice shook. "Please. Don't do this. You don't want to hurt me, or my baby. Please, don't hurt my baby."

It had been a calculated risk to talk about the baby. Her belly had only really popped over the last couple weeks. Because of it, she'd been wearing much looser clothes to accommodate her growing bump, except tonight when she'd pulled on yoga pants and a tunic.

She felt the difference in him immediately. He hadn't known.

He'd been vibrating with anticipation. Like he had all kinds of pent-up energy just waiting to be unleashed. Now he went stone still.

Time seemed to grind to a halt as they stood among the trees. He held her tightly in his arm with the knife to her cheek. She barely felt the slice of the blade across her skin and the blood that ran down her face. The sirens in the distance faded behind the blood rushing in her ears. Her focus shrank to the quiet solitude beneath the canopy of tree branches and the man on the verge of doing something terrible.

The stillness gave way to a cry so feral she didn't recognize it as the man completely losing his mind, and screaming, "Noooo!"

She was connected to *him*, belonged to *him*.

He'd felt it at the party.

He spun her around and held her by the shoulders. The evidence of her betrayal couldn't be denied. All this time he'd prepared to show her she belonged to him, and she'd gotten pregnant with another man's bastard.

He shook her. "You were supposed to be special. You weren't like the rest of them."

He'd used those other women, but Brooke was supposed to be the one who really wanted him. She'd seen into him. She knew how he felt inside.

She'd seen past what everyone else saw and looked deeper.

Blood rushing, rage rampaging through his system, he couldn't think or hear anything. He could only see Brooke and how she'd betrayed him. "You were supposed to be mine!"

He rushed her, plunging the knife down in a wide arc. She tried to turn to get away, to run, but the knife sank into the front of her shoulder with such power, it forced her to turn back toward him. He pulled the knife free and stabbed her again in almost the same spot.

Her eyes went wide as she screamed in agonizing pain.

He didn't care. He wanted her to hurt the way she made him hurt. "You were mine! Why? Why would you do this, you spoiled bitch." He pulled the knife free again, slashing at her several times, but something came over her and she fought back, blocking him from stabbing her again. "You ruined everything!" He backed her up as he brought the knife down on her again and again, slicing up her arms and hands. The more times he hit her and the more blood he saw, the greater the need to make her pay.

"Betrayer!" He sliced her again. "Bitch!" He stabbed her arm. "Whore!" He cut her across her fingers.

The adrenaline that had run through his system making him want to fuck her had turned into a red haze of rage.

He wanted her dead.

Instead of trying to back away this time, she came at him, grabbing his ski mask and smacking him in the face. He shoved her back. The ski mask pulled free in her hand and for the first time, she saw his face.

He looked right at her, his breath coming out heavy against her face. He held her bloody arm in one of his hands and the knife in the other poised above her. She had her hand on his chest ready to push *him* away.

"Adam?" she said, shocked.

Without thought, blinded by rage and panic, everything tunneled in, focused on her, he plunged the knife down and buried it in her. The slippery blood ran over the knife handle, oozing through his fingers and making the knife slip from his grip.

She came after him with a vengeance. She hit him in the face and raked her nails down his cheek.

He grabbed her wrist to keep her from scratching him again. Off-balance, they fell to the ground, her arm hitting a large rock and snapping under the force.

Despite the broken arm, she kept struggling.

With blood on his gloves, he couldn't hold her.

She slipped out of his tight grip, scrambled up, and tried to run. He grabbed her ankle and held tight as she got up, twisting her foot and bringing her down again. She kicked and struggled, but he gripped her legs and climbed up her body as they fought in the dirt.

Adam rolled her onto her back and stared down at her, shocked.

Brooke looked down, her eyes went wide, and a scream rose up out of her and echoed through him.

They both stared at the knife handle sticking out of her swollen belly.

Stunned, Adam's world stopped. He couldn't believe what he saw. Blood covered her shoulder and her arms, but it was the blood pumping out of the wound on her belly that left him reeling. Dark red oozed freely out from under the pulsing handle of the knife. Her rounded belly, a reminder of the small, innocent baby inside her.

Sound exploded around him and echoed in his head. Sirens squealed and people yelled Brooke's name.

Fear washed through him, along with agonizing remorse. He needed to get away.

He leapt up and ran through the trees, leaving her lying in the dirt, blood flowing out of her with every beat of her heart winding down. She couldn't survive that.

Oh God. What have I done?

Brooke's head fell back and thudded in the dirt. She stared up at the stars peeking through the tree branches and felt a wash of numbness come over her.

Someone yelled her name.

Afraid to die alone, she sucked in a breath and rasped out as loud as she could, "I'm here!"

Tears streamed down her face. She knew the life inside her had extinguished. She felt it all the way to her soul.

Emptiness like a deep chasm opened up inside her and swallowed her whole.

Moaning in anguish and trying to catch her breath, she sobbed. She didn't speak when the officers found her. She couldn't manage more than, "My baby's dead."

The look on their faces said it all. They agreed with her. She couldn't take it.

Passing out would have been a blessing, but the blackness she wanted to welcome refused to come. She was forced to look into the sad and devastated faces of the policemen and paramedics as they quickly wrapped her bloody arms, strapped her to a board, and carried her out of the trees.

The last thing she saw was Mindy Sue in Tony's arms as they approached before the paramedics put her into the ambulance. She could only manage to tell Mindy Sue one thing. "Don't let them c-call h-home. P-promise."

Mindy Sue gasped at the sight of the knife sticking out of her belly. "Brooke, you need your family."

"N-no. C-call your d-dad."

Brooke lost track of time after that. First she was in the ambulance, then she was surrounded by a team of doctors and nurses all calling out information and orders before she was rushed into an operating room and some nice man did what she really wanted and knocked her out.

She woke up in recovery, aching with a loss so profound and deep and dark she wished she'd never woken up at all. "W-where's my b-baby. I want to s-see h-her."

The nurse put her hand on Brooke's good shoulder. "I'm so sorry for your loss. You need to rest now."

Brooke fell into oblivion again.

"Brooke, sweetie." Mindy Sue touched her cheek sometime later. "Are you awake?"

Brooke couldn't stand to open her eyes and see the damage Adam inflicted on her body. "Where is she? I need to see her. Why won't they let me see her?"

Mindy Sue brushed her hand over Brooke's hair. "I'm so sorry. You're going to be all right."

She'd never be okay again. "He killed my baby." The wail filled with all her pain and agony tore through her and made everything else hurt more. Every wracking sob compounded her pain.

"Brooke, please. Calm down. I don't want you to hurt yourself more."

She couldn't hurt any worse.

"I'm so sorry, sweetie." Mindy Sue leaned over her and gently held her close while she cried. Brooke felt her friend's tears drip onto her cheek.

She cried herself back into a fitful sleep, filled with agonizing images of Adam attacking her. She heard his voice. She felt him all around her and coming at her. She remembered how hard she fought to save herself and the baby.

But she lost.

And now she didn't want to live without her little girl.

She woke again later. Hours. Days. She didn't know how much time had passed. She didn't care. It didn't matter.

Mr. Wagner walked into her room. He pulled Mindy Sue up from her chair and hugged her so close and so tight it choked Brooke up just seeing it. "I love you so much, honey. The thought that it could have been you in that bed... I'll never forget the fear I felt when you called last night and told me what happened to Brooke. Did she say anything?"

"They won't let her see her baby, Daddy." Tears fell down Mindy Sue's cheeks.

Her father gently wiped them away.

Brooke closed her eyes on the tender scene, too emotional to watch anymore. She didn't have a father anymore.

Her mother would be devastated when she heard what happened.

Cody used to be her friend. Now they only spoke through text. Well, except for her birthday. He'd hate her for not saving his child.

He'd lost two now.

She ached for him as much as she hurt for herself.

The doctor came in and updated Mr. Wagner and Mindy Sue on her condition. Most of the cuts on her arms were stitched up; the two stab wounds to her shoulder required surgery to repair and close; she had a broken arm requiring a removable cast thanks to the pins they put in and the deep, stitched cuts that needed to be tended, and a severely sprained ankle. Her leg was in a walking brace. Her abdomen had suffered the worst injury—besides her shattered heart.

The surgeon had performed an emergency C-section to stop the massive bleeding, and repair the damage done by the six-inch blade. The doctor assured them she'd heal.

Right. Everything but her heart would mend itself back together.

Mr. Wagner asked about her daughter. "Can she see the baby?"

She could barely hear the doctor's reply. "The baby was injured quite badly. The psychiatrist believes seeing the trauma the baby suffered would only traumatize Brooke more than she's already been."

Brooke didn't want to hear that. She wanted to hold her child and see her grow up into a beautiful woman. She wanted to put the baby in Cody's arms and watch him light up with joy. But she couldn't hold her baby. She couldn't give him that happiness.

And Adam needed to pay for all of it.

Brooke turned and opened her eyes. "Mr. Wagner, please." The tears came again. It seemed they were never far from spilling over.

"Yes, honey. What can I do?"

She beckoned him to come closer so only he'd hear her request and whispered in his ear. "Get to Adam Harris before the governor does."

His eyes went wide. "It's too late. It's all over the news. He tried to commit suicide. His mom and dad found him just in time."

Too late. They'd cover it up. She turned away from him and lost any hope she'd ever get justice for her little girl.

Chapter Thirty-Seven

C ody had crashed in Brooke's bed. Again. Another long workday. Another night thinking about Brooke and a future without her that had him dreaming about her. Only this time, things turned dark.

Kristi was holding his hand as he tried to reach for Brooke, who stood just out of reach of him, facing a bright, sun-filled horizon, while Kristi stood behind him, a turbulent storm approaching.

Even in the dream he understood the imagery. If he was with Brooke, he'd be happy. If he stayed with Kristi, he'd forever be fighting to get to Brooke and living in a storm of emotions and a life fraught with conflicting feelings about Kristi.

They were good together, but their relationship wasn't easy. He was forever trying to be what she needed him to be and falling short in her eyes. With Brooke, he could simply be himself.

Both of them loved him for who he was.

But Brooke loved him as is.

Kristi wanted him to be more and do more. He tried. But in doing so, he failed because it was never enough.

The cold hard truth was that Kristi fit him and his life in many ways, but she wasn't the woman he loved and wanted to be with forever.

Over the last many months it had become clear he and Kristi could have a good marriage. One built on mutual appreciation and support of the other. But that would only take them so far and make the things lacking between them more obvious and necessary. The marriage would fall apart, leaving them both bitter, more than likely.

And it would be his fault because he loved another. More than anything.

Kristi felt it. She knew it.

Both of them had spent the past six months ignoring it.

He couldn't do that anymore. Not when he felt this emptiness growing inside him. Not when the closer it came to Brooke graduating and coming home, the more he thought about what a life with her could be like.

Not when he woke up from that dream of him trying desperately to escape Kristi's grasp, so he could grab hold of Brooke and hold on to her forever in the light and warmth and love she offered that left him with her name on his lips and tattooed on his heart and soul.

He knew what he needed to do.

Maybe Brooke had someone else. Maybe she didn't anymore. He didn't know. All he knew was that he needed to go after Brooke, tell her that he loved her, and only her, and do whatever it took to get her back.

I can't live without her.

She's mine.

I hope you enjoyed the first half of the SHE'S MINE duet.

Order LOVE ME to find out what happens next!

Here's a sneak peek...

LOVE ME

Chapter One

The silence might kill her.

Where was the wail of her baby crying?

When would she feel something other than the smothering of her grief?

Heartbreak. That's just how it started.

Agony was where she was stuck between the physical and emotional pain writhing inside her.

She could hear the scream lodged in her throat. Feel the emptiness in her belly like a living thing clawing at her.

She couldn't escape the loss she felt of someone there, then gone, but never here.

The agony crashed over her, then receded into a throbbing ache before it built again as she considered what was gone. What would never be. Hopes and dreams and a life barely lived.

The spark ignited by love and passion snuffed out by twisted desire turned to rage.

He killed my baby!

The words were a scream in her mind. An echo that sounded over and over again with each tear that fell.

She's gone, and I am empty.

The deep, dark pit of despair held her locked tight against its silent, heartless soul, aching to be free of the pain and resigned to feeling it forever.

Chapter Two

Adam winced at the bright light in his eyes and the pain in his wrists. He tried to lift his arm to see why it hurt and discovered the padded band around his forearm was actually strapped to the bedrail.

What the fuck!

He was restrained to the bed by both arms and ankles. He struggled against his bonds. A sense of déjà vu came over him.

Someone trying to get away from *him*.

Oh shit!

It all came back in a flash of nightmare images. Brooke! His beautiful Brooke.

His heart thrashed in his chest, pounding so hard he could barely catch his breath.

He'd almost had her. She was right there. His for the taking.

I was so close.

She wanted it.

He knew she did.

She'd been waiting for him.

But no. She fought him.

Fury seared through his veins. The cunt! She'd given herself to someone else. He tugged at the restraints again, wanting to flee this place and find her, hunt her down and get his hands on her.

More images flooded his mind. She fought him, trying to push him away. Holding her hands up to ward him off. But he kept attacking.

Blood. Dripping down her arms. Soaking her clothes. His vision a red haze of rage.

Oh God, no. More blood. Pumping out of her round belly.

Her agonizing screams echoed in his ears.

He hurt her.

He never wanted to hurt *her*.

"What have I done?" Shame. Guilt. Utter sorrow washed through him.

He'd killed a baby.

Her baby.

Tears leaked from his eyes, down his cheeks, and drenched the hospital gown he wore.

He didn't deserve to live. Not now. Not after what he'd done to her.

Trapped, he flailed in the bed, desperately trying to get free so he could end it. He didn't deserve to live. Not after what he'd done to the woman he loved.

Brooke. His beautiful Brooke.

He spotted the bandages over his wrists, sat up, and tried to lean forward enough to bite them off.

Monitors shrieked.

The door flew open.

His father stood there, his mother behind and to the side of him.

She looked shocked and anguished. Sad. Lines wrinkling her forehead and around her tight lips.

He looked pissed and horrified.

Can't have this, can you, asshole?

What will people think?

How many votes will this cost you?

That's all he'd think.

"Adam. Stop struggling," his father commanded. Like his order, his rule, was law.

"Fuck you! Untie me and get out." Adam pinned his mother in his gaze. "Why the fuck did you save me?"

"We love you," his mother wailed, tears raining down her face.

"Bullshit. I'm nothing more than a prop." Adrenaline cleared even more of the fog from his mind. "Where is she? Is she here? Is she alive? I need to see her. I need to tell her I'm sorry. I NEED TO SEE HER!"

A nurse burst in holding a syringe.

He leaned forward, his arms drawn tight by the restraints. "Don't even fucking think of coming near me with that," he snapped at the nurse, staring down his father. "You can make this happen. I need to see her."

"Calm down." His father eyed the nurse. Then Adam again. The silent message: *Not in front of witnesses.* He cocked his head at the nurse. "Please excuse us. We'd like to be alone with our son."

The nurse hesitated but ultimately followed his order and scurried out.

Adam wondered what fucked-up tale he'd told everyone about what happened tonight. "Is she alive?" She had to be alive. *Please.*

"Yes," his father bit out. "Though I guarantee she doesn't want to see *you*." His father stepped into the room, his mother following, then leaned against the door, barring anyone from coming in. Voice low, his eyes narrowed, he gave Adam the cold, hard truth. "You fucked me."

"Of course you think this is all about *you*." Adam fell back in the bed, exhaustion clawing at him. Probably from the blood loss after he tried to end it all.

"Why didn't you just let me go? It would have been so much easier for you to use your fake heartbreak over your loss to gain voter sympathy. And don't think I don't know you've already ordered your lapdogs to tell the press how distraught you are over your son's mental health and how hard it's been on *you*. You'll be able to milk this for weeks. Because I know you'd never let it get out that I was the one who went after those stupid girls and nearly killed Brooke."

"Why?" His mother's anguished voice broke him out of his sorrowful fury.

"Because I love her. I wanted her. She saw me for who I really am." He glared at his father. "Not your fucking son. Not some actor in your fucking political play. She liked *me*."

"So why go after those other women?" his mother asked, seeing that she got him talking when all he wanted to do was rail at his father.

Not that he liked her much better. She played her part and it usually meant her making him go along with everything his father wanted. She was his fucking puppet.

"I wanted to be my best for her." He settled back into the pillow, unclenching his fists to relieve the pain in his wrists. "I need to see her."

His father left the door and came to his bedside. "You will never see her again." *Because you can't be linked to her*, his eyes said.

He held his father's hard gaze. "I *need* to see her."

"You will keep your mouth shut about what you did. You will tell the doctors, anyone who asks, that you tried to take your own life tonight because you've been overwhelmed by school and struggling with depression that you never disclosed because you feared what people would say."

He glared his father down. "I could give a fuck what you or anyone else thinks. I. Need. To. See. Her!"

"If you don't follow this order, there will be nothing I can do. You'll either play along and stay in this very *nice*, very *expensive private* hospital for the rest of your life, or you'll go to prison, where God knows what you'll suffer."

"I. Need. To. See Her."

His father stared him down, thinking of all the possibilities and ways this could play out. He liked control. He needed it. And he forced others to his will with a smile, a few direct words that left others clamoring to do his bidding, and a handshake.

"She's asked to see me."

Adam gasped. "When? I want to go with you."

He shook his head. "I'll go alone. If she decides to go public, I won't be able to help you."

"No, you'll do and say whatever you have to do to distance yourself from me. Your son. Because we both know all you care about is your fucking career and getting more power."

His father grabbed the guardrails on the bed, his knuckles going white as his eyes narrowed. "Believe it or not, Adam, I love you. Maybe I didn't always understand you, or give you what you needed, but I did the best I could." He rubbed his hand over the back of his neck, tension around his tired eyes and body. "I know, I should have made more time for you. But I can't change that now. All I can do is help you." He dropped his hand and pinned Adam in his gaze. "But that doesn't mean I'm going down with you. So you'll have to do what you've always done and get on board with the plan before your fate is out of my hands. Please." For a brief second, Adam saw the fear and concern in his father's eyes before he locked it down and turned for the door.

"Take me with you. I need to see her," he begged, tears welling in his eyes.

His father walked back to him. "Get this straight. You are never getting out of here. You are never going to see her again. After what you did, she's never going to want to see you again. *You* did that. Now accept it and play your part before you end up locked in a cage the rest of your life."

I'm already in one.
But I will get out.
I will see her again.

Acknowledgements

I hope you enjoyed the first half of Brooke and Cody's tumultuous love story. For more information about upcoming releases and sales, please sign up for my newsletter.

I wrote this book many years ago. I loved it, but never thought a publisher would go for the dark plot. So I left it sitting on my computer while I wrote a whole bunch of other books. When I decided to start self publishing my books, this was the first one I thought to do after I finished the Dark Horse Dive Bar for my fans.

The best thing I ever did was hire an amazing developmental editor. Thank you, Susan Barnes (www.susanbar nesediting.com), for seeing the potential in the very rough draft. Your suggestion to make it a duet was brilliant. It allowed me to really dive deeper into the characters and separate the tough road Brooke and Cody had to travel from being separated, to healing, and finally getting their happy ever after. These books are everything I didn't know they could be until you showed me the way.

Melissa Frain (www.melissafrain.com), thank you for another great copyedit filled with all the words I don't know need to be hypenated. It is the bane of my existence. I appreciate your hard work. I was so happy to give you and the readers that surprise at the end.

Angela Haddon (www.angelahaddon.com), you are an amazing cover artist. Thank you for the beautiful covers!

To my amazing agent, Suzie Townsend, thank you for always having my back, guiding me through this crazy business, sharing your insights and expertise, and always cheering me on. I couldn't, and wouldn't, want to do this without you.

Steve, I love you. What else is there to say after all these years of support and encouragement, kids, laughter, fun, and everything else that goes into a life together. I can't imagine doing any of this without you by my side.

ALSO BY JENNIFER RYAN

Chasing Morgan – The Right Bride
Lucky Like Us – Saved by the Rancher
Short Stories
"Close to Perfect" (appears in Snowbound at Chrstmas)
"Can't Wait" (appears in All I Want for Christmas is a
Cowboy)
"Waiting for You" (appears in Confessions of a Secret Ad-
mirer)

Also by Jennifer Ryan writing thrillers as JENNIFER HUNTER
The Ryan Strickland Series
The Lost Victim – The Rose Reaper

About the Author

New York Times and *USA Today* bestselling author Jennifer Ryan writes suspenseful contemporary romances about everyday people who do extraordinary things. Her deeply emotional love stories are filled with high stakes and higher drama, family, friendship, and the happy-ever-after we all hope to find.

Jennifer lives in the San Francisco Bay Area with her husband and three children. When she isn't writing a book, she's reading one. Her obsession with both is often revealed in the state of her home and how late dinner is to the table. When she finally leaves those fictional worlds, you'll find her in the garden, playing in the dirt and daydreaming about people who live only in her head – until she puts them on paper.

Please visit her website at www.jennifer-ryan.com for information about upcoming releases.